The
Sandalwood
Fan

Also by Diana Brown

The Emerald Necklace
Come Be My Love
A Debt of Honour
St. Martin's Summer

The Sandalwood Fan

Diana Brown

St. Martin's Press   New York

Library of Congress Cataloging in Publication Data

Brown, Diana.
  The sandalwood fan.

  I. Title.
PR6052.R58943S2   1983   823'.914   83–2894
ISBN 0-312-69909-3

Design by Laura Hammond

First Edition
10 9 8 7 6 5 4 3 2 1

For Ralph, Pamela, and Clarissa,
who make all things possible

Author's Note

The Cockney rhyming slang used by Albert Watkins in *The Sandalwood Fan* originated in the London underworld in the early part of the nineteenth century and spread to Ireland, Australia, and some parts of the United States.

The slang consists of two or more words of which the last is a rhyme or assonance of the word it represents, such as bees and honey (money), cat and mouse (house), ivory pearl (girl), pot and pan (man), frying pans (hands), hot cross bun (run), butcher's hook (look), linen draper (paper).

Occasionally one word may suffice, as in greengages (wages), or the phrase may be shortened to the use of one word alone, for example, rabbit, for rabbit and pork, meaning talk. The word represented may also be slang in itself—grasshopper (copper) or Noah's ark (nark).

Often, proper names are used. Edna May (way), Charlie Freer (beer), or Jim Brown (town).

The explanation of other expressions used in this book is left to the reader's conjecture.

D. B.

1

*Those English who are lovers of liberty will one day lament
with tears having gained the battle of Waterloo.*

Napoleon, 1818

And still his head ached. Lord, how it ached! He turned
gingerly on the pillow and immediately regretted the move
as the bright sun shone directly onto his eyes; its glare was
insupportable. He tossed in impatience. What fool had
opened the bed curtains?

Unwillingly he raised his eyelids to discern the wiry frame
of Glossop profferring a glass filled with a vile-appearing
concoction.

"What the devil are you doing here? Get out!"

"Yes, me lord, after you've taken of this."

"Take it away."

"When you've drunk it I'll take the glass away, me lord."
Glossop's voice was singularly calm and even. It served to
irritate him even more.

"Take it away, I said. Dammit, are you deaf?"

"No, me lord," Glossop replied without moving a muscle.

"Leave me alone. What are you, a blockhead, don't you
understand me?"

"I do, me lord. I also understood what you said when we
was in Spain where you got the recipe for this devil's brew—
you said whenever you was the worse for wear I was to
make sure you drunk it down, no matter what. And this
morning, me lord," Glossop surveyed his master's bleary

1

countenance dispassionately, though his stare was not entirely devoid of pity as he repeated, "This morning, me lord, if you'll pardon me saying so, you're very definitely the worse for wear."

"Then give me the bloody stuff, if that's the only way to be rid of you."

Lord Charles Mortimer seized the glass Glossop held out. He glanced down briefly at the dark potion and immediately regretted his action; on top floated a bright, glutinous egg yolk which stared back at him impassively as it slowly circled the glass. Mortimer shuddered and closed tight his eyes to shut out the nauseous prospect before performing what he considered his most courageous act, an act his stomach warned him was an impossibility—he choked down the contents of the glass and thrust it back at Glossop.

"Ugh! Poison, bloody poison, that's what it is."

"It's just senna, Epsom salts, a little bruised ginger and coriander seeds mixed together with a dram of brandy—not forgetting the egg, o'course."

"Who could possibly forget the egg!" Mortimer's stomach rebelled at the very thought.

"You'll be right as rain in a trivet, me lord, you'll see."

"And you'll shut up and shut the curtain if you know what's good for you," his master growled.

"Yes, me lord, but I'll be back. Last night you told me to be sure you was up and on the road afore noon. I regret to tell you that's barely more than an hour away."

Glossop's voice contained precious little regret, in Mortimer's opinion, and though his long-time manservant closed the bed curtain in what *he* considered his quietest, most discreet manner, it was a manner his master, turning over on the other side of that curtain, considered quite boisterous and unfeeling.

But though Mortimer groaned, the potion was already beginning to take effect and, as it did, he remembered where he was and the events of the previous evening, all of which made him groan once again.

It was she who had suggested the meeting. Her husband was leaving for his plantation in the Indies; she could get away, she said, so would he *please* come to her. The Blue Boar at Gerrard's Cross was comfortable yet a place where one's actions went unremarked, or so she had heard. She implored him to be there. She longed to see him, but, of course, he knew that.

He'd come, cursing himself for his lack of resolution. He'd waited what had seemed an eternity for her, with the chamber appropriately warm, the wine appropriately cool. Then that blasted messenger had come with her note, so prettily worded, full of impatient dashes—her husband's departure had been delayed hence she was unable to join him. Would he not come on to London so she might see him at Lady Lambourne's ball on Thursday evening? She sent him her love. She missed him terribly since he had buried himself away at Chenwyth. She longed to be with him, but, of course, he knew that. She knew he understood.

Well, damn it, he hadn't understood. It was *she* who had chosen the meeting place and he who had come hurrying down from Shropshire at her bidding—when he had forsworn returning to town—hurrying at her beckoning, cursing himself all the way for a fool. And all he had to show for his frantic haste was a stuffy room and a ghastly wine that he'd chosen only because it was her favourite.

Yet even in his anger his mind went back almost a decade to that time he had first seen Georgina. She'd been the talk of London that season, he the impoverished holder of an inferior Shropshire estate without prospects, nothing, in fact, to show for himself but an old and respected name and a favourable appearance. Still, those attributes had held him in good stead, particularly with the ladies, who had flirted with the rather shy youth, she the most outrageously of them all. Yet she had laughed, laughed outright at his audacity in the proposal of marriage he had tendered with all the passion of his one and twenty years. He forgave her laughter, for even he had to admit it was preposterous to expect the season's brightest debutante to settle for a man with nothing but a title to offer, no prospects of fortune. He forgave her, too, because he was hopelessly in love, yet he couldn't bear to continue to see her when, soon after, she became engaged to Sir Philby Staverton, a foppish, silly fool if he ever saw one, but owner of the finest town house on Brook Street and due to inherit vast sugar plantations in the Indies.

Mortimer had mortgaged, pawned, and borrowed to purchase a commission in the Fifteenth Hussars, his grandfather's regiment. To do so he had been forced to turn to the only source from which he knew that money would be forthcoming—at usurious rates yet forthcoming nevertheless—his detested Shropshire neighbour, Samuel Trueblood, who had catered to his father's weaknesses for wine and cards and held the Mortimers in the palm of his grasping, miserly hand. Well, Mortimer didn't care anymore; he vowed never to return to England and left to fight in the Peninsular wars.

Perhaps because he cared so little for his own life, he rapidly became known for his dauntless gallantry, his unshakable calm under fire, his unhesitating willingness to enter the most impossible situations, to expose himself in the thickest of battles without a sign of fear in the face of the most devastating opposition. And through it all, he, who cared so little for preserving his life, who believed he had nothing for which to live, rode unscathed, suffering not so much as a sprained finger.

He acquitted himself with such valour at Sahagun and later at Benevente that his name, mentioned time and again in dispatches, soon became the subject of discussion in those London drawing rooms he had vowed never again to frequent.

It was an irony on which he long pondered that he, who cared not one whit whether he lived or died, was spared from enemy fire, from injury, from disease, while those around him succumbed, and he bore witness to the most gruesome spectacles. He learned to live only for the moment, to take what he could from it, to expect nothing and, because of that attitude, he came to enjoy his life, to love the army, to admire the endurance, the doggedness of the common soldier under his command. He never coddled his men, often demanding more of them than his fellow

4

officers, yet invariably he treated them with respect and saw to it that they received their just due, complaining on their behalf at poor rations and late supplies. In turn, they accorded him a devotion seldom found. Whether he was leading a battle charge against an intransigent foe or rallying men caught in impossible straits, his scarlet shako, which had replaced his fur cap on the battlefield, his figure unbowed even when mount after mount was shot from beneath him, inspired esprit and confidence. He appeared to lead a charmed existence occasioned not, he insisted, by pluck, but by a quixotic Lady Luck who had denied him what he most wished and spared his life only, he swore, because he would so willingly have given it away. This very insistence, carried back to England by his fellow officers, served to make of him a legend in his time.

As he rose from the rank of lowly subaltern to colonelcy, none was more surprised at his rapid advance than himself; and when, after Waterloo, his exploits the subject of song and story, a grateful country bestowed upon him the Order of the Bath and an annuity of twenty thousand it was said, by all who knew him, to be only his due.

Though cursing himself for a charlatan, Mortimer accepted the honours and, having done so, returned to England determined to enjoy them. Yet he could not forbear to conclude that life was futile for sparing him while so many husbands and fathers had perished, that he was unfairly rewarded for remaining unscathed. It was somehow ludicrous, yet, having been spared, having been rewarded, he determined to live as he had learned to live, for the pleasure of the moment, nothing more.

The hero who returned to England was by no means the young man who had left; he had aged by more than years. He was debonair, charming, witty, cynical and at times quite ruthless. He ignored the obsequities and flattery which a society that had once barely tolerated him bestowed upon him. Those matrons who had considered him unworthy of connexion with their lines now lay in wait for him, pursued him, offering up their charges like sacrifices to a god. And he, who had a word and a smile for the least of his men, haughtily ignored those hypocritical *grandes dames* and the simpering charges who followed in their wake.

While he refused all entanglements set in his path, he did not refuse to amuse himself with the more beautiful, the more charming, the more available ladies who boasted of his attentions. But there was one lady he took care to avoid: Lady Georgina Staverton, who, though he would gladly have denied it, still held a place in his affections that the intervening years with their countless casual encounters had not dimmed.

When at last they met, as inevitably they must, Mortimer recognized her ascendancy over him to be unchanged. He found her charms not one whit diminished, but rather enhanced by having been so long held in his memory and then at last witnessed in their all too tangible, all too desirable form.

She laughed when she saw him, but no longer at his audacity, only with the sheer joy of their meeting. Though he would feign have ignored her he could not, particularly when she confessed to having loved him always, that her marriage to Philby Staverton had been a monstrous mistake promulgated only by ambitious parents. It was, she assured him, a marriage in little more than name, and Mortimer, older and wiser though he was, was quickly conquered once again, and London knew that while he might continue to amuse himself, his attentions to Georgina Staverton were somehow different.

Yet Mortimer could not long endure the sight of his love at the side of her husband. He had fled, from her, from all of London's sycophants, back to Shropshire, to regain Chenwyth. To Samuel Trueblood's chagrin he now had money enough, not only from his annuity but also from a distant relative who had been all too delighted to bequeath a generous fortune to a branch of the family he had previously scorned.

It had been satisfying to free himself from Trueblood's grasp, a man he hated not only for the harm he had done to his own family but for all the times he had supplied the army overseas with shoddy goods, always overpriced, while he warmed his narrow and fleshless backside before his home hearth. Never again would Mortimer ask anything of him, never!

Yet Mortimer's restless energy demanded outlet, more than the usual country sports, more than the visits to his sister, Eunice, and her husband and those nephews and nieces whom he adored, could afford. He set about restoring Chenwyth, then urging the use of the new road surfaces developed by Telford and Macadam. He designed his own coaches with all four wheels of equal size. The coachmaker at Bridgnorth had insisted it could not be done, that the front wheels of necessity must be smaller to allow them to pass beneath the body of the coach in turning. But Mortimer had shown him that if the central pivot for the wheels was placed near the centre of the perch, between the front and rear wheels rather than over the front axle, the front wheels would not lock around the perch-bolt but stay clear of the body of the coach in turning despite their larger circumference. He also insisted on the spokes of the wheel being conical rather than flat and having the outer tire shrunk onto the rim wheels while hot, a process that made a wheel virtually indestructible.

Driving south in answer to Georgina Staverton's summons, choosing the closed carriage rather than the curricle in the event she might wish to ride back to London with him, his design was vindicated by the smoothness of the ride. Yet that thought did not cheer him as he sat alone at the Blue Boar. He re-read her letter before throwing it aside in disgust. He'd come, but he'd be damned if he'd go any further at her bidding.

He threw out the wine and went down to the taproom to call for porter. There he recognized Reginald Palfry, a gentleman of decided fashion and even greater obtuseness who fancied himself a great one for the ladies. They fell into desultory conversation, but after their glasses had been refilled for the third time and Palfry suggested a pursuit of local lightskirts for their joint enjoyment, Mortimer, no novice to the coarse obscenities of the field, found Palfry's manner of speaking guttersnipe language in smooth and

cultured tones abhorrent. He excused himself and fortui-
tously ran into Rodney Bullerton, with whom he'd spent
time in the Peninsula; his friend's pugnacious expression
and plain attire, his obvious pleasure at the meeting, were a
welcome contrast to Palfry's unsavoury presence. Bully, on
his way to visit his mother at Malmesbury, was only too glad
to find an excuse to delay a visit to a matriarch—who, despite his years, always managed to make him feel like a
naughty schoolboy—and he decided to order a room for
the night.

Thus they had spent the evening together, dining in the
taproom on the finest turtle soup, rump steaks, Hambro
sausages, pigeon pie and a magnificent wedge of Stilton,
with porter followed by claret, claret by brandy, and brandy
by champagne that was pressed upon all and sundry by a
besotted young gentleman who was to marry the next day.
Mortimer caught only one more glimpse of Palfry conducting a young woman upstairs; it was apparent that the Blue
Boar, while catering to the gentry, was a free and easy establishment where no questions were asked, no answers expected.

He and Bully entered into a lengthy and, as time pro-
gressed, lugubrious discussion on the dismal state in which
they found England, agreeing that the true victor of Waterloo had not been Wellington, nor any of the statesmen who
had earnestly pondered territorial rights at the Congress of
Vienna, and most certainly not the foot soldier who had
fought long and hard for his country. No, they concurred
bitterly, the victor was his English counterpart, the mer-
chant who had stayed at home, lining his pockets while
others did his fighting for him.

Mortimer could never forget Waterloo, the sheer hell it
had been, the smell, the dirt, the hail of fire—great iron
balls, ten pounds and more, smashing men and horses indiscriminately, heads, limbs shot from bodies, the cries, the
carnage. There had been no glory in that battle—except for
the maker of munitions. Mortimer drank to those who had
fallen; he drank to remember them, but mostly he drank to
forget.

And his head the next morning bore ample testimony to all he had consumed, yet gradually it cleared as Glossop's potion numbed the pain. He turned again in bed. The Blue Boar boasted big beds, solid beds, beds designed for use by more than one. His thoughts returned to Georgina; if she had been there with him, it would have been a delightful night instead of a disaster of remembrance. Oh, the futility of it all!

Mortimer sighed on hearing a graveyard cough from the other side of the curtain. Glossop had returned and was practicing what he always insisted was his most delicate method of awakening his master—it was a cough capable of awakening the dead, and Mortimer stretched, knowing his moments of rest were numbered.

Glossop had been with him ever since Sahagun, where he'd been left for dead on the battlefield. Mortimer had discovered him the following day, and when the surgeon had refused to treat him, saying he was so close to dead there were others who could better use his services, Mortimer had found an old midwife who promised to take care of the soldier at Mortimer's expense. Glossop had recovered and thereafter attached himself to Mortimer, insisting upon serving him. Mortimer has been equally insistent that he could not afford a private servant, but Glossop stayed nevertheless, and it had become an arrangement that suited them both admirably. He was now amply rewarded for his efforts, and over the years he had come to know Mortimer's moods, needs, and desires often before Mortimer himself was aware of them.

"Time you was astirring, me lord," Glossop announced apologetically yet with not a little triumph, deftly drawing the curtains aside after finishing another bout of coughing.

"I hear castor oil is excellent for the throat," Mortimer suggested malevolently.

"No use to change the subject, me lord, it's time."

"What, is Brutus sick, and will he steal out of his wholesome bed to dare the vile contagion of the night?"

"'Ardly, me lord, at 'alf past heleven in the morning," Glossop sniffed—whether in disparagement at the Bard or

9

at Mortimer's dawdling was difficult to say. "Be noon afore long and you said. . . ."

"I know, I know." Mortimer swung his long legs over the side of the bed. "I know, my dear Glossop, what I said. You seem to think because I indulged in a little Bacchanalian revelry that I remember nothing. I promise that we shall be on the road by noon." He glanced blearily out at the brilliant mid-day sun and added hastily, "Or reasonably soon thereafter."

"The road back to Shropshire?"

Mortimer glanced over the assortment of meats, cheeses, and fish on the breakfast tray sent up from the kitchen and shuddered slightly. "Just coffee, I think, will do this morning." He caught sight of Georgina's note, which lay on the table beside the tray. "No, not Shropshire. Since we're so close, we might as well go on to town. I'm expected at Lady Lambourne's on Thursday. We can return to Chenwyth after that."

2

Art, glory, freedom fail,
but nature still is fair.

Byron
Childe Harold, 1812

They entered London by way of the Tiburn Road. It being such a fine afternoon and there being no necessity to preserve a lady's privacy after all, Mortimer regretted that he had not brought his light curricle. He chose to join Glossop on the box, taking the reins and setting the horses to a strong, steady pace. The rhythm of the wheels, the fresh April day, the songs of birds returned to enjoy an English spring all contributed to make him forget his disappointment of the previous day. As they neared the metropolis, he realized that his head was considerably cleared and his stomach would appreciate a good dinner.

On an impulse, thinking to shorten his route to his new establishment on Aldford Street, he turned into Hyde Park. But it was approaching the fashionable hour and the crush of carriages decided him to turn into a little frequented lane leading by the Serpentine. As they neared Knightsbridge, the peace of the bucolic scene was broken, quite suddenly, by a fracas in the path ahead of them, and an incredible sight met Mortimer's eyes.

A rough, burly man was struggling with a dark-clad woman of slight build who, despite her small stature, was striking repeatedly at the man's arms and chest—to little avail, for the man was far stronger and held her arm in what must have been a cruel grip. Beside the struggling pair cowered a young girl, a crossing sweeper apparently by the broom she held, though whether it was she who held the broom up or the broom which kept her thin frame from falling was unclear. A small urchin, with some article tucked beneath his arm, was looking on with interest, but as soon as he caught sight of Mortimer he took off like a bolt from an arrow.

The horses shied violently as Mortimer, with an oath, jerked them to a halt. Throwing the reins to Glossop he jumped down, grabbing the man by the shoulders as he descended, thereby forcing him to release his hold of the woman. A glancing blow to the side of the man's head followed by a swift jab that landed squarely on the jaw of his startled face sent him sprawling to the ground, and a restraining boot placed across his chest prevented him from rising. Only then did Mortimer turn to see how the woman had fared. He had taken her for some associate of the man, but as she stood rubbing her arm where the man had held her, Mortimer could see that she was a lady—not a London lady, to be sure, for her plain, neat, definitely drab attire was more serviceable than fashionable. A governess, he surmised, or perhaps a maiden aunt on a visit to the capital.

"Are you all right, ma'am?" he enquired solicitously, handing her her bonnet which had fallen in the fray.

She looked at him directly for the first time, and though he saw he had been right in his assumption that she was no beauty, still her eyes were interesting, clear, golden, like sherry freshly poured. Her hair was lustrous and of like colour, or so it seemed before she quickly covered it with her cottage bonnet.

"Quite all right, sir," she replied breathlessly but matter-of-factly, as though they had met in the normal course of events and would go on to discuss one another's well being and, perhaps, proceed to ascertain the health of any mutual acquaintance they might have.

"You must pardon me, ma'am, for, perhaps, seeming inquisitive, but it did seem as I approached you were in need of some help. Might I ask," and Mortimer looked down at the robust form squirming beneath his foot, "might I ask whether this person is an acquaintance of yours?"

"Indeed not!" was the sharp rejoinder.

"Then why, then how . . ." Mortimer stopped short, noting the remote area of the park in which they found themselves, then adding, not without a sense of horror, for the lady before him in her plain attire without the slightest adornment appeared so obviously the soul of respectability, "Surely he was not attempting to abduct you!"

"Of course not!" Her sharp reply echoed his own disbelief. "It was the child he was harming." She looked down at the man. "You are a great beast and a bully to beat this poor child so. You must never touch her again. Do you understand? You are to leave her alone."

The man wriggled under Mortimer's boot, growing even redder in the face.

"She's me own soap and water. No one can do anyfing to me for wot I do wiv 'er—I don't 'ave to 'ot cross bun from the grass'opper fer it," he growled, until the pressure of the boot on his chest caused him to desist.

"Soap and water . . . hot cross bun . . . grasshopper," the lady repeated in puzzlement.

"He means she's his daughter, ma'am, and he doesn't have to run from the copper for what he does to her. It's a sort of slang used by Cockneys," Mortimer explained before warning the ruffian, "You may have authority over your child, but the law will have something quite different to say about your laying hands on this lady, that I can assure you."

"She weren't 'urt. She said she weren't 'urt. Tell 'is nibs yer weren't 'urt, missus," the man pleaded.

"He's right. I am unhurt, and I'll press no charges against him as long as he promises to leave the child alone in the future."

"Do you think his promises are worth anything?"

"Perhaps not, but to bring charges against him can help no one. Promise me you'll not hurt her again, and I shall make no complaint of your conduct."

"Oh, no, missus, no. I wouldn't think of it. Wouldn't do no 'arm to me little saucepan lid."

"Kid . . . eh, child," Mortimer put in.

"Sometimes I don't reelize me own strenth." The man appeared to be considerably cheered by her forgiving attitude.

"Then I shall make no charges. You may release him."

"The lady deals more kindly with you than I would have done in her place. I recognize a scoundrel and a blackguard when I see one. You'll treat your child with greater care if you know what's good for you, and don't let me ever hear of your laying a hand on this lady, or any other for that matter, for if you do I'll have your cobbler's awls no matter who pleads for your release, do you understand?"

"Yus, yer honour, to be sure. All I wus doin' was takin' a ball of chalk by the Turpentine and the lidy attacks me, came between me and me soap and water, no one can do that to an old pot, now can they."

"I'm not a father, but if I were it would be all the more reason to find your conduct reprehensible. Go about your business then." With that, Mortimer released him.

He scrambled anxiously to his feet with an alacrity that belied his girth and retrieved his cap, which had fallen by the water's edge. He popped it on and off his head several times first in the direction of Mortimer, then to the lady, before beating a retreat.

"I'm on me old Edna May. Yer can count on me, yer honour."

"I can count on him to put a knife in my back for a shilling," Mortimer said grimly, watching the retreating figure.

The lady also watched him as she asked, "Could you explain, taking a ball of chalk by the Turpentine?"

"A walk by the Serpentine."

"And cobbler's awls, was it?"

Mortimer flushed slightly. "It's a rather crude anatomical expression, you must excuse me, but it was necessary to make my point."

The lady reached on her arm for something and then looked around.

"What is it? Have you lost something?"

"My money, it's gone."

"So he did harm you after all."

"My purse, it's nothing, but I wanted to give something to this child. She's half starved, I'm sure of it. I expect it was the small boy who was watching who took it."

"The brute probably runs gangs of them, little monkeys, thieving for him."

"If he does, it's hardly their fault."

"No, I suppose not." Mortimer eyed her curiously. "You must excuse my curiosity, ma'am, but I am at a loss to understand what a lady is doing here on her own."

"I came to paint the fritillaries. Early morning or late afternoon is the best time, when the low sunlight passes through their delicate, checkered petals to show such an elegant blending of pink and plum purple. We have them in Oxfordshire, but these I find brighter in hue, more graceful."

She bent down to gather up her paints, which had been scattered during the fracas. The young girl, who had remained, turned to help her while Mortimer went to retrieve her pad of paper beside the water. He held her unfinished painting at arm's length.

"Exquisite, really exquisite, quite perfect, in fact. I dare say we have these little flowers in Shropshire, but I can't lay claim to having noticed them before. It takes a trained eye to show them as you do, ma'am. You are a true artist."

"Not an artist, merely an illustrator. An artist interprets while I only try to relay what I see in nature, though given her beauty, her symmetry, her regularity, her order, it becomes well nigh an impossible task. Occasionally I may tend to exaggerate the shape, the colour or the texture of the leaves or petals, but that is not interpretation, only an attempt to draw attention to details that may be overlooked. And, unlike most illustrators, I find it preferable to sketch or paint the flower in its setting rather than a single, perfect bloom, stark and alone."

"Your eyes, if you will pardon a compliment from a stranger, are not merely fine to behold, but they possess the ability to observe with greater precision than the ordinary variety such as my own."

"There is nothing ordinary in nature, be it plants or eyes,

anybody's eyes." The lady snapped the paintbox closed. "There, all is in order and I am ready to leave. I thank you for your assistance, sir. Good day to you."

The girl stood by, watching them, and Mortimer, reminded that the lady had wished to recompense her, reached his hand into his pocket to draw out a half guinea and give it to her. It was the lady who thanked him, rather than the girl.

"I shall return the money to you if you will give me your direction."

"May I, perhaps, take your painting in its stead?"

"But of course." She was clearly surprised. "It is scarcely worth such a sum."

"It is worth far more. Many people would be delighted to own such work and would willingly pay highly for it."

"You jest. You mean that people would pay for something which is done for pleasure?"

"Pleasure is well worth paying for, either in giving or taking. But has no one before told you that your work is very good?"

"It has been used by a friend of my father's who teaches botany at Oxford. I was told that my work was accurate, suitable for the purpose."

"It is far more than merely accurate. Call yourself an illustrator rather than an artist, but I believe you have few equals."

But the lady's attention had turned to the girl, who continued to stand by, clutching the gold piece in her hand as though it might take wings and fly away.

"Are you sure you are quite all right?" And, dissatisfied with the child's nod, she took a sheet of paper from her pad and, after writing on it, folded it and gave it to the girl.

"Take this. If your father ill treats you again, come to me—you may count upon me to do whatever I can."

"God bless you, mum, and you, kind sir." Then, perhaps afraid that the coin might be taken from her, she caught up her broom and took off at a run.

"Poor child!" the lady murmured.

"Poor, miserable little slattern!" Mortimer gazed after the thin waif. "I'll bet she'll not keep that piece for long."

"But why not? It's hers."

"Not once that father of hers lays eyes on her it won't be, I'll be bound."

"Perhaps I should follow her to see he does her no further harm."

"My dear lady, you cannot expect to protect every child in London from harsh and grasping parents. Besides, I should only have to rescue you again, and more than one rescue a day would be difficult even for St. George. I am, besides, not in the best condition."

"You are ill, sir, I'm sorry."

"Not ill, ma'am, just a trifle white about the gills, from my own doing, but there's nothing like a set-to to make one forget such trivia. My carriage is at your disposal. Allow me to take you home."

The lady glanced dubiously from Mortimer to his closed carriage with Glossop sitting patiently at the reins.

"I think I prefer to go on foot," she said stiffly, awkwardly. "That is, if you would kindly indicate the direction of Devonshire Place. The map I had with me was in my reticule, and I'm not sure that I remember the way."

"Surely you can't believe I can allow you to walk back alone, not after what has just happened. If you insist on returning to Devonshire Place on foot, then I shall have to also, though there are, in my opinion, other forms of exercise vastly superior to walking." One glance at the lady's determined face made him add quickly, "Dancing, for instance."

"I rarely dance, but I do walk a great deal."

"To walk when one might ride bespeaks a spartan nature, but, sobeit, I resign myself to my fate."

"There is no need, sir, I asked only for an indication of the direction."

"I will not allow you to return alone and will brook no more discussion on that point. But may I not give Glossop your paintbox and paper to put up beside him?"

"I am really quite used to carrying them."

"Then give them to me, for it would be most uncomfortable to walk beside you while you carried the burdens."

Brushing aside her demur, he took the articles from her,

and, ordering Glossop to follow at a snail's pace, they set off.

The lady, now more at ease, volunteered, "It is, indeed, a handsome coach, and of such unusual design, wheels of equal size, I have never seen the like before."

Mortimer could not help but feel a flash of pride as he owned, "I designed it myself," adding not a little hopefully, "and I can assure you it is most comfortable."

But the lady's reply, "I am quite sure that it is," gave no encouragement that she might relent and step into the coach. He took consolation in explaining to her the details of its construction.

"Quite ingenious," she said when he had finished, which gave Mortimer the opportunity to wonder whether ladies lacking in fashion and beauty made up for it in their ability to listen and understand.

"If we are to share this expedition together, it is only proper to present myself. I am Mortimer, Charles Mortimer."

The lady acknowledged his introduction with a nod, but they might have continued in silence had not Mortimer prompted.

"If I may make so bold, ma'am, might I enquire your name, for I judge we have more than an hour's walk before us. To cover the distance with your knowing my name while I am quite ignorant of yours seems hardly just."

"I am Mrs. Bransom."

Though her tone did not encourage further comment, Mortimer persisted, "Ah, so it is *Mrs.* Bransom. Somehow I had not taken you for a married lady."

"Why not?" Mrs. Bransom asked quickly and just as quickly seemed to regret that she had shown curiosity regarding whatever he might think about her.

"There is something innocent about you, and, if you will pardon my saying so, you appeared just now to be one of those fearfully earnest, benevolent ladies who thrust upon the world their good deeds. And they, from my observation, are almost always of the single state, perhaps because . . ." He paused briefly. "But I have no right to speculate on that score. Does not your husband object to these long rambles you take on your own, quite unprotected?"

"No."

She was a most uncommunicative lady, and Mortimer, glancing longingly at the empty coach keeping pace with them, began to think it was going to make for a very long walk indeed. Without great interest, he interjected,

"He must trust you implicitly. But then, you are not from London I take it."

Mrs. Bransom, at his side, was walking quickly, at a far steadier stride than any ladies of his acquaintance could claim. Nor would any of those ladies ever wish to be caught dead in the sensible, sturdy shoes she wore.

"It hardly takes a sage to recognize that I am from the provinces," Mrs. Bransom said at last, with more than a hint of sarcasm in her voice.

"I believe you mentioned Oxfordshire. At least you said that the fritillaries here in the park were superior to those found there, brighter in hue, but since, as you pointed out, there are no common eyes and no common flowers, I suppose it may depend on the soil, the moisture, the angle of the sun at the point of Oxfordshire of which we speak."

"I believe you are laughing at me." Mrs. Bransom smiled.

"I wish we might laugh together at something to pass the time pleasantly."

"I may appear to be lacking in discernment, in subtlety, but I am simply not used to the ways of society, of being in the company of those of, of—what do they call it—*le beau monde?*"

"*Le beau monde, le haut ton, le cercle merveilleux,* there are, I suppose, a dozen or so hyperbolic names by which London's society describes itself. I don't consider myself a part of any of them. Chenwyth, my home, is in Wrexford, a Shropshire village, not London."

"Yet everything about you bespeaks the gentleman of all those magnificent French epithets far more than the country squire."

"By this I see that you are determined to discuss me and not yourself. We must have covered a half mile—judging by the pace you are setting rather than my own, for though I hate to confess it I find myself hard put to keep up with you—and all I know is that you are Mrs. Bransom from some unnamed part of Oxfordshire, a county noted for its magnificent stone mansions and perpendicular churches, its university of which I must proclaim its superiority being a product thereof, and its beneficent and artistic matrons."

"Now I know you're laughing at me, but I am determined not to be put out by it. Oxfordshire is, indeed, an important county, not only because of the university, certainly not because it is my home, but the wool from the Cotswolds close to where I live has been one of England's chief sources of revenue."

"Ah, yes, England's revenue. That, it seems, is our country's greatest concern, far more than the men who have died defending her." He hastened to obliterate the bitterness in his tone with a lighter vein. "Well, now it has been narrowed considerably. Since the Cotswold hills barely enter Oxfordshire, my task may not be so difficult after all. Wasn't Burford the centre of the wool industry, or there's Taynton, or perhaps Chipping Norton, or . . ."

"I'm from Mayfield, not far from Taynton. I had no intention to make a secret of it."

A short silence ensued, broken at last by the lady.

"I must apologize if I appear rude, but I confess I greatly detest making conversation. I suppose it is for that reason I much prefer my own company—if I bore myself, I have no one but myself to blame for it."

"How very singular! You are indeed not a lady of London, though I can scarcely think of any lady of my acquaintance, and I include my dear sister Eunice, who does not enjoy conversation for its sake alone and who would not prefer to hear her own voice to any other."

"I must take it that you do not think very highly of the female sex."

"On the contrary, I don't know where I should be without them. I am fond of the company of ladies. I believe that in light conversation they excel. But a discussion between like minds cannot be surpassed, and like minds, from my observation, denotes like gender. I cannot imagine that you are as reticent with other ladies as you are with me."

"You sir, can scarcely be said to be reticent at all."

Mortimer eyed her thoughtfully. "I believe I am to take that as a rebuke."

"Excuse me, perhaps I had no right to speak so, especially after you delivered me from a difficult situation. That poor girl." Mrs. Bransom sighed. "I wonder what will become of her."

"She will probably do her father's bidding until she marries, if, indeed, the man who gets her with child can be brought to do so. Thereafter she will do *his* bidding."

Mrs. Bransom's face became grave, even bitter. "I hate it when the strong prey on the weak."

"It has always been so. It will always be so. It is nature's law."

"You, sir, if you will forgive my frankness, are a cynic."

"I cannot disagree with your assessment of my character, Mrs. Bransom. But it occurs to me I still do not know the events which preceded my coming upon you in the park."

"The little girl, I gather, had been sweeping crossings since early morning and had wandered into the park to rest from her labours. She saw me at work and watched me, but was much too timid to speak, though I tried to draw her out, to show there was nothing to be afraid of. I was explaining to her, just as I do to my brother's children, the enduring values I enjoy from the beauty of the world about me, the perfect relationship of parts one to another, the harmony which shapes nature—all of which was broken by the arrival of that awful man, swearing at her for neglecting her work. He would have taken the very life from her, I believe, had I not intervened."

"You may be lucky that he did not take yours instead."

"My life is not so very valuable."

Mortimer was nonplussed by hearing a remark he had often made, coming from the lips of a woman. They were passing through Knightsbridge with its crowded establishments, when a shopkeeper—bustling from his haberdashery, proudly boasting the Royal Warrant over its door, his attention upon an armload of boxes—walked into the lady's path and might have collided with her had not her companion grasped her arm to pull her aside.

"Take care, clumsy oaf, watch what you're about!" Mortimer snapped.

The shopkeeper, flustered, hastily drew aside and, recognizing Mortimer, made to tip the tall hat he was wearing, causing the boxes to wobble wildly.

"I beg your pardon, me lord, I didn't see you. Excuse me, madam. And a good day to both of you," he called after them though Mortimer, still keeping his hold of Mrs. Bransom's arm, strode on without a word.

"It wasn't his fault. He couldn't see with all those boxes."

"Too intent on his trade to have a care for passers-by, unless he can entice them to buy his wares, then it's all smarm and civility. I'm fed up with English shopkeepers grown fat while others died that they might prosper. I hate their veneer of patriotism covering a rapacious greed. I hate . . ." He broke off and laughed abruptly, as though he had said too much, revealed too much, and resumed his nonchalant air. "But my demure companion from the provinces, Mayfield in Oxfordshire, to be exact, champions a world which must be entirely foreign to her with a frankness, an innocence I don't think I ever possessed. I have no right to ruin it for her."

"Why should this world appear differently to you?"

"We have already established that you observe the world of nature with eyes of greater discernment than mine. I bring my own experiences with me to this world, to these shops, these people, these streets, the costers with their barrows, the very muck in the gutters. You champion causes. I champion nothing."

"Yet you were willing to risk being hurt to protect someone completely unknown to you. I scarcely know how to thank you for your brave act."

He smiled mischievously. "Had you been a man, or a young lad, perhaps I might have ridden by and ignored your difficulty. But I adore to assist ladies, for, who knows, perhaps one day I may demand a kiss as recompense."

Mrs. Bransom flushed. "Are you never serious when speaking to ladies?"

"Never. For a gentleman to speak seriously with a lady can only lead to him being taken seriously or being found an object for ridicule. With an unmarried lady the result is a trip to the altar, one I have no desire to make. With a married lady . . . but that, I am quite sure, is never discussed in Oxfordshire except within the confines of under-graduates' lodgings where they talk of little else."

She made no comment, and as they passed the corner turning into Wimpole Street a flower girl thrust her wares before them.

"Lovely and fresh they are, sir. Flowers to remember you by. Buy some for the lidy."

Mortimer carefully selected a bunch of violets and presented them to Mrs. Bransom.

"For you," he said solemnly. "A bunch of violets for your thoughts—so much less mercenary than a penny, you must agree."

"My thoughts were of the little girl and the terrible life she must lead with such a father." She shuddered slightly. "Men are so barbarous towards those over whom they have dominance."

"You rebuked me for my attitude towards your sex, yet your sentiments are equally harsh towards my own. Are not women often barbarously cruel towards men over whom they have dominance?"

"Ladies with dominance over gentlemen—I know of none."

"Come, come, it is so whenever a gentleman is so foolish as to lose his heart to a lady."

"You lose your heart often?" she questioned and flushed immediately at her own temerity.

"Often." He smiled lazily at her confusion as she turned away to smell the violets.

"I do wish there was something I could do to help the child, but I doubt I shall see her again."

"You need not worry, the city is full of objects for your philanthropy."

"Better a philanthropist than a philanderer," she retorted.

"Perhaps, though at the moment my sympathy is all for myself. I don't know when I've walked so far on hard pavements and cobblestones."

They had reached the corner of Devonshire Place, and Mrs. Bransom slowed her pace.

"This is where I live. I thank you for your company, but there is no need to go any farther."

"I quite understand. The very proper Mrs. Bransom does not wish to be seen accompanied to her door by a perfect stranger, a situation which might lead to misunderstanding, though I should be most happy to explain that you quite exhausted all of my energies with the pace you kept in walking."

Mrs. Bransom smiled. "I have no pity for you, sir, for you chose to walk. Any soreness of foot you may have suffered as a result must be lain at your door."

"Ah, cruelty, thy name is woman," he mocked. "The trouble with philanthropic ladies is that they have no sympathy except for the poor and downtrodden. A blister concealed within a well-made boot invites no charity from them."

"I advise you to bathe your feet in strong alum water, as hot as possible."

"I could expect little gentleness in the cure from such a determined lady. But now we are arrived, confess, were you not more afraid of me than that bully in the park, was that not why you refused to ride as I so sensibly suggested?"

"Perhaps, but all gentlemen are not to be trusted."

"Believe me, with a lady of your obvious respectability and decorum I should long hesitate before overstepping the bounds of propriety." He bowed. "Your servant, ma'am. Perhaps I shall have the pleasure of seeing you again while you are in London."

She retrieved her paintbox from him.

"It has been an instructive afternoon, sir, and I thank you for it. Good-day."

3

A violet in the youth of primy nature,
Forward, not permanent, sweet, not lasting,
The perfume and suppliance of a minute.

Shakespeare
Hamlet, 1601

Penelope Bransom was unaccountably relieved to find, when she entered Lady Halstead's Devonshire Place house, that her hostess, dissatisfied with the gown her daughter, Emmeline, was to wear to Lady Lambourne's ball the following evening, had set off for the dressmaker to demand that she lower the neckline to provide provocation and then set in lace gatherings to conceal such provocation for the sake of propriety. Melissa Woodard, Penelope's younger sister, though quite happy with her own dress, had accompanied them. All the ladies being gone, Penelope was able to gain the seclusion of her room without making any explanation of her late return, nor would the fact that she had been in the company of a strange gentleman cause question.

Before removing her bonnet to don her cap of India muslin, Penelope filled a small vase with water and there arranged the bunch of violets she had been given. On an impulse, she chose two of the largest purple-blue flowers and placed them between the pages of the volume of Thomson's *Seasons*. This book, which her mother had given her, contained two wild columbine from the wreath she had laid on her mother's grave together with a sprig of baby's breath she had carried at her confirmation at St. Anne's the following year when she had assumed responsibility for the disposition of her own soul. The lily-of-the-valley from her wedding bouquet was no longer to be found. Carefully she flattened out the small, fragrant blossoms of that flower Shakespeare had so favoured in his plays and sonnets.

"It came o'er my ear like the sweet sound that breathes upon a bank of violets, stealing and giving odour," she murmured as she finished her task.

She was about to put away her paintbox when, struck by the fascination of the light from the window shining across the delicate nosegay, she set it down and opened it. She began slowly, carefully, though with increasing excitement, to attempt to transfer that colour and translucence onto paper.

Violets stood for modesty and faithfulness. Both were qualities quite naturally hers. She had always been timid as a child, content with her role of passive onlooker to the world, content to be told what was expected of her, what she should do. Possessed of brown hair without the slightest tendency to curl, a nose too short for fashion and a mouth more rose than rosebud, she had frankly admitted to her reflection in the mirror that she would never be chosen as Queen of the May, nor would a prince ever fit a glass slipper on her foot. Yet neither of these realizations completely quelled her romantic imagination, which found an outlet in the world around her—not the world of people but the world of nature. It was not, however, until her father's friend, a botanist from Oxford, presented her with a copy of Mrs. Trimmer's *Easy Introduction to the Knowledge of Nature* that she began to take more than a spectator's interest in that world. She studied its illustrations more carefully than those in the lesson books she shared with her brother, Arthur, thereafter always carrying a sketchbook with her on the long walks she took. For consolation on her mother's death she had been given a paintbox containing only the basic colours: cobalt, sepia, yellow ochre, vermilion, viridian green along with black and white. With these the world of colour was opened to her eyes, a world she had, ever since, been attempting to interpret but never to imitate; that was impossible. Colour, vibrant and exciting, added emotion to her careful outlines. Thoughts she was unable to share with anyone became expressed in the passion of the purple iris, in the flamboyance of the red oriental poppy, in the serene blue of the forget-me-not. She learned to use an old brush and colour stipple on dry paper to give texture to a leaf, drawing its veins precisely with the fine point of a brush kept for such intricate work.

Her work was all consuming, yet her father considered it no more than a suitable pastime for a young girl until his friend took some of her watercolours to illustrate a botany lecture he was delivering at Balliol and thereafter placed requests for specific illustrations. Neither of them considered it necessary to compliment her on the finished illustrations; she received gratification enough from having a useful, enjoyable task to accomplish. She neither expected nor received anything more and was, therefore, unperturbed by lack of praise.

She achieved her utmost serenity in interpreting nature. She would gladly have devoted her life to that task, but when one day her father informed her she was to marry, she had accepted his decision without demur, waiting only to be told the name of her future husband. If she felt any surprise to learn that it was Josiah Bransom of Greystone Hall—a gentleman who held an enviable position in Mayfield, possessor of its largest estate, renowned for his breeding, his piety, far closer in age to her father than her own seventeen years—she did not express it. He was, of course, well acquainted with the Woodards. Penelope had, in fact, known him all her life, though only in that way in which children know adults, with reserve and respect.

The proposal had been made and accepted in the presence of her father, who had been so well pleased that Penelope was sure that she must be also. When repeatedly told that having precious few endowments and precious little fortune, she was lucky to have been chosen by Mayfield's most eligible bachelor, she at last began to feel she had, contrary to her expectations, been fitted with the glass slipper.

That had been a decade ago, a decade which seemed a century, yet she remembered her wedding day at St. Anne's so clearly, it seemed only yesterday. She was sure that it would always be so.

The sound of Lady Halstead's return in the hall below broke into her thoughts. After a cursory yet critical, unsatisfied scrutiny of her unfinished painting, she reluctantly closed her paintbox, glanced in the looking glass to make sure that her cap was set properly on her head and, satisfied that her hair was respectably covered, hurried downstairs.

"Really!" Lady Halstead railed. "Really, Penelope, the dressmaker would argue that the waistline should be gathered in front, but I wouldn't have it. If Emmeline's waist were as tiny as Missy's, it wouldn't matter so, but you know she's far too plump."

"A pleasing roundness is all, Henrietta."

"Plump, downright plump. I dare say she may outgrow it, and of course, once married she will very likely be with child and it would be expected, but in order to reach that pleasant state her waist must be disguised as much as possible, not emphasized with frills and ruffles."

Penelope was glad that Emmeline had gone upstairs with Missy and was not there to hear such criticism. She hastened to console her friend, who had taken on what Penelope considered the arduous duty of bringing out not only her youngest daughter but Penelope's sister also.

"Emmeline doesn't suffer from the awful freckles I had at her age, she has such a lovely colouring that I'm quite sure her glowing cheeks will catch all attention even if her waistline is not exactly the size fashion demands."

"Emmeline is healthy all right, but men, I can assure you, seldom pine over robust health. Their looks are on a woman's form. Besides which, she's so horribly shy, she'll probably not be able to string two words together tomorrow night at her first ball. It's hard being a mother, perhaps it's as well that you will never know how hard it is."

"I suppose," Penelope responded thoughtfully, "although there are times when I believe my feelings for Missy

2 8

are more maternal than sisterly. I suppose it's because almost ten years separate us, or perhaps because she was only thirteen—little more than a child—when she came to me."

"I always thought your father showed remarkably good judgement in sending Missy to live with you on your bereavement. Goodness knows you took your husband's death badly enough; at least it gave you something else to think about. Not that I think you've ever recovered from the shock of his passing. I must say I had hoped when you came to London that you might finally be persuaded to discard that dreadful mode of dress. But no," Lady Halstead eyed Penelope's deep grey cambric with some distaste, "I suppose nothing will ever get you to do so."

Lady Halstead had marvelled at Penelope's continued appearance in mourning so long after the prescribed period— a year had been quite enough for her after Percival had gone, enough for any widow except Penelope Bransom. It was the sign of a man well-loved, a man not to be forgotten was the opinion of Mayfield's inhabitants at such a visible sign of continued grief. They had watched and waited for a pink shawl, a bonnet trimmed with anything but black velvet; none came. And they remembered that melancholy scene at the Hall with the splendid oak coffin displayed upon a bier in the great hall—she, poor thing, had left almost immediately to take up residence in the Dower Lodge, long before it was necessary, but it was said she could not bear to remain there for a single night with his lifeless body. They had craned their necks for a sight of her face at the high mass said for his soul at St. Anne's, but they had been disappointed; it was impossible to see anything beneath her heavy widow's veil. Eventually—some said only because those forbidding weeds of deepest black wore out— she adopted a half mourning, occasionally wearing dark brown or grey, but never again did she resume her normal garb.

And there had been that marble monument marking Josiah Bransom's final resting place, magnificent it was, fit for royalty. But that was not all. She had had installed, above the Bransom pew, a splendid stained glass window depicting, in brilliant hue, their patron saint, Saint Anne, gazing piously down upon the dear departed, whose hands were clasped in everlasting prayer. No, his widow would never forget Josiah Bransom, nor would Mayfield.

She never spoke of him, but the outward manifestation of her grief needed no words. She was quiet, she concealed her feelings, they knew that, so it was natural that she should say nothing. She rarely visited the Hall now that it belonged to his nephew; too many memories, they said. But there were always fresh flowers on his grave, a grave carefully tended by a caretaker well-rewarded for the task of ensuring that no weed dared to trespass on that sacred soil. Yet even as time passed, his widow could not bring herself to look upon that grave without emotion; she always entered St. Anne's by the south portal away from the churchyard. As she sat between Mr. Edward Bransom and her sister, Miss Melissa Woodard, in the Bransom pew with the rainbow hues from the new stained glass window pouring across her face, there was a solemnity about her that defied approach. Not so with Miss Melissa Woodard, who laughed out loud at life, but from Penelope Bransom nothing more than a quiet smile was ever forthcoming.

"Such a pity," Lady Halstead repeated as she had so often before. "Really, Penelope, there is something depressing about that drab garb of yours."

"I'm sorry you feel so. For my part, I don't."

"I know you don't, more's the pity."

Emmeline came down the stairs wearing the pale pink silk with its lowered, lace-trimmed neckline, now lacking the offending gathers.

"There!" Lady Halstead proclaimed in triumph. "Isn't that an improvement?"

"I like it either way," Penelope said.

Melissa Woodard, who had accompanied her friend downstairs, quickly agreed with her sister. "The pink suits Em to perfection. I couldn't wear it nearly as well."

Missy, as Melissa Woodard was known to family and friends, was one of those unusual young women who combine great beauty with an admirable disposition. She had been filled with gratitude when Lady Halstead had offered to bring her out with her own daughter; her sister had not come out and she had never counted on having such an opportunity. Nor would she have it that she was doing a favour to her friend, who was hopelessly timid on her own, though Emmeline would brave anything, or almost anything, even a dreaded introduction to a world of important strangers, with Missy, her best friend, at her side.

Missy, standing beside her elder sister, was taller by far. She had a softness not found in Penelope who, gentle though the lines of her face might be, gave evidence of a core which no one, not even her dearest Missy, might penetrate. Seeing that shadowed darkness in the depths of her eyes, one was never quite sure what she was thinking. With Missy it was exactly the opposite. Not that she chattered inconsequentially, but she did love to talk, to laugh, to enjoy all social occasions which made the visit to London such a pleasure.

Though she had never before left Mayfield, Missy had a natural air of fashion about her: she knew just how to carry herself to show her figure and long, slender neck to perfecton, what to wear to heighten the blue of her eyes, when to smile sweetly, and how to respond to comments from dowager ladies who could be so important to a young lady making her bow to society. She knew without guile, without being told; she was, in fact, a born diplomat, quite unlike her sister, who often said what was in her mind without weighing her words.

"Do stand up, Emmeline, look at Missy, even though you're not as tall as she is—in fact because you are not as tall, you must learn to stand straight and always hold your head high. And do try to be just a *little* more animated. No one will long put up with a girl who is both timid and lifeless."

Emmeline flushed as she always did at her mother's not infrequent rebukes. "I shall try, mama, really I shall."

And Penelope hastened to take her part. "I expect, Henrietta, when you were Emmeline's age you found adults equally formidable, and stuffy, too, not at all easy to talk to. I remember that I certainly did when I was young."

"For goodness' sake, Penelope, anyone would think you were around when Stonehenge was set in place to hear you talk. You've four birthdays, at least, until your thirtieth."

"Three," Penelope corrected quietly.

"Well, three then—at twenty-seven you're not ancient, and I'm sure it would be obvious to everyone if only you wore something just a little more becoming. Don't sit down in your dress, Emmeline, go up and change before you make it unfit to wear tomorrow." When the girls had left, Lady Halstead continued, "If the truth were known, Penelope, I believe you look better now than on the day you married Josiah Bransom. Oh, I know, you were a lovely bride, all brides are lovely, but you were nothing more than a sweet child then. Now there's a quiet beauty about you, though you take great pains to disguise it beneath that drab exterior of yours. Even so, there are times when I see that attractive, vibrant woman, then pouf! Like the seed from a dandelion, she's gone—it's as though you deliberately suppress her."

"I'm sure I don't know what you mean, Henrietta."

"I think that you do. You never wear anything which becomes you in the least. I suppose even those drab colours of yours, well-cut and of fine fabric, could be improved, but I have a suspicion you do it on purpose so that you will never attract another husband."

"I shall never marry again—never, you know that."

"I know, I know, more's the pity, for Missy surely will, and you'll be left at the beck and call of that brother of yours and his wife, summoned for each lying-in, whenever their children need care, or asked to dine only when they need an even number at their table. They'll always know they can count on dear Auntie Penny."

"Since I don't object, I can't see why you should, Henrietta. I have Arthur's children, I love them dearly, each one of them, Beatrice, Sally—well, all of them, each is special in the way only a child is special. If you see the girl I once was in me today, it's because of them. Whatever I do to help Arthur and Phyllis with their children, I shall do as much for Missy when that time comes." Then she added thoughtfully, "But I can't deny when that time does come, I shall miss her dreadfully."

"Well, my dear, loyalty and devotion are fine qualities in a woman, but they don't keep the bed warm, and I hate to see you living to old age with only memories for company." Lady Halstead paused, as though considering, before venturing hesitantly, "You know, Penelope, there are several gentlemen in town to whom I should very much like to introduce you, gentlemen who would appreciate—"

But she didn't finish, for Penelope interrupted with, "No, Henrietta! Please promise to dismiss any such scheme from your mind, otherwise I shall regret having accompanied you to London. I am being quite honest when I say that I never want to remarry, never! You may think my life drab, but I am happy with it. I have my painting and the world of nature all around me—an exciting new world each day. I don't deny I regret not having children of my own, but I have Arthur's children to show that world to—Beatrice is developing a fine hand in her sketching."

"So you told me," Lady Halstead put in drily.

"I'm sorry if I repeat myself, but I am so proud of her. You see, children have so few inhibitions, it takes little effort to make them aware, but it gives me great satisfaction." She paused and shook her head. "No, Henrietta, I have known marriage once; that is enough. I am satisfied with my life. No matchmaking for me—you must promise it."

Penelope's voice as well as her face gave credence to the sincerity of her wish, and her Mayfield neighbour and long-time friend sighed, "Very well. But you mustn't blame me for wishing it were otherwise."

Impulsively Penelope hugged her. "Dear, dear Henrietta. I know you have only my best interests at heart, indeed, the best interests of all of us, but do believe me, I *am* happy in my present state. I desire no changes."

Henrietta Halstead was clearly affected, yet she couldn't help complaining, "Widowed at an age when many girls are only just entering into matrimony, I think it too bad by half the way you've buried yourself alive ever since, worshipping that man's memory for how many years is it—six or seven—far too long. Even here in town you've refused every invitation extended to you. You won't even go to Lady Lambourne's tomorrow, and I can assure you you would find that vastly amusing. I know I always do—it's one of the season's gala events; even those who are only spectators find it great sport. But there, it is your business. I respect your wishes, Penelope. I shall say no more on the subject."

4

Teach not thy lips such scorn, for they were made for kiss-
ing, lady, not for such contempt.

Shakespeare
Richard III, 1592

Though Penelope had refused the Lambourne invitation, as she had all others extended to her in courtesy as a guest at Devonshire Place, she was, much against her will, obliged to attend that particular event, for on the morning of the Lambourne ball, Lady Halstead came down with chills and a temperature, a combination of symptoms that utterly precluded her chaperoning the girls. It was either a case of their not attending, which Lady Halstead found unthinkable, or of Penelope taking her place. Though that possibility was equally unthinkable to Penelope, she reluctantly agreed to do so.

"You may wear anything of mine," Lady Halstead's muffled voice reminded Penelope hopefully as the note was despatched to Lady Lambourne advising her of the change. "The midnight blue satin is not in the least gaudy and would suit you well."

"Thank you, no. I have a brown moiré silk which will do very well."

"I suppose that's the one I've seen you in for the past three Christmasses."

"It's a very handsome dress."

"Nothing is handsome that is so . . . so dismal." And then Lady Halstead sighed, "Oh, my dear, I am sorry, forgive me. I'm just feeling low today."

Penelope plumped her pillows and assured her that everything would be all right, and Lady Halstead refrained from saying anything later when Penelope came to bid her goodnight wearing the offending brown silk and an ivory lace cap. She thought of offering Penelope her new Kashmir shawl, which would have been perfect, but a look in her friend's eyes made her desist. At least she was pleased to note that Penelope carried her mother's fan of sandalwood ornamented with heart's-ease and forget-me-not, wrought in mother-of-pearl, which provided some note of frivolity to a very sombre appearance.

The evening at the Lambournes' proved long and tedious to Penelope. Apart from her sister and Emmeline, she knew no one. Though those young ladies were nominally in her charge, she sometimes thought the reverse to be the case—both of them, even timid Emmeline, were less strangers to their surroundings than was she.

From the moment they entered the ballroom Missy's beauty was remarked upon, and she was deluged with requests to sign her dance card. Emmeline, her card empty, clung to Penelope's side until Mrs. Plunkett-Gall, an imposing dowager who was acquainted with Lady Halstead, suggested that Emmeline join one of her own charges, an affable if rather plain young lady who was also having little success.

"Won't do, Mrs. Bransom," Mrs. Plunkett-Gall reproved Penelope, "won't do to have her sit too long. I don't allow mine to. Can you not find someone for her?"

"I'm afraid I know no one. I am new to London, in fact I am here only because Lady Halstead is indisposed."

Mrs. Plunkett-Gall inspected the room through her gold lorgnette, then waved it ostentatiously in the direction of a foppish young gentleman nearby.

"There's Morton Weathersbee—fifteen hundred a year, most of which he spends on his back, that or the ponies— but good stock and they say he may inherit through a cousin who, he puts it about, is in failing health though when I last saw him I thought he seemed admirably fit. It may be a case of wishful thinking on Mr. W's part, though he is convinced of it. So, judging by that rig he's got up in, is Mr. W's tailor."

"I don't know that Miss Halstead would care for such . . . such a fine gentleman. Even if she would, I'm afraid I don't know how I should go about it."

"My dear!" Mrs. Plunkett-Gall trained her lorgnette upon Penelope at very close range. "Well, since in Mr. W's case I am not interested in him for my own charges, I should be glad to introduce you, and you, in turn, may present Miss Emmeline Halstead, though whether it would result in anything I cannot say. How much has she?"

"How much has who?" Penelope was puzzled by the disconnected flow of Mrs. Plunkett-Gall's conversation.

"What is her dowry, her settlement upon marriage?" Mrs. Plunkett-Gall explained with some asperity.

"I'm afraid I really don't know."

"My dear Mrs. Bransom, that is the very first thing on which you should have full particulars. I wouldn't dream of introducing a girl without knowing it, it would be deceitful and could lead to all sorts of misunderstanding. You *do* have much to learn." Again she trained her lorgnette on Penelope for such a long time that Penelope believed she must be studying every inch of her complexion, every blemish, and she found herself flushing under the scrutiny. "Let me tell you," Mrs. Plunkett-Gall continued at last, lowering her glass, "you will have difficulties with Miss Emmeline Halstead for I can see that she won't take, Mrs. Bransom, mark my words on that point, she won't take. I've been introducing young girls for over a decade now, and she's the type who will never take. Now that other girl with you"— Mrs. Plunkett-Gall waved her lorgnette airily in the direction of Missy, who was dancing with a captain in the Lancers—"the one over there, what's her name?"

"That is my sister, Miss Melissa Woodard."

"Miss Woodard, to be sure. I've heard her spoken of before, though it's the first time I've seen her for myself. Not much money, they say, but she'll never lack for partners. For Miss Halstead, however, there is little hope. Oh, her name's all right, but no looks, no figure, and I doubt she has enough otherwise to make up for that *and* her lack of spirit.

3 7

The best advice I can offer is to take her in for some tea, for if she is seen to sit too long in the same place it will be quite decided that she is a wallflower, and then no one will ever be induced to ask her to dance for fear of being thought unable to find anything better."

Penelope, glad herself to escape Mrs. Plunkett-Gall and her strident voice, clearly audible to all around, thanked her and rose. While Mrs. Plunkett-Gall turned to relay what she obviously felt had been succinct and felicitous advice to Lady Beddows, who sat on her other hand, Penelope hastened to Emmeline to suggest they take the air on the terrace.

It had been a fortunate move, for there, also taking the air, was a young gentleman mopping his head with a large white handkerchief whom Emmeline recognized, after he had folded it up and put it away, as Mr. Gerald Wendling, a friend of her brother who was down from Oxford. Thus it was she who introduced him to Penelope who, after some civil but inconsequential remarks about the weather, the fineness of the evening and the benefits of avoiding the crowd, stepped aside to allow events to take their course.

Like Emmeline, Mr. Wendling was of a retiring nature, and the efforts he had made in merely appearing at such a social event at his mother's behest had caused him to perspire heavily; he had, therefore, been spending most of his time on the terrace. Discovering a young lady, a most pretty young lady, who felt very much the same, inspired Mr. Wendling to pluck up courage and ask whether Emmeline had any dances free and, if so, whether she might spare one for him.

After that, though Emmeline did not dance quite every dance as did Missy, still, her hand was requested by other partners, and when she did sit out, it was to have Mr. Wendling as a sympathetic onlooker beside her.

With Emmeline occupied, Penelope was left to the tender devices of her companion chaperones, Mrs. Plunkett-Gall and Lady Beddows, neither of whom was at all to her liking. No one spoke of anything of interest; there was nothing to do except sit and observe. From time to time she sought refuge outside on the terrace. It was, perhaps, a chaperone's duty to watch her charges constantly—certainly Mrs. Plunkett-Gall and Lady Beddows took obvious delight in doing just that, in fact, following not only their charges but everybody and everything else also—but Penelope could find no benefit in it. She discovered a secluded spot on the terrace from which, alone and unobserved, she might look out upon the beauty of the night, leaving behind the empty pursuit of pleasure within. There she spent much of her time until supper was announced, an insupportable meal which Penelope was forced to endure seated between the Beddows, with Lady Beddows throughout reprimanding her lugubrious husband over Penelope's head, for spending the entire evening in the card room.

It was some time after supper when, as she sat counting the hours and minutes until they might leave, Penelope caught sight of a figure known to her, the gentleman she had met in the park on the previous afternoon. She felt a sense of relief, even pleasure, at the sight of a familiar face, the first that evening. She welcomed the opportunity to talk to someone besides the Beddows and Mrs. Plunkett-Gall, but though he glanced more than once in the direction of the corner where she sat he gave no sign of recognition. It was hardly odd, she realized at last, for he was engrossed with an elegant group on the other side of the room, his attention particularly occupied by a willowy blonde lady who had been pointed out earlier as Lady Georgina Staverton.

Penelope found herself unable to contain her curiosity and was forced to ask Mrs. Plunkett-Gall, "The gentleman talking to Lady Staverton—his name, I believe, is Mr. Mortimer—is he known to you?"

On this occasion Mrs. Plunkett-Gall did not require the use of her glass to identify the gentleman in question before demanding scornfully, "How long did you say you had been in town, Mrs. Bransom?"

"Approximately three weeks."

"Well, wherever it is you are from, and during your three weeks in town, you must have led a very solitary existence indeed not to recognize Lord Charles Mortimer of Waterloo."

"I thought he was simply *Mr.* Mortimer."

"No, no, the Mortimers are an old Shropshire family, fought at Agincourt, I don't know quite how far the earldom goes back, but their fortune was dissipated some time ago. When Lord Charles Mortimer first took his place in society he had precious little to show for himself except those shoulders. I ask you, Mrs. Bransom, who could ignore those shoulders? He wasn't overlooked—a fine figure, expressive eyes and a not unpleasing manner—but none of that puts diamonds on a lady's fingers. I don't mind admitting to you, I said as much to Lady Beddows at the time, I found him attractive, but I wouldn't introduce him to the girls I was presenting. It wouldn't have been right to them or to their mamas, they might have fallen for him and he had nothing, absolutely nothing, and worse yet, no prospects of anything. Now, more's the pity, try as I may he won't have anything to do with any of them." She sighed heavily. "That's what a hero's welcome and twenty thousand a year will do. I hear, also, that some dotty second cousin once removed who previously would have nothing to do with the family, has left him everything. Now he has acclaim, money, and he can have anyone he wants."

"And yet I found him . . ." Penelope broke off. "I mean, he appears to be quite affable."

"To Lady Staverton, of course," Mrs. Plunkett-Gall sniffed. "They say, at least she has it about, that he's still mad for her. Everyone knows that he fell desperately for her when first he saw her, wanted to marry her, but of course it was out of the question at the time and she refused him."

"Yet she appears to dote on him now. I wonder why she married someone else."

"Philby Staverton has extensive sugar holdings in the Indies." Mrs. Plunkett-Gall's tone indicated that her statement explained everything.

"I suppose her parents insisted upon a good match, which makes it rather tragic."

"Oh, don't misunderstand, she wanted it. She may have been smitten with Charles Mortimer, but Georgina Staverton was never one to pine in poverty. She'd never have been dressed like that if she'd taken an impoverished earl. Take that gown she has on tonight—just look at the seed pearl trim on that silver gauze, three hundred pounds at least, probably much more. Mortimer could afford it now, but then it would have been muslin and cambray, and Georgina Staverton would never have stood for that. He took her refusal hard—left London, left England in fact, scraped together money for a commission somehow and off he went to fight in places with long, foreign names—and in doing so he made himself the talk of London. People were anxious to say they knew him. Yes, he didn't do too badly out of it, a handsome annuity for his efforts." Here Mrs. Plunkett-Gall raised her glass to scrutinize the lovely lady who, in emphasizing a point, had placed her fingertips on Mortimer's arm. "I suppose now she's sorry she didn't take him, Philby Staverton always was a dolt. Still, if she had, he'd never have gone off and made a name for himself. Anyway, she makes the best of it. By the look of it she can have her cake and eat it too."

"What do you mean?" Despite herself, Penelope couldn't resist following this gossip with an avidity quite foreign to her.

"Well, even if she didn't voice it about, anyone can see for themselves he still dotes on her. I swear it's the reason he's scorning heiress after heiress pressed upon him, all because of her. Still, mark my words, sooner or later he's going to want an heir for that estate of his—mortgaged to the hilt it was, but now he's got it back and is making a showplace of it, they say. He's going to settle eventually and when that time comes I'm going to find the one for him."

As Penelope watched the pair, there did seem to be an obvious understanding between them.

"He is clearly taken with Lady Staverton," she said, half to herself.

"Of course he is, and he can go on being taken with her. Marriage has nothing to do with that."

"Might the bride-to-be not think otherwise?"

"You are a country mouse," Mrs. Plunkett-Gall reproved.

As she talked to Mrs. Plunkett-Gall and watched Lord Mortimer, Penelope saw that more than once his eyes drifted across to them with a cold, distant stare, and she sensed he knew that he and the lady beside him were the subject of their conversation. She was relieved that he had not remembered meeting her after all and was suddenly ashamed of herself for being party to such gossip. Seeing that Emmeline and Missy were both dancing, she left the ballroom to seek solace in her secluded position on the terrace, to enjoy the music with only the clear air and the freedom of the dark, star-filled sky around her. The moon was rising, a new moon; she should make a wish on it as she always did. As she pondered her wish, she discovered her thoughts had drifted back to the ballroom and to Mortimer. She shook herself and resolutely decided she would think of him no more and wished herself freed from such banality. Yet even as she did so, Shakespeare's line—Oh, swear not by the moon, the inconstant moon, that monthly changes in her circled orb—crossed her mind to mock her resolution.

At that moment she became aware that she was not alone; two figures had come out of the ballroom and were strolling in her direction. There was no doubt who the gentleman was, the very one she had resolved not to think of, and, as they approached closer, she could clearly see that the lady with him was Georgina Staverton.

Had it been possible she would have left her niche immediately, but to do so must reveal her presence and cause possible embarrassment, especially since their closeness to one another bespoke their intimacy. She shrank back into the shadows and prayed they would soon move from her view. But instead, when they were almost immediately before her, they stopped, and with horrified fascination she watched as Mortimer took the lady in his arms to kiss her with a passion, an intensity that made Penelope catch her breath. It was scandalous that she should be witness to such intimacy, such obvious ecstasy as the lady's sighs betrayed— Penelope felt it an affront that a lady should return those kisses with obvious fervour, clinging to him as she did. She should not watch, she knew she should not, and she tried to close her eyes but found herself unable to keep them closed. If only they would go away! She was terrified she might be found, how discomforting it would be for all of them. She scarcely dared breathe as she waited for the embrace to end.

One kiss led to another. Inside the music was finishing, the dance at an end. Surely they would be missed. There was a whispered exchange of which she heard every word, a *rendez-vous* arranged for the following evening, and at last Lady Staverton tore herself away and returned inside. But still Penelope could not move, for Mortimer stood still, and when at last he moved towards the door close by, he seemed to be looking directly at her. She held her breath, waiting for him to pass, closing her eyes, and then gasped as a hand firmly and surely grasped her arm.

"Ah, so it is Mrs. Bransom after all. I thought so, though it is more the style of Mrs. Plunkett-Gall or Lady Beddows to hide themselves away and eavesdrop on others, but perhaps they gave that task to the newcomer to their gaggle of gossips. I must confess to finding myself surprised to see you among them and not a little disappointed, for I had taken you for different mettle. I've been mistaken before, however, and I don't suppose this will be the last time I'm erroneous in my judgement. You must be pleased. Your place amongst them is assured once you carry back your lascivious morsel of gossip, sure to be the *bon mot* of the evening. . . ."

"I assure you, sir, I have no intention . . ." Penelope began indignantly.

"Of course you don't," Mortimer agreed calmly. "But just to aid you in your resolve, or else to make your account more accurate—this may serve either purpose."

Before Penelope could guess—or protest—his intent, Mortimer had taken her in his arms to plant a kiss on her lips, very much as she had seen him kissing Lady Staverton moments before, though perhaps there was more deliberation, less passion in the performance. Penelope, startled, resisted little—later she could not be completely certain she had not returned that kiss, though if she had, she told herself, it was only in the shock of the moment and not simply because she had never been held or kissed in that way before.

Her embarrassment and confusion were apparent when he released her, but all he said was, "I wasn't altogether wrong in my assumption yesterday—I suspected that despite your being every inch the respectable provincial matron, or perhaps because of that, it would be very satisfying to kiss those lips of yours—but undoubtedly your husband has told you so many times."

"How dare you, sir! To mention my husband at such a moment shows, as I suspected, that you have no compunction whatsoever. I shall not discuss him." To speak at that moment of her widowhood seemed to Penelope only to invite further advances.

"I'm not particularly keen on discussing husbands myself, come to think of it," he concurred blandly. "They're a boring lot, always in the way when least required. It is a sorry thing for a gentleman to become a husband, an onerous yoke I am not anxious to assume with all of the amusements life has to offer."

"I can only hope, Lord Mortimer, that yours are not the ways of the average London gentleman, since I am with two young ladies who are at this moment being introduced to your world."

"My dear madam, I can assure you that there is nothing average about me. To be average is to be mediocre and that is not a quality to which I have ever aspired."

"There is such a thing as common decency which should guide you in your . . . your impulses. Your embraces may be welcomed in some quarters, but I assure you they will never be welcome in mine."

"I seem to think I warned you yesterday that I might steal a kiss in repayment for my aid."

"Then you have taken it, and I trust you are satisfied, for you will never receive another."

"Perhaps I may have reason to remind you of those words at some future time, my dear Mrs. Bransom. But I must not

4 4

detain you. Undoubtedly you are anxious to carry your tale to your good companions, and your story now will provide them with far more accurate fare than mere conjecture. Nothing can prevail over an eyewitness account unless it be that of a protagonist in the plot." He seemed to delight in her obvious discomfort. "I regret that my discovery of your hiding place must preclude its continued use for such illuminating, albeit nefarious, purposes."

"You, sir, are insufferable. Your audacity confounds me. I shall consider that you do me a great favour by never again addressing me."

Head high, with as much dignity as she could muster, Penelope pushed past Mortimer, ignoring his bemused smile. As she took her place in the ballroom, she kept her eyes lowered for fear they might betray something of her confusion to her companions. They must leave as soon as the dance was over. She would make some excuse to the girls, a headache perhaps; that would not be altogether wrong, for she certainly did not feel well.

Just as Penelope felt that she was recovering her composure, she saw Lord Mortimer enter the room and felt his eyes drift towards her. He bowed to her as he passed, causing Mrs. Plunkett-Gall to demand with some surprise, "But are you acquainted with Lord Mortimer, Mrs. Bransom?"

"No, yes, I mean . . . we have met," Penelope replied in a cold voice which to anyone except Mrs. Plunkett-Gall would have signalled she wanted no further discussion of the matter.

"But, my dear, how very fortunate for your girls!"

"Why, how can it affect them?"

Mrs. Plunkett-Gall became exasperated. "Is it not obvious? He's such a catch, why did you not present them to him the moment he walked into the room? I should certainly have done so had I been in your position. After all," she sniffed, "he did acknowledge you."

"As you pointed out earlier, he has been occupied since his arrival. Besides, from all that I know . . . that you have said, it would appear he is hardly a fit companion for young ladies."

Mrs. Plunkett-Gall laughed. "You owned it yourself, Mrs. Bransom, and every word confirms it, you really are a newcomer to town. Because Lord Mortimer finds pleasure with ladies such as Lady Staverton has nothing whatsoever to do with his being a fit companion for young, marriageable ladies. There, I can assure you, he behaves most decorously, more's the pity, for it makes entrapment virtually impossible."

"Entrapment!" Penelope protested. Her companion suddenly lifted a finger to her lips to silence her, and an over-eager smile wreathed her face. Turning, Penelope saw that Lord Mortimer was approaching them.

"Mrs. Bransom," he greeted her, his manner all charm and dignity. "How delightful to meet you again. You did not mention that you would attend the Lambournes' ball. Perhaps you might do me the honour of presenting me to the charming young ladies who are with you."

He smiled down at her, sure of himself, enjoying her annoyance and discomfort as a thousand retorts rose to her lips, none of which she dared to utter before Mrs. Plunkett-Gall, Lady Beddows and the other ladies in their corner of the room who all had their eyes upon her. She watched the twinkle in his deep blue eyes as she swallowed her anger and presented him to Emmeline and Missy, whereupon Lord Mortimer asked Emmeline to stand up with him for the Devonshire Minuet. Though thoroughly intimidated, she dared not refuse, and when she returned to Penelope's side it was to say how very kind her partner had been at her clumsiness.

"I thought you acquitted yourself beautifully, Emmeline. Now, where is Missy, for we must leave."

But Missy's hand was already being requested by Lord Mortimer for the next dance, and Penelope could do nothing but give her approval. To do otherwise would surely have caused a scene; as it was, there was a murmur around the room at Lord Mortimer choosing to dance with eligible ladies.

"How I underestimated you," Mrs. Plunket-Gall murmured *sotto voce* at her elbow, watching Missy's grace and beauty coupled with Mortimer's debonair form. "What a splendid turn of events! Who knows where it may lead."

"Nowhere, for we must leave immediately after the set is over."

"How very clever—to remove your girls now that their names are on everyone's lips; it can only serve to enhance qualities which are otherwise quite unremarkable. You are far more astute, Mrs. Bransom, than I had thought."

Penelope ignored her. She was determined also to ignore Mortimer when he returned. She stood aside, pretending to be intent on Lady Beddows long description of her eldest daughter's labour pains, but to no avail, for he intervened with,

"Mrs. Bransom, if I may claim your attention—I must tell you how charming I find your sister and her delightful friend."

Penelope acknowledged the compliment with the barest nod, but he made no move to leave.

"Now, perhaps, you will do me the same favour. It is a country dance next, I believe."

Penelope flushed. He was determined to torment her for having unwittingly been a witness to his conduct with Lady Staverton. She would gladly have cut him yet every eye was upon them. The only pair of eyes she herself was aware of were those of unholy blue, inscrutable in expression.

"I thank you, sir. I seldom dance, and it was certainly not my purpose in coming here this evening."

"I did not enquire your purpose, merely whether you would do me the honour of standing up with me."

"We are on the point of leaving."

"Another time, perhaps."

She made no reply but, summoning Emmeline and Missy, made her departure. At the door she realized she no longer had her sandalwood fan; perhaps she had dropped it on the terrace or beside her chair. No matter, nothing would induce her to return to search for it among those clacking tongues and that insufferable gentleman.

5

Maidens must be mild and meek
Swift to hear and soft to speak.
           James Kelly
           Complete Collection of Scottish Proverbs,
           1721

It was her habit to rise early, but having returned from Lady Lambourne's at an unusually late hour, by the time Penelope descended the stairs the following morning she found that Lady Halstead had preceded her to the breakfast room. She was greeted by, "But my dear, I simply can't believe it. However did you manage it?"

"Manage what?" Penelope asked from the sideboard where, rejecting the potted meats and smoked haddock, she selected only a hot roll and sliced apple to have with her coffee.

"Why, don't be sly now," Lady Halstead went on as she sat down. "I couldn't credit it, but already I've received two notes mentioning oh so casually that Lord Mortimer stood up with both Emmeline and Missy last night. How did you bring it about?"

"I'm quite sure I had very little to do with it."

"But he never asks young ladies to dance, young, single ladies that is. It is well known that he chooses his partners among certain ladies—how should I say—ladies who have husbands already. His dancing with our girls has caused quite a stir."

"Perhaps." As she sipped her coffee, she remembered his words on the terrace and unwittingly repeated them. "He may not be mediocre, yet I'm not at all sure that he is a good influence."

"What can you mean?" Lady Halstead laid down her knife and fork and turned to Penelope in astonishment. "How on earth could England's hero be mediocre or a bad influence? I fail to understand you this morning, Penelope."

"Well, you said yourself the ladies with whom he spends his time are ladies of some experience. . ." She broke off abruptly, wondering if he had taken her for such a lady— was that why he had behaved towards her in such a fashion? Her cheeks flushed at the thought.

Lady Halstead, misunderstanding that flush, responded, "Despite being married and widowed, Penelope, there are times when you are quite naive. Perhaps it comes of spending all your life in a village the size of Mayfield though, goodness knows, neither your father nor your husband drew their acquaintance solely from the village. Surely you must know that a gentleman may amuse himself where he chooses."

"That, Henrietta, I surely do know," Penelope replied wryly. "And Lord Mortimer did amuse himself last night, of that I am assured, though whether his amusement was confined to dancing with Missy and Emmeline is another matter."

As much to divert Lady Halstead's attention as anything else, Penelope turned to Emmeline to ask, "Did you enjoy dancing with Lord Mortimer?"

"It was quite pleasing," Emmeline replied.

"What did he say to you?" her mother pursued anxiously.

"That I was very light on my feet, mama, and that I looked very well in pink."

"Very well in pink!" Her mother beamed. "You were right, Penelope, about that dress. And what did you say, dear?"

"Nothing, mama."

"Nothing! Emmeline, how many times must I remind you of the importance of casual, spontaneous conversation— you really must master it. First you may speak of the size and crush of the room; next you may comment on any mutual acquaintance you may have—only most generally, mark you, for you don't want it supposed that you gossip; then, if all else fails, you may speak of the weather. What could be more simple than that, I ask you?" Her mother's lips pursed in annoyance.

"I forgot, you see, I was concentrating on my steps, mama. You know that dancing does not come naturally to me as it does to Missy. I have to think about it, and I cannot think about my steps and talk at the same time."

"What *am* I to do with her?" Lady Halstead turned to Penelope in exasperation, and Penelope, contrite that she had brought about this turn of the conversation, put in quickly, "She danced very prettily, Henrietta, indeed she did. Mrs. Plunkett-Gall remarked to me how well she looked on the floor."

"And Lord Mortimer didn't mind not talking, mama. He said that most ladies talk a great deal too much and that silence is more eloquent than words."

Lady Halstead was mollified. "Well, if he said so and if Mrs. Plunkett-Gall thought you pretty, you must have acquitted yourself quite well. And Missy, I've no doubt, gave a good account of herself?"

"It would seem so," Penelope agreed quietly.

"Wouldn't it be marvellous if he developed a preference for one of them," Lady Halstead mused, before demanding, "But you haven't yet told me how you brought it about. Mrs. Plunkett-Gall says in her note that you were already acquainted with him—though her information rarely errs, on that point I am sure she is mistaken."

Penelope carefully finished buttering her roll before replying. "I did meet him in Hyde Park the day before yesterday—I had gone to paint the fritillaries, there is one spot where they grow in profusion—and he offered to escort me back to Devonshire Place."

"He saw you all the way back from Hyde Park in his carriage?"

"No. Actually, we walked."

"*Walked* all the way from Hyde Park to Devonshire Place! He accompanied you, and you said nothing of it?"

"I forgot," Penelope said lamely.

"Forgot! Why, you must have been in his company close to two hours."

"No, it was hardly more than an hour, really. You know I prefer to walk at a steady pace."

"You're splitting hairs, Penelope. One hour, even, the point is that you made no mention of it."

"It seemed of little importance. I didn't know who he was; he introduced himself, but I didn't recognize his name. It just didn't seem noteworthy."

"Not noteworthy, the hero of Waterloo! Surely you must have heard of him."

"I heard a great deal of him last night. His name was on everyone's lips, but until then I had not. I'm afraid I bury myself in nature to the detriment of current events."

"Well, perhaps it was refreshing to him that you refrained from fawning all over him—I know he detests the way Mrs. Plunkett-Gall does so. That lady, by the bye, has written specifically asking that I bring you to her afternoon assembly next week. It seems she must have taken a liking to you."

"I was unaware of it. I'm afraid I must refuse. You know I don't attend these things. I wouldn't have done so last night had you not been indisposed—I wish it had not been necessary then, indeed I do."

"Well, in view of the way the evening turned out, I can hardly agree with you. I am glad you went."

"And I am glad to see that you are feeling better today. I hope you remain in good health."

"Thank you, dear, I am much recovered." Lady Halstead rose from the table. "You won't mind my leaving you to finish alone, but I think I should take Emmeline to have a new bonnet made, a bonnet trimmed with pink daisies or roses—I suppose pink roses would be more suitable. And perhaps a pelisse of a matching shade. She does look well in pink."

Penelope lingered over the coffee after Lady Halstead had left the table, her thoughts returning involuntarily time and time again to the previous evening. She was still wondering whether Lord Mortimer had behaved in such a fashion because he treated all ladies so, when the footman came in to announce, in disapproving tones, that there was a young person below who refused to leave without seeing her.

"Where is she?" Penelope asked.

"In the servant's quarters, madam."

"Well, do show her up."

"Very well, madam, if you say so," was the reluctant reply.

Even more disapproving was his expression as he showed into the breakfast room an angular, dirty waif whom Penelope immediately recognized as the street sweeper she had met in Hyde Park. She took her by the hand.

"My dear! I am so glad you came. Are you all right?"

"Well, yes and no, mum. 'E's worse to me now, worse than before, so I come, you said I could."

"Indeed I did, and I meant it. Sit down. A cup of hot chocolate I'm sure will not be amiss."

As she gulped the hot chocolate and the potted meat Penelope had given her, the girl explained, "I didn't keep that bees and 'oney more than ten minutes afore 'e took it off me," and seeing Penelope's puzzlement, "the money, the gold piece the gentleman give me. It's gone, course, and 'e tole me to get out on the streets."

"Back to your sweeping," Penelope prompted sympathetically.

"Not sweeping, mum, 'e wants money for blue ruin, so 'e's gone to find something to wear to show me thousand pities," her thin hands indicated her barely burgeoning breasts, "to put me on the streets as a Jane Shore. 'E says I'll get a sight more from Friar Tucking than I will from sweeping, but I'm scared. I don't want to."

Though she could not understand the girl's words, there could be no mistaking her father's plans for her, the very thought of which horrified and revolted Penelope.

"What is your name, my dear?" she asked gently.

"Meg Watkins," the girl said, biting off a large piece of bread spread with potted meat as though fearing unless she swallowed it whole it might be taken from her.

"And how old are you?"

"Thirteen," was the muffled reply.

Thirteen—and her father wanted to send her out on the streets to—why, it didn't bear thinking about. That was the age Missy had been when she'd come to live with Penelope at the Lodge after Josiah Bransom had died. Missy had been a child then, a mere child, and this girl, despite her knowledge of the world, was no more.

"You'll not go out on the streets, Meg. I shan't allow it," Penelope affirmed.

"'E's set on it, mum. 'E's me dad. I got to." The girl swallowed the food in her mouth before going on. "'E wants the money. I can't cross 'im. I got to do what 'e says."

There was no arguing with that—fathers were to be obeyed. Even though Missy had lived with her, up until his death her father had ruled on every matter, however small, just as he had with Penelope until her marriage. It was a role her father had expected to resume after she became widowed, but then Penelope had been firm; if marriage and subsequent widowhood had done anything for her, it had given her a measure of control over her own life.

She looked with compassion at the waif sitting across from her, reaching for yet another slice of bread. She was half-starved, and looked even younger than her thirteen years. Penelope couldn't bear to think of her on the streets.

"You shan't, Meg, you shan't go out and . . . and sell yourself."

"But I got to get money fer 'im, 'e'll kill me if I don't. Sweepin's not enough—a few coppers a day is all. But 'e says even though I'm skinny and young there's lots of gents like 'em like that."

Penelope shuddered. "Look, Meg, my sister and I are in need of a lady's maid. How would you like the position? We can train you and pay you ten shillings a week. You may give your father some of that, but I'll not allow you to part with all of it. What do you say?"

"Cor, a lidy's maid!" The girl's face shone with pleasure and just as quickly it clouded. "I don't know if I could."

"Of course you can. I must warn you, however, that when the season is over we shall return to Mayfield, where we live;

that's in Oxfordshire, quite far from London, and very small by comparison."

"Oxfordshire!" Meg's face lit up. "Me mum come from there—she's dead—died when I was born, but me dad's mum told me that."

"Then perhaps it wouldn't be so strange for you. We'd take good care of you."

"Oh . . . do you reely mean it?" Meg's face flushed and her hands trembled as she spoke.

"You will do us a great favour by agreeing to stay with us," Penelope said gravely.

So it was that Meg Watkins came to stay at Devonshire Place to learn a variety of skilled and difficult duties under the watchful, often supercilious, gaze of Lady Halstead's maid. Unlike a valet, who was aided in his task of caring for his gentleman by the tailor, the hatter and the linen draper, the lady's maid assumed full charge of the care of her mistress's wardrobe and toilet. Meg learned that while wool dresses might be brushed, the same method would ruin silk, and only the merest rubbing with a piece of merino of similar shade would restore its lustre; muslins and similar light materials required a simple shaking. She learned to dust bonnets with a feather plume and to take special care of that mark of a lady, her *chausserie* or footgear. After ruining several of Penelope's muslin caps, she found that in ironing it was essential to have an immaculately clean ironing blanket and that the fire to heat the iron must be neither too hot nor too cold. She cleaned silk ribbons with a mixture of gin, honey and soft soap, thinking all the while how her father would deplore such waste of blue ruin. But it was in dressing the hair that she excelled. She made hairwash from a pennyworth of borax mixed with rosemary water, and a pomade for after washing from lard, olive oil, castor oil and elder-flower water. Her fingers worked so nimbly with curling papers, bandeaux, and frizettes—brushing, parting, crimping, curling, and braiding the hair into elaborate coiffures—that on special occasions her services were sought by Lady Halstead and Emmeline in preference to their own maid.

With good and regular nourishment, Meg's slight, angular frame gradually filled out, her eyes lost their hunted, melancholy air, and her hair, once clean, was found to be an attractive shade of auburn instead of mousy brown. She learned to speak in a clear, modulated voice, and to carry herself erect and tall in her new grey and white uniforms and the dimity dresses Penelope showed her how to make.

If Meg loved her life at Devonshire Place, it was no more than Penelope loved having her there. As with Missy and with Arthur's children, Meg's was a young life placed, for a time at least, in Penelope's hands, to cherish, to mold. No greater gift could have been hers.

6

Visits should always give pleasure—if not the coming then the going.

Portuguese proverb

Much as she tried to eradicate all thoughts of Lord Mortimer and what had occurred on the terrace at Lady Lambourne's, Penelope could not. At most inopportune moments these would recur: when morning visitors called at Devonshire Place and his name arose, as it so often did; during a pause in conversation at table; or, as on this morning, while she was writing letters. When, lost to her immediate surroundings, her thoughts turned back to that moment, her cheeks would become diffused with the brightest pink at the remembrance. It was unthinkable that a gentleman, a virtual stranger, had embraced her in such a fashion—utterly unthinkable, yet she thought it and blushed at the thought. Lady Halstead might demand, with some concern, whether the room was too warm or might she not be coming down with a nasty spring cold, forcing Penelope to make excuses, to speak less than the truth. It was all too provoking.

In writing to her brother that morning, her thoughts drifted from her assurances that she would be home for Phyllis' lying-in—her fifth in as many years of marriage to Arthur, though fortunately there was plenty of room for their ever-enlarging brood since Arthur had inherited Kerswell at their father's death. As she momentarily forgot the domestic scene at what had once been her own family home, again she experienced that pang of anger mingled with something else, shame perhaps. The thought that Mortimer had dared to kiss her, as though his exalted status as a military hero gave him that right—more than that, that she had allowed it, even for a moment—made her heart beat faster, her cheeks grow crimson, so that she was glad she was alone, her confusion unseen, without fear of intrusion since she had instructed the servants never to admit visitors when Lady Halstead was out.

The sudden opening of the door to admit the footman, immediately followed by the very gentleman who was the cause of her confusion, accompanied by one other, was therefore a total surprise.

"Not all the ladies are abroad then, I see," Lord Mortimer began with infuriating assurance. "I am glad that I insisted on being shown in. Mrs. Bransom, please allow me to present Colonel Rodney Bullerton, an old and trusted friend of mine. Having seen your sister, Miss Woodard, at a rout the other evening, and discovering it was within my power to effect an introduction to her, nothing would do but that we come to Devonshire Place without delay. Is that not so, Bully?"

Colonel Bullerton's murmured words of assent, swiftly followed by apologies for their intrusion, convinced Penelope that the idea had not been wholly his.

"Your visit, I fear, is in vain. Did the footman not tell you that my sister has accompanied Lady Halstead and her daughter on their morning calls?"

Penelope's tone could not have made her reluctance to receive Lord Mortimer more plain. Yet it seemed lost on that gentleman who, after the merest pause in which he searched out the chair closest to her, agreed, "He did. But we have no objection to waiting, do we, Bully?" And he proceeded to seat himself opposite her, motioning his friend to take a seat also. Penelope was enraged. How dare he inflict his presence upon her?

"I have no idea when they may return. Lady Halstead is at home on Tuesday," she said pointedly, making no effort to disguise her coldness and unwillingness to receive them, but it went unheeded by Lord Mortimer, as did his friend's obvious discomfort at their cool reception.

He replied with all aplomb, "I know Colonel Bullerton will be abysmally disappointed if we rush off; for my part, I have no objection at all to awaiting their return."

Though convinced that Mortimer did nothing except what he himself wanted, Penelope felt obliged to call for refreshments since he showed no sign of departing. Determined, however, to do nothing more to add to their welcome, she returned to her letter.

Lord Mortimer was not easily discouraged. "I have frequently seen Miss Woodard and Miss Halstead since the Lambourne ball, but nothing of you, Mrs. Bransom. I trust you have been quite well."

"Quite."

"You do not go out much in society?" he pursued.

"I prefer not to."

"Yet you went to the Lambournes'. Did something there discourage you from continuing to frequent London's amusements?" His eyes, those startlingly blue, penetrating eyes, questioned her as much as the deliberation of his words.

"I daresay nothing that happened at the Lambournes' differed greatly from what happens at other such events," she replied with asperity. "I was obliged to accompany the young ladies that evening since Lady Halstead was indisposed."

"But you miss a great deal. I must say I am finding this season livelier than last."

Having heard from Lady Halstead that Sir Philby Staverton had recently departed to tour his Jamaica plantations, leaving his wife in London, Penelope did not doubt that Mortimer was, indeed, finding amusements particularly to his liking.

She returned to her letter and, had it been possible, would have completely ignored him, yet he kept up a steady flow of conversation, asking her opinion of the court dresses with the new hoops—she had none—or whether she had read the article on calumny in the *Ladies Monthly Museum,* which he had picked up from the table—she had not. Undaunted by her terseness, he continued blandly, "But the weather, surely you must consider it exceptionally fine, for I swear the sun has shone every day this week. In fact, for one disinclined to rise before noon, I have, at times, found it particularly obtrusive in announcing its presence."

Recognizing Lord Mortimer was resorting to that most innocuous of subjects, the one Lady Halstead recommended when all else failed, Penelope responded tartly, "It is indeed fine, sir, and tomorrow it may rain, and the summer may be short or long—it seems it is only of import if it causes one's feet to get wet, or one is unduly warm, or perhaps in need of a greatcoat when none is at hand."

"But as a nature lover I should think, Mrs. Bransom, that topic would be of interest to you where others have failed."

"Only insofar as the sun affects light and shade, or heavy dew causes a drop to form upon a rose. Since, this morning, I am endeavouring to complete a letter to my brother rather than to paint an object from nature, it is of little import."

"But you wish it were otherwise, is that it? And you wish me at the devil, is that not so?"

"I am always at my most serene when I am alone with work I enjoy. I have told you earlier, I am not a social person. Perhaps I should apologize for not entertaining you in better fashion. I did, however, warn you that Lady Halstead was out."

"But I am not in the least bored." And again, as those deep blue eyes fixed themselves upon hers, Penelope felt he spoke no more than the truth—that he was greatly enjoying himself, and her discomfort and annoyance grew.

In the light of this strained situation, Penelope longed for a diversion, though not the one that occurred, for when the ladies arrived at last, they were not alone. Accompanying them were two gentlemen, one of whom, Sir Reginald Palfry, was known and quite plainly disliked by Lord Mortimer; the other, Mr. Edward Bransom, was only too well known to Penelope.

On being presented to Mr. Bransom, Mortimer made it clear his dislike of Palfry extended to his companion also. Cursorily his eyes travelled critically from Edward Bransom to Penelope and then back again. Bransom, recognizing in Mortimer the hero of Waterloo, proceeded to wax eloquent on his bravery for his country. Such effusions were never welcomed by Mortimer, and that particular panegyric appeared to please him even less than usual, for, with Bransom in mid-sentence, he announced his departure.

This sudden decision, after having waited so long to meet the charming Miss Woodard and finding her every bit as delightful as he had supposed her to be, caused Colonel Bullerton to entertain a certain degree of grievance. But despite Bullerton's grimaces and Lady Halstead's cajoling, Mortimer was not to be prevailed upon to stay. Indeed, while he had professed to be awaiting the return of the ladies, their arrival seemed only to signal his departure. Not a little of his displeasure, however, could be placed at the door of Mr. Bransom's effusions; the other gentleman, with whom Mr. Bransom was staying, was also little to his taste. Bowing to the company, Mortimer withdrew, leaving Colonel Bullerton little choice but to follow reluctantly in his wake.

7

Second marriages are lawful, but holy widowhood is better.
                         St. Augustine
                         On the Good of Widowhood, ca. 413

"**M**y dear Lady Halstead," Mr. Bransom began as soon
as the door closed behind them, "why, I had no idea you
numbered Lord Mortimer among your acquaintance. You
never mentioned it before. Your reticence on such a lofty
and inspiring connexion does surprise me, though your
modesty on that score does you credit."

"I am afraid I can make no such claims," Lady Halstead
protested. "It is Penelope who introduced us to Lord Mortimer."

"Indeed!" Mr. Bransom's eyebrows shot up in astonishment as he directed a none too kindly gaze upon his uncle's
widow. And though she would have preferred to say nothing, she knew that to leave his implied question unanswered
would only further strain an already tenuous relationship.

"I had been sketching in Hyde Park, and Lord Mortimer
assisted me in finding my way back, that is all."

"That is all indeed!" Lady Halstead interposed. "He
walked all the way home with her, walked, mark you. And
at the Lambournes', apart from dancing with our girls, I
have learned from Mrs. Plunkett-Gall, requested the favour
of her hand in a dance; is that not so, Penelope?"

Penelope knew that Lady Halstead's remarks were well
meant, but she wished they had never been uttered. More

than that, she wished Mrs. Plunkett-Gall's gossiping tongue would remain forever silent in regard to her affairs. She responded as calmly as she could, "I explained that I did not dance."

"For a widow it would hardly be seemly." Her late husband's nephew pursed his thin lips in disapproval.

"Really, Mr. Bransom, after all these years, I wonder you don't persuade Penelope to dispense with that horribly drab manner of dressing."

"It's hardly my place to rule on such matters," was his unctuous reply. He turned to intervene in the conversation underway between Missy and his uncle's friend, Sir Reginald Palfry, who appeared quite as taken with that young lady as had Colonel Bullerton earlier.

The sight of Edward Bransom leaning across to pay heavy compliments to her sister, following her every move, her every word, brought back to Penelope only too clearly the main reason why she had been glad that Lady Halstead had insisted upon this London visit. Initially when the proposal had been made to bring out Missy in London with Emmeline, Penelope had not been overly enthusiastic, for theirs was a quiet, uneventful life. But her last painful visit to Greystone Hall the previous month had quite abruptly decided her in favour of the plan.

It had been Lady Day. She rarely visited the Hall except on quarter days when she was required by Mr. Edward Bransom to do so in order to receive the settlement bequeathed by her husband, which he punctiliously, precisely, and begrudgingly doled out to her. It was just as though the money was his instead of rightfully hers; it would, of course, revert to him should she remarry or break the terms of her husband's will, but she would never do either, never.

The smile of welcome Mr. Bransom had extended to her on her arrival that day, half-hearted at best, had disappeared entirely on finding that she had come alone.

"But your dear sister is not with you—I trust she is well."

"Quite well, I assure you; however, she is busy today."

"Preparing clothes for the charity basket, no doubt."

"No, this time Missy is making clothes for herself. She has

been invited by Lady Halstead to go to London with Emmeline, and though it is as yet not quite decided, she is making arrangements should it come about. If she does go, she will need many things, and for that reason I should much appreciate an advance of next quarter's allowance together with the one I am here to receive today."

"Indeed!" Mr. Edward Bransom, settled into the leather armchair her husband had always occupied, was clearly unhappy. For Penelope, facing him from the small Chippendale chair that had been hers while the Hall was her home, the surroundings were filled with memories.

"I cannot recommend the plan. No, London is not at all the place for so young, so delicate and charming a creature as Miss Melissa Woodard. To go to that iniquitous city, to be introduced to . . . to goodness knows who, to go without the protection of a gentleman. No, I cannot agree to it at all."

"Mr. Bransom, while your concern is appreciated, I should point out that I shall be with my sister. In truth, even if I were not, I am quite convinced that Lady Halstead would not introduce anyone to Missy whom she would not also present to her own daughter. I have implicit faith in her judgement." And when Edward Bransom's frown showed no sign of vanishing, she went on, "I venture to say, too, it is hardly for you to agree or disagree on the worth of the plan. You may, under the terms of my late husband's will, have some measure of control over my activities, but you have none at all over my sister's."

"Mrs. Bransom! My dear Mrs. Bransom!" he interjected. "Why must you always misunderstand me so? I think only of the welfare of you and your dear sister, whether required by law to do so or not. I feel it is my right, indeed my duty, to guide you. Don't, I pray, misunderstand."

"You have neither the right nor the duty to intercede. As executor of my husband's will, you may control the allocation of my portion, but why I must come to you each quarter to beg for what is legally mine is beyond my comprehension." Her sharp tone evidenced the number of times this had been a matter of dispute between them.

"Since you speak of what is legally yours, I must remind

6 3

you, while we are being so very frank this morning, that it is yours only so long as you comply exactly with the terms of the will."

"That I could scarcely forget," Penelope scorned. "But while my husband's will states I am to reside at Dower Lodge, a place that well pleases me, nothing therein states that I may not travel occasionally should I so desire."

"My uncle, I think you must admit, was extremely liberal. He doted upon you, and everything in his will indicates that he wished that caring to go on beyond the grave. He was a thoughtful, considerate man, a man I greatly admired. I try to follow his precepts. His request at death was that I assure his will be carried out to the letter. I do not mean to shirk that responsibility. If it seems to you restrictive, I can assure you he had only your good in mind. He had a reason for each and every stipulation."

"I am quite sure that he did." Her tone caused Bransom to cast a sharp glance in her direction.

"As a woman, you may not understand. . . ."

"But I do," Penelope interceded. "I understand perfectly."

"In the matter of remarriage, for instance—"

But she did not allow him to finish, saying abruptly, "I shall never remarry."

"No, of course, I know that no one will ever replace him." If there was a suspicion of a sigh in Mr. Bransom's voice, it melded to perfection with his mournful tone. "As for the matter of asking you to come each quarter day to receive your allowance, I think I do not ask too much—that is my means of assuring that you are acting in accordance with his wishes. Otherwise, I rarely see you, though barely three miles separate our dwellings. You never call on me—I hesitate to think of the number of invitations I have extended to you and your dear sister, yet you seldom grace my table. I, on the other hand, relish each opportunity to visit the Lodge. Be honest, would you be here with me this morning were it not Lady Day?"

"I am sorry, sir." Penelope's expression softened slightly. "If I seem rude, it is not personally intended. It is simply

6 4

that it is not entirely pleasant to come here . . . there are memories."

"I know, I know. Such devotion. I shall never forget the magnificence of his funeral, but then there is always that splendid stone to remind me of it, not to speak of the window you had installed at St. Anne's." Penelope turned away. "Perhaps some of his testamentary wishes might appear to outsiders to be a trifle whimsical, but I believe we both know that everything there stemmed from his deep regard for you and his desire for your continued comfort and protection. I do my best to carry out his wishes, onerous though it may be at times. I try not to complain even when I consider you quite wilfully ignore enquiries which are hardly those of idle curiosity. For instance, when I ask what becomes of your allowance, it is not because I wish to interfere, but merely to assist you—finance is, after all, a gentleman's sphere. Five hundred a quarter is a liberal sum; on that, I think, we can agree." He paused expectantly until she nodded. "Yet what becomes of it? We have few frivolities on which to spend such a sum here in Mayfield. At Dower House you live frugally; your table is well but most plainly served, as I have remarked on those few occasions when I am invited to sit down with you. Your clothes are . . ." here his eyes swept her slim figure in its grey cambric dress decorated only by a tatted collar of matching grey, "are quite adequate, but less than stylish."

"Sir, I did not come here to listen to your opinion on fashion, but I would say that my mode of dress is in no small part due to your uncle's testamentary wishes."

"Mourning is a mark of respect. It is true that he specified you were to wear the darker shades, but there is nothing necessarily unfashionable in them. In this matter, as in others, my uncle sought to guide you, for remember, you were still comparatively young at the time of his death, and your father, as he so rightly surmised, was not long in following him to that place from which none returns." A lugubrious sigh accompanied this dismal thought. "But though you must refrain from wearing brighter hues, there is no reason that dark garments may not be quite as handsome, as sumptuous, as others, or indeed that you might not possess a wardrobe of changing styles. You must have worn that particular dress for several years past to my recollection. Your money is most certainly not spent on clothes. And it is not put aside, as one might expect, for the proverbial rainy day, for here you come demanding an advance of next quarter's allowance for this foolish notion of yours—which can only indicate that you have no other resources on which to fall back."

Penelope Bransom closed her lips sharply to prevent an unkind rejoinder. The conversation with her husband's nephew was proceeding much as had others on previous quarter days. These days were always difficult for her, but there being only four in the year, she must learn to contain her temper. She did, after all, depend on the draft she received from him, not only for her own well-being but for that of others also.

"If you will but give me my allowance, I need trouble you no further. I can manage without the advance on next quarter."

"Still you refuse to answer me on what you do with my uncle's money."

"It is no longer your uncle's—it is rightfully mine. I am his lawful widow. I have no need to explain to you or to anyone how I choose to spend it. If it is your concern that it may be wasted, I can assure you it is not."

"I wonder." He eyed her speculatively. "One day I may make it my business to discover what you do with it."

The turn of the conversation had increasingly determined Penelope on the worth of the London plan.

"Since we may still be at Devonshire Place on next quarter day, may I ask that you forward the draft there when it is due?"

"I would suggest it would be to your advantage to be here in Mayfield on Midsummer Day. In fact, it would be greatly to your advantage never to leave Mayfield at all. You are a lady of some experience. By that I mean that certain things are not unknown to you, but when I think of that fair sister of yours exposed to the vagaries of town life, I shudder."

"Under Lady Halstead's care I think your apprehension is entirely unwarranted."

"Lady Halstead is a fine lady, but she has her own daughter to care for. I dare say it will be you who will be called upon to chaperone your sister, and I cannot be reassured by your judgement in all matters."

Penelope rose from her chair. "Well, Mr. Bransom, since Missy is my sister rather than yours, I find your dire concern misplaced."

"But I have a great regard for Miss Woodard, though not necessarily fraternal in nature." He fidgeted awkwardly. "For some time now I have been thinking of marrying, of providing an heir for the estate. It was, I believe, the underlying reason for my uncle's marriage, though he, God rest his soul, had the misfortune to contract a union without issue. It has been on my mind to speak to your brother, as Miss Woodard's legal guardian, on the matter. Your plans precipitate that talk." He noticed that the colour had drained from Penelope's cheeks and added, "I know that this is unexpected. Your sister is not a wealthy woman, but I can overlook that for those assets she does possess, sweetness of disposition and fairness of form."

Penelope found her tongue at last. "I'm afraid it will not do, Mr. Bransom."

"Won't do—what can you mean? Though your sister resides with you, I hardly see it as a matter in which you have any say, nor should you try to influence her, which would be unfair, most unfair, to her as well as to me. I am not one to boast, but there are a score or more of ladies who would welcome my addresses. It is your sister's good fortune that I have decided upon her."

"But Missy is only just turned eighteen—surely there is too great a disparity in your ages."

"I am barely forty. Need I point out that you were younger than your sister when you married my uncle, and he then older than myself by several years? You cannot deny the happiness of your union. Your objection is spurious. It is not the matter of age which upsets you; you know from experience that an older man may provide wise guidance for a younger woman, may dote upon her as another would not." His eyes narrowed. "You resent the thought of another woman in this house, presiding at what you still continue to think of as my uncle's table. You resent my presence here, and that resentment is quickened by the thought of a lady here in the place you once held. That's it." His voice rose in triumph.

"That is not so, Mr. Bransom. As my husband's heir, the Hall is yours by right. I think only of Missy."

"As I do, and as I am sure your brother will."

In the silence broken at last by the chimes from the ormolu clock on the mantel—those chimes that had been the signal for her husband to wind his watch and say, "Put away your embroidery, Penelope, time to retire"—she reflected that the nephew was not entirely wrong in saying she still thought of Greystone Hall as his uncle's house. She saw and heard her late husband everywhere. Was she, in fact, being fair to Edward Bransom, who spoke no more than the truth in saying he was the neighbourhood's most eligible bachelor? Once the offer was made there would be pressure from all quarters for Missy to accept him.

"There is some justice in what you say, Mr. Bransom," she began at last. "When I said Missy was young and you older, I intended no insult. There may, at times, be an advantage in a difference in age, though when I married I held the position of being the oldest child of the family, whereas Missy is the youngest—I'm afraid I still think of her as the baby. You are right in saying I should not interfere in your proposal, but may I ask that you wait until our return from London to make it? She will then have seen something of the world besides Mayfield and be better able to know her own mind."

"Yet you knew nothing of the world when you married. I believe that may have been an advantage. You wanted for nothing, but neither did you come with ideas which might lead to dissatisfaction. We live quietly in the country, but after London may your sister not long for constant distraction?"

"May she not be equally glad to settle back to the serenity of country living?"

Mr. Bransom rose to pace back and forth before the portrait of his uncle, which hung above the mantel. Their similarity in appearance was remarkable—the same elongated features, the same red-brown hair, the same pale eyes—yet perhaps it was only in appearance they resembled one another.

"I shall speak to your brother," he decided at last. "I shall confide in Arthur, one gentleman to another. I have no wish to be harsh, Mrs. Bransom, but there are things to which you do not give due consequence, perhaps because you are a woman: financial security and status. Your brother, on these and other matters, sees life much as I do. I shall confide my intentions to Arthur."

That Arthur Woodard saw matters in the same light as Edward Bransom was made plain by his call on Penelope only hours later. It had, in fact, been that call that had decided her, with no further hesitation, to espouse Lady Halstead's plan.

Arthur had come just as she was forwarding the draft she had received that morning to her solicitor—instructing him to make the usual payments and deposit the rest to her account—a letter she quickly covered at the sight of her brother's sturdy figure dismounting from his horse at her gate.

"I just talked to Edward Bransom," he began as soon as he entered. "And he's quite upset about this rackety scheme of yours—going off to London. I should have thought you would have mentioned it to him before you made any such plans."

He flopped into a velvet-covered armchair by her side.

"And why should I?"

"Well, Pen, he is your husband's nephew after all, and he does, in a manner of speaking, hold the purse strings."

"But it is *my* money, not his. I am quite sure that if I had had adequate legal advice in the matter I shouldn't have to beg for it each quarter, but you insisted it wasn't necessary."

"All Edward wants is to help you, Pen, but you're so stubborn. He's asked me time and again what you do with your money, and I'll be darned if I know. Must admit I'd been hoping you were putting it aside for my brood, but he tells me you don't even have enough saved to cover this hare-brained scheme of going off to London—he said you wanted an advance from next quarter. I couldn't believe it. I don't blame him for being annoyed. How on earth do you manage to spend it?"

Arthur Woodard looked around the small front parlour with its cretonne-covered easy chairs and chintz curtains, its plain wool rug and well-polished but ancient oak tables, then back to the desk at the bay window where his sister sat.

"I can see you don't want to talk about it, but even though I'm younger than you, Pen, you must remember I am the head of the family."

"Yes, Arthur, I know."

How was it possible to forget that Arthur had stepped into their father's shoes—he reminded her of it at every turn. He meant well, she kept reminding herself. He had assumed what he felt to be his duty of protector to his sisters as well as his own wife and children, but, always unsure of himself, he carried it out as a pale imitation of his father with alternating pomposity and obduracy. All too often it was friends like Edward Bransom who made his decisions for him, men he admired for their position rather than for their intrinsic worth. Because he was weak in himself, his dominance over those he considered weaker, particularly the women in his family, was diffuse but palpable. Even though Penelope understood he was only attempting to carry out a role for which he was quite unsuited, she found his meddling into her affairs onerous.

"Since you agree, then, perhaps you wouldn't mind explaining to me just how you manage to dispense the five hundred pounds you receive from Edward each quarter. I see no sign of waste or frivolity, yet how else can it disappear?"

She sighed in clear exasperation. "Arthur, again you make it sound as though my allowance is a gift. It's my money, and I've said all I have to say in the matter to Mr. Bransom this morning. I've no doubt that every word I uttered has been relayed to you—I've nothing to add to that. As for setting it aside for your children, it's not my intention to complain, but I would remind you that apart from Missy's portion, everything in the family estate went to you—father left me nothing."

"And why should he? Though your husband was dead when father departed this world, he knew Bransom had taken good care of you."

"Just so, Arthur. I only raise the subject to explain why I see no reason you cannot provide quite handsomely for your family without expecting any help from me."

Her brother fidgeted impatiently. "I didn't ask for help, Pen. It's just that, who are you going to leave it to? You know, Edward's right, five hundred a quarter is a generous sum, a magnanimous sum, even, given the way you live."

"Arthur, I've told Mr. Bransom that I don't intend discussing this matter with him, nor do I feel it necessary to discuss it with you—not unless I come asking you to support me. *That,* I promise, I shall never do."

"I should hope not," was his huffy rejoinder. "Not with an income like yours."

"I would ask you to stay to tea, Arthur, but I have some letters which must be written. So, unless you have something else on your mind . . ."

"As a matter of fact, I do, and damned important it is, too. I think when you hear what it is you may change your plans completely about London."

"Oh!" Penelope dreaded what she felt was sure to come.

"Edward's made an offer for Missy!"

Arthur's triumph was sorely taxed by his sister's noncommittal, "So."

"So! Is that all you have to say—Edward's the most eligible man in the neighbourhood, and all you can say to our sister's good fortune is 'So'!"

"He intimated to me that that was his intention this morning."

"Well, you don't sound overjoyed, but I was, I can assure you. Missy can't do better anywhere."

"I think she should come out first. I told him so, I asked him to wait until our return. She's young, she's met no one—you know what a quiet life we lead. Let her see a little of the world, then let her decide."

"Edward thinks exactly the opposite, Pen, and I agree

with him. Let her stay and marry, not go off on some wild caper. Only think, if she asks him to wait there's the risk she might lose him altogether."

"If he's that easily lost, perhaps it is well to discover it now. It's a poor attachment that can't survive one season."

"You're a romantic, Pen, that's your trouble. Just because you found someone to devote your life to, you think there can be no marriage without love. That's not necessarily so. Phyllis and I barely knew one another before we married, and we settled well enough. I think Edward and Missy would suit, really I do; so does Phyllis."

One look at the obstinate jut of her brother's jaw made Penelope desist from further argument. She knew that look only too well.

"Perhaps you're right, Arthur. Anyway, Missy is the one who must decide, not you, not me, not Phyllis, not even Mr. Bransom. And so far she hasn't been asked."

"Edward's going to do so on Sunday. He'll call after mattins, and Phyllis and I will come with him so we can take you aside while he proposes—it's all decided. He wants to marry before Whitsun."

But when Mr. Edward Bransom, assured and resplendent, had called at the Lodge that Sunday it was to discover, to his great chagrin, that the ladies had departed for Devonshire Place the previous day.

It was the widow's doing, there could be no doubt of it. A self-righteous indignation rose in Edward Bransom's chest, fanned in no small part by Arthur Woodard's repeated apologies, which he thrust aside with a benevolence he was far from feeling.

"No matter, Arthur, no matter. I am quite sure that your *younger* sister has no part in this, which is all that matters."

But one day, he vowed, Penelope Bransom would regret having defied him.

His anger was revived on seeing his chosen one the object of attention from other gentlemen in Lady Halstead's drawing room. Only with reluctance did he leave Devonshire Place to accompany Sir Reginald Palfry, the great friend of his late uncle with whom he was staying in London. Theirs had been a friendship that Edward Bransom had never understood: his uncle had been such a virtuous gentleman, while it was impossible to be with Sir Reginald for five minutes without recognizing him for what he was, a lascivious lecher. Edward Bransom could only think that his uncle had remained loyal to their friendship, begun when both were undergraduates at Oxford, in the hopes of redeeming a soul lost to carnal pleasures.

Because of his own abhorrence of libidinous behaviour, Edward Bransom was shocked to hear that jaded, if elegant, gentleman singing the praises of Miss Melissa Woodard. As they descended the steps of Lady Halstead's town house, he hastened to cut short the remarks by letting Sir Reginald know that the lady was spoken for.

"Though the engagement is not yet announced, we shall marry as soon as Miss Woodard returns to Mayfield."

"My dear Bransom, why did you not say so earlier? Far be it from me to intrude on another man's turf. You are indeed fortunate for she's a lovely creature, such eyes, such a soft line to her neck. I must confess I find myself discovering a latent desire to settle with some understanding lady, a lady of some passion, some charm, yet not of a jealous disposition. Quite naturally, I should always insist upon being free to pursue my own inclinations."

Mr. Edward Bransom grew thoughtful as they strolled towards Portland Place.

"I believe I know just such a lady who would suit you well."

"Indeed, and who might that be?"

"The lady you just met, Mrs. Penelope Bransom, my uncle Josiah's widow. She's older, of course, and perhaps no match in looks for her sister, but that lacklustre quality hides a passionate nature—still waters run deep, you know what I mean."

He laughed at a jest he thought would appeal to his companion, but Sir Reginald merely nodded. "I suspect you may be right. I knew Josiah well, he was a man who chose everything with care. Undoubtedly Mrs. Bransom is a woman of passion and understanding."

8

Oh, I have pass'd a miserable night
So full of ugly sights, of ghastly dreams.

Shakespeare
Richard III, 1592

The night after Edward Bransom's visit to Devonshire Place, Penelope had that dream again.

She was at home, trapped, horribly, desperately trapped, and though there were no visible bonds, try though she might and try though she did, she could not escape. She wanted to run, but her feet were made of lead, they would not move; she wanted to scream, but no sound would come from her mouth—she was struck dumb. She was being suffocated, something was over her face, something was pinioning her down, she was helpless . . . and the worst of it was they were all there, her family and her friends, talking and laughing just as though nothing were wrong.

She awoke, bathed in sweat, entangled in the bedclothes, crying out in her fear. It *had* been a dream, though, hadn't it?

Lady Halstead came hurrying in, candle in hand.

"What is wrong, what happened, Penelope?"

Behind her was Missy. "Did you have that nightmare again?"

"Yes, that's all it was, a silly old dream. I'm sorry I woke you up. I'm all right, really, but I'll light the candle and read since I am awake."

But when the door was shut, when she was alone with her

book, *The Seasons,* clutched in her hands, she made no move to open it. She just lay there, remembering—remembering everything.

Mayfield's parish church, St. Anne's, on her wedding day ten years ago. It had been decorated in foxgloves, poppies, hedge-parsley and wild-arum; she herself had collected and arranged the flowers. She had been shy on that day, pretty, but only in the sense that all brides are pretty, and very young—Edward Bransom had been right in saying she was younger then than Missy, for she was just seventeen.

She'd been surprised when her father had told her she was to marry Josiah Bransom, whom she had known until then only as her father's friend. He was highly respected in Mayfield. She had liked him as children like an adult who remembers them and sometimes favours them with sweet-meats, for which she always dutifully thanked him with a curtsy or sometimes, when she was quite small, a kiss on the cheek. She had called him Uncle Josiah, though they were unrelated, until he proposed marriage. Thereafter she hadn't quite known what to call him. Mr. Bransom was far too formal, yet she felt a certain awkwardness in using only his Christian name.

She had never thought of him as a husband, but she much preferred marrying him to marrying a stranger. He was quite handsome in the way of the Bransoms with their red-brown hair and pale complexions. He was much older than she was, which made her defer to him quite naturally, just as she deferred to her father. She had never questioned her father over his choice of a husband for her. Her father knew what was best for her and so, she was sure, did Mr. Bransom . . . Josiah.

When Josiah told her he considered the new notion of taking a wedding journey a foolish one, she had agreed with him. They had thus returned to Greystone Hall im-mediately after the ceremony at St. Anne's.

The servants had stood in line to greet the new mistress on their arrival. She had felt shy and awkward and had been glad when her husband suggested showing her her new home. He had taken her to the large drawing room, the dining room with its gate-legged dining table and silver candelabra, then upstairs to her room, small and pleasant, and then to his own, adjacent to hers, large enough to accommodate its huge four-poster bed.

It was there, to her astonishment and utter confusion, he told her to take her clothes off and get into bed. She had not understood him, assuring him that she was neither sleepy nor unwell, at which he answered her quite sharply,

"We are man and wife now, Penelope. It is for me to instruct you in that matter. Come along, hurry up."

She had done as she was told, though horrified at being seen in broad daylight, quite naked, and by one of the opposite sex, even though that one had been pronounced her husband. She hurried to hide herself between the cold sheets, but he pulled them back to look at her, an odd light in his eyes as they ran across her naked body. She had turned her head so she might not see his nakedness, but she could not ignore his hands feverishly touching her. Then, this man she had known since childhood quite suddenly became a terrible, formidable stranger, falling upon her, breaking into her. She cried out in pain, in horror, in humiliation, not understanding what was happening.

"Quiet—the servants!" he reminded her tersely.

When she struggled to free herself, he ordered her to be still.

So she lay still until, with a last groan, he lay still too, no longer moving. It was done. Without a word, he got up and dressed and bade her to do likewise, becoming again the person she knew, commenting on the fineness of the afternoon, promising to show her his butterfly collection.

Not a word was said of what had happened between them. She was to discover that it was something he never discussed, nor could she mention it.

Outside the bedroom he was much as he had always been, jovial, polite, considerate, whereas during what became a nightly ritual he was anything but. She loathed his touch; worse yet, she sensed that he was ashamed of performing this act and concealed his shame in belligerence. There was never any kindness in what passed between them, no attempt at affection, no gentleness. She felt brutally used, yet if she made any protest she was sharply reminded of a wife's duty to submit to her husband. The husband Josiah Bransom became in the bedroom was the antithesis of the kindly Josiah Bransom known in Mayfield, and that husband terrified her. The shame she sensed he felt became her shame too, and there was no one to whom she could turn. Her mother dead, her brother and sister far younger, there was only her father . . . and so it was in desperation that at last she spoke to him.

"Please let me come home, father. I don't want to be married any more—it's, it's . . . I don't like it."

Her father avoided looking at her as he asked, "What can you mean, Penelope?"

"I hate it. Being married, that is."

"Why?"

"It's Mr. Bransom, he's not nice, in fact, he's a monster."

"Josiah Bransom! Surely he doesn't beat you?"

"No," she admitted.

"Well, then, what is it?"

"It's the way he . . . he . . ." She broke off, not knowing what to call what happened between them—she'd thought it was called making love, but there was no love in what took place. The Bible was more accurate in describing it as "to know," for she really did know Josiah Bransom as she had not known him before. "It's when we're alone, the way he . . . well, I don't like it."

Her father smiled in relief, putting his arm around her shoulders. "Oh, that's all it is—you had me worried for a minute. You're not supposed to like it, Penelope, so don't be upset on that score. A wife submits to that . . . that business, but she doesn't enjoy it. I'm sorry, your mother no longer being with us, that there was no one to explain that to you."

"But father, I can't just go on letting him, I mean, it's horrible the way he . . . well, it's as though I weren't a person at all but just an object for his use. And it's to be done whenever he says, and I'm not allowed to speak of it. He won't talk about it either. I am so distressed, I just had to tell someone. That's why I came to you."

"But, Penelope," he soothed, "you've said he does not beat you, nor raise his hand to you. Many husbands do, it is their right, so you see you are lucky."

But when Penelope burst out in despair, "Why do women ever marry?" her father replied angrily, "Really, I shan't listen to such silly talk. Josiah Bransom is my friend, but more than that he is a decent and devout gentleman."

"I had always thought him so, indeed, so he is outside, but it is when we are alone that he changes—it's the way he looks at me, the way he touches me—well, it's so . . . so degrading, that's all." With that, she burst out crying.

"Come, come, Penelope! Really, all you have told me is that Josiah Bransom is consummating the marriage, as is his right. You must allow him to do so, that is the meaning of those vows you took together at St. Anne's. Rather than commiserate with you, I think you a lucky woman—Josiah is far closer to my age than yours and with time the desire, the ability fade, but it would seem he has lost none of his virility. A gentleman has . . . let me see, how should I put it . . . he has certain urges that women, or rather ladies, don't. Allow him his way; when the first passions pass all that will change. And if, perhaps, he seems more persistent than you would wish just now, it is probably because he wants an heir to succeed him, otherwise Edward will inherit the estate. Even though Josiah likes his brother's eldest, he would surely rather that Greystone Hall should pass to his own son, just as I'm glad to have Arthur to succeed me here at Kerswell. You can understand that, now, can't you? Give it time. Give him a son. Then you can rest on your laurels, having fulfilled your role. All will be different then, mark my words. Now, I've said enough. All of this is between a man and his wife. I never again wish to discuss these bedroom matters."

Could all men be so? Penelope wondered. Was that why her father sided with his friend?

Afterwards, she sensed that her husband knew that she had spoken to her father about him, possibly they had even discussed her visit. Rather than improving his attitude towards her when they were alone, it seemed only to make him more aggressive, as though certain that his dominance over her had been sanctified.

She followed her father's advice, however, submitting without a word, without a sound, praying only to conceive and thus free herself from him by giving him what she, too, had always wanted, a child. Yet her very passivity seemed to increase his demands. It was as though he wanted to force some response from her when she had none. Besides, had her father not warned her that ladies were not supposed to like it? On that score, at least, he had been right.

She longed for her monthly course, for then she was free of him for a few days. Her husband took an avid interest in its coming, yet it was something she knew as little about as she had her marital obligations. Thus she felt a sense of surprise when it failed to arrive at its appointed time, and he informed her she must be with child. She began to feel happy again, for he left her alone, much of her bitterness towards him faded; he was, after all, her husband and forever would be, he was the father of the child she desired more than anything. She began to draw and paint again, to feel a certain pleasure in living. But the pleasant truce was not to last, for just as unexpectedly as it had stopped, so one day her menstrual blood reappeared. Its cessation, she was to discover, had been caused by fear and anxiety rather than impregnation, but once relaxed her body had returned to its normal functioning.

In cowardly fashion, she said nothing, allowing her husband to believe she was still with child until, noticing no increase in girth, he had called in a physician to examine her. Great had been his fury when he had received that gentleman's report.

"You are barren, madam, barren. Do you understand the word? You seem to understand little enough of anything else. A fine wife I chose when at last I made that step— young, healthy, no beauty but comely enough, I thought, to provide me with an heir and warmth and comfort in my old age. The doctor tells me that, given the regularity of our union, he believes you incapable of conception. And I can assure you the fault lies with you and not with me—that I can and shall prove to you! As for warmth and comfort in my old age, there's little enough hope for that either, such a cold fish you've been with that glum face of yours ever since I married you. Now I am going to show you something unknown to anyone. I do it to prove beyond any doubt that the fault is yours,ther, such a cold fish you've been with that glum face of yours ever since I married you. Now I am going to show you something unknown to anyone. I do it to prove beyond any doubt that the fault is yours, not mine."

He had taken her to a dismal cottage on the outskirts of Shepleigh, a town some miles from Mayfield. There, without alighting from the carriage, he called for the woman of the house, who answered his summons with willingness if not alacrity. She was a blowsy woman in a grubby dress of low neckline revealing a large and swaying bosom. As soon as she recognized the carriage, she began to pull off her soiled apron and attempted to straighten her hair as she came towards them.

"Never mind all that," Bransom snapped impatiently. "I've not come to see you but those two bastards of mine. Bring them out and show them to this fine young wife I married."

The woman, noticing Penelope for the first time, made to protest, but Bransom cut her short.

"Hurry up, we haven't all day. I'll make it worth your while."

She reappeared with two small ragamuffins, one a head taller than the other, otherwise both equally thin and dirty, who gaped at the elegance of the coach and horses.

"Say hello to the fine gentleman and lady," the woman prompted sharply.

They had done so, nodding, all their attention on the fine equipage. The smaller of the two ran his hand across the carving on the door and was sharply told to remove it. Allowing time only for Penelope to observe their unmistakable Bransom features—their pale eyes and shocks of dirty reddish hair—their father, who spoke not a word to them, reached reluctantly for a handful of coins which he tossed in their direction before pulling off. Penelope, looking back, saw boys and woman grovelling in the ditch at the roadside, desperately searching for each and every one.

"Mine, madam, mine," Mr. Bransom fumed as they sped back to Mayfield. "By a slut, to be sure, but one with a body capable of reproduction, unlike yours, more's the pity. I brought you here so you might, without any possible doubt, know the lack of progeny in our union to be your fault and yours alone. You must live with the burden that God did not make you as he made other women—fruitful vessels able to bear annual tribute according to the laws of nature. My seed, on the other hand, is the good seed, the fertile seed, for apart from these lads I have others too, in Covey, in Brampton, possibly others from women I've known," he boasted before continuing bitterly, "A fine bargain you were. I might have been willing to overlook your lack of spirit, but not the infertility that marks you forever as a flawed and unfit woman. It's a pity your father wouldn't have you when you ran back to him, nor can I besmirch my good name and reputation by tossing you out as you deserve."

From then on, though Penelope was no longer afraid of her husband as she had been before, she was convinced of the truth of his often repeated taunt that she was a defective vessel, taunts delivered in the privacy of his bedroom where, barren or not, her presence was still required. She bore them in silence, feeling he spoke no more than the truth. He was right. God had not made her as he had made other women.

In Mayfield, theirs was regarded as the perfect marriage, yet as time passed and no child came, there was sympathy in the village that a marriage, so happy in itself, should remain unblessed.

And if Penelope's guilt for her infertility never left her mind, neither did the picture of the starving waifs— uncared for, unwanted, unloved—she had seen.

"Why not choose one of them as your heir," she ventured to her husband one day. "I should have no objection."

"I always thought you wanting in sense, now I know it is so—to expect me to bring in a bastard born of a slut to replace me!"

"Your blood is in their veins. You were instrumental in bringing them into the world. You owe them something, yet they have nothing."

"I paid the woman for the use of her body, though not as heavily as I am paying for yours," he snorted. "Why has God inflicted upon me a barren wife when I have supported His works? I have always done my Christian duty."

Penelope was slow to anger, yet Bransom's invoking God's name on his behalf infuriated her. "Surely, as a Christian, is it not demanded of you to clothe and feed progeny you admit to be your own? You speak often of charity—should you not extend some of it to those poor souls? Surely it is their due."

"How dare you speak to me so!" His face grew so dark in anger that Penelope was sure he would strike her. "If I divulged their existence to you, it was only that you might know beyond any doubt the fault was yours. I have proved my virility; I have proved that with a woman properly formed my seed undeniably reproduces. But because I have been frank with you, I'll not have you besmirching my name. You will swear to me here and now, never, ever to divulge the existence of these bastards. You must never speak of them, nor attempt to see them, not now nor later after I am gone—for sickly looking creature though you are, it's my luck that you'll survive me. I'll have your word on it."

She had given her word, and it was a vow she had kept, though daily conscious of the hypocrisy not only of her husband, but of herself and of their life together. For she continued to be the envy of Mayfield, with a husband who doted on her though she bore him no heir.

Josiah Bransom, his place in the community assured during his lifetime, had arranged that it should be preserved thereafter, planning every detail of his funeral—Norwich crepes and black gauze, the hearse to be drawn by horses with tall black plumes, the coffin of an air-tight metallic, all to be supplied by Gabriel Douce's warehouse of mourning on The Strand. And his monument, how lovingly he had worked on its design with a stonemason from Oxford. All was to be a tribute to him from his deeply grieving widow of whom, by the terms of his will, he would make a living memorial. When he died of apoplexy two years later, when Penelope was only twenty-one, she discoverd she was to wear full mourning for not one but two years, and half-mourning thereafter; she was to use black-edged paper and to continue to seal her letters with black wax; she was to ensure that her husband's final resting place was perpetually tended and to arrange for an annual service in his memory on All Souls' Day. She was to oversee exactly as planned his funeral, the placement of his monument, and the stained glass window in the church above the Bransom pew.

As long as she obeyed the terms of her husband's will to the letter—together with those private vows made to him in his lifetime, solemnly swearing to speak of them to no one— as long as she kept entirely faithful to his memory, living in the diligent, worthy manner that had been shown to her while he was on earth, then she was to be allowed her own home and a handsome allowance for the remainder of her life. She was, of course, never to remarry. To break any stipulation of the will was to forfeit all claim to her portion of his estate, which would then pass in its entirety to his nephew, Edward Bransom.

Penelope recognized in the testament her husband's determination to control her in death as he had in life, yet strangely she objected to none of the will's terms. She much preferred the comfort of the Lodge to the immensity of the Hall, which had nothing but unhappy memories for her. As for the mourning she was to wear, she had never cared for fashion, nor had she any reason to wish to appear attractive. If her husband's intention had been to preclude any possible attention from members of the opposite sex, the stipulation did her a favour, for she feared and distrusted all of them. Even had the will not forbidden remarriage, she would never again willingly enter that estate.

Penelope Bransom was happy in her widowhood, far happier than she'd ever been in marriage, happier even than when single, for she was—despite her brother's interference—quite independent. Painting the beauty of nature's ever-changing world around her, awakening the eyes of children to that world, remained her enduring joy.

Her main concern lay in being forced to carry out her husband's wishes as though they were her own; in that she felt she became as great a hypocrite as Josiah Bransom had been. Such hypocrisy she hated above all. It was a quality she believed she saw in Edward Bransom; for that reason his plan to propose marriage to her dearest Missy sorely troubled her. That her sister—who had lived with her ever since her husband's death six years ago, whom she had watched grow into womanhood, beautiful, kind, loving, and gentle—might have to endure at the hands of the nephew what she had had to endure from the uncle, was unendurable in itself.

Yet Penelope was troubled. Might she not be unjust in attributing the faults of the uncle to the nephew? Yet to reveal her fears, her reservations to Missy was to break her sworn vow of secrecy in the matter; her words could, if ever discovered, be used to break her husband's will, so that everything that was hers would revert to Edward Bransom, an eventuality she had no doubt that gentleman earnestly wished to bring about.

Penniless in her own right, since her father had considered her adequately provided for by Josiah Bransom and had bequeathed her nothing, she would be left to rely upon Arthur's charity. She might have swallowed her pride and borne that, yet what of the others whose welfare lay in her hands?

The sight of the starving children her husband had fathered had never left her. After Josiah Bransom's death, privately, cautiously—for by disobeying his implicit instructions to have anything more to do with them, she risked disclosure of the secret he had told her and thereby losing her allowance—she had searched out those children and an astonishing number of others whom he had brought into the world and left destitute. It was a risk she had had to take, for she could not live in comfort on his money knowing the innocent offspring of his illicit liaisons starved. Through her solicitor, she was now taking care of all of them, or as many as she had been able to discover, giving enough for food, clothes, and an education sufficient so they might eventually be able to provide for themselves.

She never met or saw any of his illegitimate children, though she often wished she might. If she did, there was a chance that everything would become known, and the world could never be told Josiah Bransom's true nature. With his will written so as to preserve his good name and his widow handsomely provided for only as long as she specifically carried out his wishes, to disclose what became of an income designated for her support alone would be to lose it, to render destitute not only herself but those other poor, helpless creatures. What she did for them was her secret.

Though the candle was low, the room was bright, and Penelope realized the light came from the rising sun; she rarely returned to sleep after that recurrent nightmare.

She opened the book that was still in her hands, and out fell the violet she had pressed from the bunch Mortimer had given her the day she had met him. All men were despicable, and he had proved himself equally so. She made to crush the flower, but her eye was caught by the deep blue as the morning sunlight fell across its petals; she had seen that self-same colour the previous day, though not in a flower. She again saw Mortimer's fixed gaze directed upon her—his eyes were of a blue of the same value and intensity.

Gently, she replaced the violet between the leaves of her book, not, she told herself, because it reminded her of Mortimer's eyes but because she could not destroy an object of natural beauty.

9

Art alone supplies an enjoyment which requires no appreciable effort, which costs no sacrifice, and which we need not repay with repentance.

J. F. C. Schiller
Essays, Aesthetical and Philosophical,
1796

It did not take Edward Bransom long to return to Devonshire Place to put that question which had been the purpose of his first coming there. The very next morning found him at Lady Halstead's door, spurred to such haste, perhaps, by the attention Missy's charm and beauty were drawing from other quarters.

Penelope saw him as he entered and their eyes met—apprehension on one side, defiance on the other. She would not, indeed she could not, prevent his speaking. Missy must decide for herself what her answer would be.

Penelope went upstairs to her room to complete a sketch of columbines she had begun earlier, detailing the construction of the flower minutely to keep from her mind the interview in progress below. There, half an hour later, a flushed and flustered Missy burst in with her not unexpected news.

"I was never more surprised, for I had never thought of him in such a light," Missy concluded. "But he said he had long made up his mind to offer for me, that he had spoken to Arthur, and that Arthur most heartily agreed on the wisdom of the match. He also implied that you knew of his intention, but in that I believe him mistaken, for you said nothing of it to me."

"But I did know of it, Missy," Penelope acceded.

Missy considered her sister's face. "Since you said nothing of it, Pen, does that mean you do not approve?"

"I . . . it is not for me to approve or disapprove, Missy. I am not your guardian."

"But you know me better than anyone else. If you are not my guardian legally, you are in fact."

"What was your reply?" Penelope said, ignoring what she felt to be justifiable criticism.

"I told Mr. Bransom—oh dear, I forgot, he asked me to call him Edward, but it seems somehow disrespectful to address him so—anyway, I told him I must speak to you."

"I see. And what did he say to that?"

"He seemed to feel it unnecessary. I had the impression he was not in favour of my doing so, though I don't know why. Do you and he not like one another? I thought the only reason we didn't visit the Hall more often was . . . well, its associations."

"That is so; there are memories of which I prefer not to be reminded. Regarding Mr. Edward Bransom, I neither like nor dislike him, though that is hardly the point at issue. What are *your* feelings for him?"

"I . . . I like him, I suppose. At least, I know him."

"But do you, Missy, do you really know him?" Penelope pressed.

"Well, I know as much of him as of any other gentleman, except Arthur. But as I said, I was taken aback by his offer, for I never thought of him as a husband. He pointed out to me all the advantages I should have in marrying him, and they are many. Arthur told me it's a superior offer, one I was lucky to receive, one I could not refuse, and I suppose he's right, he has only my interests at heart."

Penelope was forcefully reminded of her own position ten years previously, of her father confidently giving his blessing while he enumerated the advantages of her match, and she hastily turned away from her sister's earnest gaze lest she betray her apprehensions.

"Marriage lasts a lifetime, Missy. Material advantages are important, but you must live with the man you accept each and every day of your life. You must not make a hasty decision or allow yourself to be persuaded by anybody. You must examine your feelings and the man himself, everything you know of him. Study him, not as a friend or neighbour, but as one who may become your husband—and lover. No material comfort can ever make up for a life with one for whom there is no love and no respect."

"Well, you loved and respected Mr. Josiah Bransom, and I daresay there is no reason I should not be equally happy with his nephew. One great advantage that I see to the match is that we should continue to be as close as we are now. Of course, I should be up at the Hall, but that, I hope, would make you visit there more often. Certainly we could meet daily."

"Missy, whomever you marry and wherever you live, I shall be there whenever you need me," Penelope assured her, though she knew that Edward Bransom, should he be her sister's choice, would probably strive to disrupt their relationship.

"I just thought, Pen," Missy asserted, "we should even share the same name—Melissa Bransom. Do you think it sounds well?"

"Mmm," Penelope uttered noncommitally.

"But what am I to do? Mr. Bransom . . . Edward wanted an immediate reply, but I said I couldn't—not this morning, not until after I had spoken to you. I'm in a quandary, for he's to return tomorrow and I don't know what to say. Tell me what to do, Pen," she pleaded.

If only life were that simple, Penelope thought, looking at the distress in her sister's face. If only it were made up of clear choices, of well-defined roads to follow. If only she could say with certainty this or that was the course to take.

"It is your decision, Missy," she counselled gently. "No one else can make it for you, not Arthur, not me, not even father if he were here. You must be the ultimate judge of whether Edward Bransom is the man with whom you wish to spend your life."

"But you see, I don't know. I just don't know."

"Then think on it, let the matter rest, for a time at least. While you say you know Edward Bransom, you know him

8 8

only as a neighbour, or as a relation by virtue of my marriage to his uncle. You must begin to look at him in a new light, as a man with whom you might spend each day . . . and each night. In marriage you would be closer to him than you have been to any other human being. While there are certain things we may not know until we enter into marriage, we can, perhaps, establish a man's character, his sincerity and honesty, beforehand. If you find him truly worthy of your respect, then he will probably be a good husband to you. My advice, since you press me for it, is not to refuse Mr. Bransom, but to ask him to wait for your reply until we return to Mayfield at Midsummer. Leave yourself free until that time to meet and assess other gentlemen in the same manner as you will assess Mr. Bransom. In such a way you may discover his true worth. If he truly loves you, I think he will agree to your decision."

Missy hugged her. "You're so wise, Pen, and I love you so. Truly I didn't want to leave London just now, for I'm having such a wonderful time with Emmeline. Everyone is being so kind to me—I'm sure I don't know why, but they are. Of course, I couldn't say that to Mr. Bran . . . Edward, for I'm sure it sounds frivolous."

"You are young, Missy; you deserve to enjoy yourself before you become staid and matronly like me. And people are not just being kind to you." She smiled at her sister's eager expression. "They appreciate a young lady who is not only gentle and considerate but very, very beautiful."

"Oh, Pen, you'll make me conceited."

"But that is what is so particular about you, Missy. Though you are, in my opinion, far more beautiful than many of the London ladies I have seen, or even those depicted in famous works of art, you are not in the least conscious of it. And speaking of works of art, are you inclined to accompany me to the showing at the Royal Academy this afternoon? Henrietta is taking Emmeline to the dressmaker again, and anyway, she says she hates crushes and craning her neck to see the paintings, but I do really want to go and she won't hear of my going alone."

Though Missy willingly accompanied her, Penelope

might well have been alone when they entered the great Exhibition Hall at Somerset House, for they became lost in the fashionable throng, whose interest was concentrated more often upon one another than on the lofty walls crammed to the ceilings with canvasses of varied dimensions. There were portraits of the beautiful and the illustrious, and some scenic views, but the majority were enormous paintings depicting recent English military and naval victories over Napoleon.

Penelope found a corner isolated from the throng, where she assiduously studied the catalogue she had received on entering. She read that the Academy had been opened by Royal Charter in 1768, and it consisted of forty members, Royal Academicians, twenty Associates and six Associate Engravers. The first President had been Sir Joshua Reynolds, followed by Benjamin West, while Sir Thomas Lawrence presently held that office. It possessed a fine collection of casts and models; lectures were delivered by Professors in their various branches during the winter season; and medals were given annually for figures and drawings, paintings, sculpture and design. The Exhibition opened on the first of May to display works of art consisting of paintings, sculptures, models, proof engravings and drawings, all available for viewing between two and five for the cost of one shilling. There followed a long list of the names of exhibitors, with those of Lawrence, Opie, Wilkie and Turner the most prominent. Intently Penelope searched for a painter whose work had increasingly caught her attention, though he had little national renown, and at last she found it, number 487, Flatford Mill by John Constable.

It was while in search of this painting that her glance was captured by a bust cast in bronze, the head and shoulders of a male figure she immediately recognized though it bore only the caption Hero of England. There was the slender nose with its flared nostrils, the deep-set eyes, in which the sculptor had dexterously captured their owner's aloof independence mingled with nonchalance. Yet it was the lips which held her attention, lips of generous proportion, firm yet oddly sensual even in the cold, impersonal metal.

"Do you find it a fair likeness?" a voice at her elbow questioned.

She hoped he might not have noticed how long she had stood before that likeness and wished she had moved away from it sooner, yet it had held her fascination as did the voice at her elbow. She might have feigned ignorance of the subject of the bust or pretended it was the battle scene of Trafalgar on the wall above that was the object of her attention—but to make such a pretence, a pretence he would undoubtedly recognize, was unworthy of her.

"Yes, it is a very good likeness," she replied gravely.

"It has been remarked that the muscles of the neck and shoulders are not entirely lifelike. Are you of that opinion?" Mortimer's eyes twinkled, though his face was impassive.

Penelope's eyes fell on his high coat collar and crisply starched neckcloth tied in triangular form. "I have no idea whether they are lifelike or not, not having . . ." She broke off her sharp retort, flustered, as she became aware of the teasing mischief which gradually spread across his face.

"Not having seen the original?" he questioned lightly.

"I am no expert on human physique; my domain is the world of nature."

"Yes, I remember. I am enjoying your painting of the cluster of fritillaries." He looked about before asking, "Are you unaccompanied?"

"No, my sister is with me, but we became separated in the crowd." Penelope looked about her. "I expect she is looking for me. I must find her."

"Miss Woodard's attention has been irrevocably claimed by my friend, Colonel Bullerton. He is most horribly smitten by her, but I suppose that was obvious to you yesterday."

"I had supposed that he might behave so with all pretty ladies."

"No, not Bully—you might cast that at other men, at me perhaps, but not Bully. I've never seen him so taken with anyone. Your sister has, however, attracted a great deal of attention, though I would forewarn you of the gentleman who accompanied your husband yesterday."

"My husband!"

"Yes. He is here today also, perhaps?"

"My husband is dead, sir," Penelope replied briefly, flushing at being caught in a half truth.

"But I thought . . . you said nothing of the sort before. Then the gentleman by the name of Bransom I met . . ."

"Edward Bransom is my late husband's nephew."

"His nephew!" She found the expression that accompanied Mortimer's exclamation difficult to understand, but then he caught himself up. "Excuse me, Mrs. Bransom. Allow me to convey my sympathy."

"Thank you, but it is many years since he died, not a recent event."

"Many years?"

"Seven to be exact."

"Seven years, and you still continue in mourning!" Mortimer ejaculated. "You must pardon me, Mrs. Bransom, but it is unusual."

"It would appear to be a personal matter."

"Of course, yet still I find it hard to understand."

"What is it, Charles, that you find so hard to understand?"

For the first time Penelope saw Lady Georgina Staverton at close range, and as Mortimer introduced the ladies she could not help but remember all Mrs. Plunkett-Gall had told her of Mortimer's infatuation for that lady. It was not at all difficult to understand with that finely structured face of flawless complexion and exquisite colouring.

"But you haven't answered my question, Charles. What were you saying was hard to understand?"

"I find it hard to understand why your likeness is not hanging in this hall. Don't tell me it is, for I've searched everywhere for it."

"Had you been here earlier, instead of chasing Boney all over Europe, you would have seen the quite charming portrait Sir Henry Raeburn did—but then, I forgot, of course you have seen it, haven't you!"

She laughed and a complicit glance passed between them, making Penelope suspect that portrait did not hang in the *public* rooms of Staverton's Brook Street home.

"But what think you of this sculpture of England's hero, Mrs. Bransom?" Lady Staverton enquired.

"It is very good."

"Good, yes, but to me the muscles of the neck and shoulders are those of a ploughman, not at all as they . . . as they should be."

So, Penelope thought, Lady Staverton was the critic, but she might have guessed. Feeling intrusive, though not understanding why the obvious intimacy between these two people should concern her as it seemed to, Penelope looked down at her catalogue and murmured, "I really must go and search out these paintings I have marked."

"Let me see what interests you." Mortimer grasped the edge of the catalogue Penelope was holding. As he did so his fingers touched hers, whether by accident or by design she couldn't be sure, but she felt his touch as though her hand had brushed against burning iron. Just as quickly, as though it had, she moved her fingers away from his.

"Number four hundred and eighty seven is the one I am particularly interested in," she said stiffly.

"There is a lady of sense and discrimination. Will you not present me, Mortimer?"

The newcomer, a gentleman with graying hair and hawk-like features, appeared not to please Lord Mortimer, but Lady Staverton greeted him with a charming smile.

"Samuel, I didn't realize you were in London."

"Had to come down since Lady Radcliffe's fete is benefiting my own society."

"Why, of course, the waifs and strays are your particular interest—I had forgotten that."

"I am still waiting an introduction to the lady who favours Constable, the only decent piece in this conglomeration of poor taste."

"Mrs. Bransom, this is Mr. Samuel Trueblood. Mr. Trueblood, Mrs. Bransom." Nothing could have been colder than Mortimer's tone.

"Perhaps, Mrs. Bransom, since I am searching for that particular piece, we should endeavour to find it together."

"I'm sorry," Lord Mortimer intervened, "but I have already arranged to show the Constable to Mrs. Bransom."

"Very well, Mortimer," said Trueblood and left, plainly annoyed.

"Oh, Charles, you are so rude to him, and you two from neighbouring estates in Shropshire," Lady Staverton chastised. "He's quite a powerful man and always giving money to charities. He's President of the Society of Waifs and Strays now."

"He does it to assuage his conscience for all those inferior supplies he furnished the army. I know of at least a score of deaths to be laid at his door because of them, and I suspect that's only the tip of the iceberg. He was handsomely rewarded for shoddy uniforms and rotten foodstuffs, and now he seeks to expiate himself by becoming a benefactor of this society and that."

"His taste in works of art does not seem inferior, however," Penelope interjected.

"No, but that is the only point on which I may be forced into his corner. In truth, I wish his taste were appalling."

"Now, Charles, you're getting into one of your moods, and I shan't have it," Lady Staverton cajoled. "Especially when I was about to ask you to take the part of Paris to my Helen in the tableau at Lady Radcliffe's."

"If you expect me to stand around Kitty Radcliffe's garden shivering in a bedsheet, you're sadly mistaken, Georgina."

"But it is for the benefit of the waifs and strays, Charles."

"I don't care who it's in aid of, you can search elsewhere for Paris—try Bully over there, he'd make a good one. Anyway, I expect your tableau is primarily for the purpose of providing a display of female pulchritude, and I can so much more readily admire that as an onlooker."

"You are a spoilsport," she complained, yet in a jocular vein. "Well, I'll try Bully, though I suppose he'll give me the same response. By the bye, who's the beauty with him, he hasn't taken his eyes from her since she came in."

"That happens to be Miss Melissa Woodard, Mrs. Bransom's sister."

"My goodness, I should never have guessed," she remarked, in such obvious amazement that Mortimer frowned. "I meant no offense, it's just they don't look at all like sisters."

"Perhaps if you ask Miss Woodard to take the part of Helen, Bully may agree to be Paris. You, my dear, would make a quite astounding Venus."

"Mmmm, that's rather a good idea, for Lady Radcliffe is taking the part of Juno in her tableau."

"What could be more appropriate, since Venus and Juno were also mortal enemies?"

She laughed. "I don't intend to let you off completely. We are to compete for the best tableau, and I intend to raise the most money for the society. I warn you, I expect your full support."

"You know you always have it."

"My dear Charles, what should I do without you, even if you won't be my Paris. Oh dear, there goes Kitty. I'd better catch Bully and his delightful companion before she approaches them."

"Now for the Constable," Mortimer said when she was gone. He smiled, and Penelope noticed the crevices deepen at the corners of his eyes and then chided herself for her interest. He put his hand under her elbow, deftly guiding her across the crowded hall.

"It is in the farthest, darkest corner, away from these great monstrosities, and I find him as true in his depiction of nature as you are. Whereas these gentlemen of the Academy, never within sight nor sound nor smell of a battlefield, hardly let truth disturb their artistic efforts. With all aplomb they depict the scene as they think it should have been, all flag and glory, but where is the dirt, the sweat, the confusion, the gore, the fear, the death. . . ." Mortimer broke off with an impatient shrug. "But perhaps they are right. Why should the truth of war be shown in all its stupidity? Let the illusion remain, for that, after all, is what England wants to believe."

For an instant Penelope thought she saw beyond his calm, nonchalant exterior, but as quickly as she sensed his bitterness it was gone and he smiled again. He indicated a canvas high on the dimly-lit wall.

"There is your Constable, deserving of a much better

9 5

place, but at least it is hung, not always the case with those who deserve it."

"Is it the Academy you think unfair, or life in general?" she asked with interest.

"I don't believe just rewards are given."

"Yet you yourself have been well rewarded."

"That, possibly, is the most unjust of all," he said sardonically and then smiled again. "Since, however, I was so handsomely rewarded for being spared, I am determined to enjoy every minute of everything life has to offer. It is something I might propose for your consideration, Mrs. Bransom."

10

The gods have no time to attend to small matters.
                                        Ovid
                                        Ars Amatoria, ca. 2 BC

"**I** told Mr. Bransom—Edward, I mean—when he called
this morning," Missy announced the following day. "But it
was difficult, Pen, and I'm still not sure that he completely
understood that I wished to delay the matter until our visit
is over, for he was full of plans. He insists on coming to
escort us home in June, to which I agreed, but not to anything else. I said I would let him know my feelings when he
came, but though I asked him not to, I am not at all sure
that he is not going to talk to the rector about calling the
banns. What should I do?"

"If you feel, in your own heart, that you have been entirely frank with Mr. Bransom, any premature actions on
his part can be no fault of yours."

The sisters were sitting together in the morning room
devising a costume for Missy's role of Helen, that she had
accepted to play opposite Colonel Bullerton's Paris in the
garden fete, though she had agreed to do so only after
ensuring a part would be given to Emmeline. A note from
Lady Staverton had just been delivered offering Emmeline
the role of Minerva, an offer gladly accepted by Lady Halstead over her daughter's protests; indeed, a more timid
goddess of warfare would have been difficult to find.

"What about this?" Penelope held up an illustration in a

Child's Book of Mythology showing a tearful Helen, in a long flowing robe, bidding farewell to her love. "We could get simply yards and yards of fine gauze, for it must be full, gather it at the shoulders, drape it across the neck and then cinch the waist with a silken rope tie—the art of understatement. You'll look gorgeous, but you always do. Em's costume is going to be more difficult. I must think about that."

Penelope had offered to make the costumes since both young ladies would be busy with rehearsals in the week that preceded the fete. The results of her handwork—Missy's soft Grecian gown and a simple but elegant Nile green tunic decorated with a border of Minerva's symbol, the screech owl, for Emmeline—were pronounced so successful the participants insisted that Penelope attend.

Missy was obdurate. "If you won't come to see us, then we shan't go, shall we, Emmeline?"

"No, indeed. Do come, Penelope. I need you to give me courage."

"And it is in the afternoon, and outside, too," Lady Halstead, who was following the event with keen enthusiasm, put in. "Lady Radcliffe has such a lovely garden, and magnificent hothouses where she grows the most exquisite orchids of which you've never seen equal, I'll be bound."

It was impossible for Penelope to refuse such blandishments and temptations. So, on the afternoon of the fete, all four ladies set out from Devonshire Place, the costumes having been carefully packed and carried over earlier by Meg, who had also taken along donations from each of them to be auctioned for the cause. Penelope had had framed the watercolour painting she had done of Mortimer's violets; even she had admitted that the result in an oval blue lacquer frame was pleasing.

"I'm sure I shall just die when I have to stand before all those people out there," Emmeline whispered to Penelope as their carriage stopped in front of Lady Radcliffe's. "Even though I know they'll be looking at Missy and not me, I shall feel so conspicuous."

"I certainly expect you to be conspicuous," Penelope returned, "for you look so very lovely, positively regal."

"Do I really look regal?"

"Really."

Yet it was not only Penelope's encouragement but also the encouragement of a certain young gentleman who stood close to the door as though waiting for them and turned so very pink at the sight of Emmeline that her own timidity vanished at such evidence of her power over Mr. Gerald Wendling.

Lady Halstead was immediately taken aside by Lady Beddows, who had pressing information to impart, the young ladies were quickly ushered behind the scenes to change into their costumes, and Penelope went in search of the hothouses and Lady Radcliffe's magnificent orchids. There she was not disappointed, for she found a profusion of exotic blooms, carefully labelled, the purple and pale mauve cattleya, the green and white lady slipper, the bright yellow dendrobium, and the small but spectacular moth orchid. Not only the beauty and fragrance of the flowers fascinated her but also the luxuriant and heavy foliage everywhere, and the moist, cloying air enervating but oddly exciting in its strangeness. She wondered how it might be to live in such warmth and humidity, never found in England, what difference such an environment might make to character and susceptibility. Would people, like plants, become exotic?

It was as she was admiring a particularly beautiful cattleya, bending down to examine its irregular perianth, that she was startled by a male voice behind her.

"Lovely, isn't it? So delicate, so pale, so smooth, so very vulnerable; one must take care, for orchids are easily crushed."

Turning, she recognized Sir Reginald Palfry, who had been brought to Devonshire Place—a friend of her husband, Edward Bransom had said on introducing him. There was something unpleasant in his voice and a veiled expression in his eyes; his lips were red and moist . . . too red, too moist. She thought of Mortimer's warning and, realizing they were quite apart from the rest of the company, tried to conceal the terror which rose in her breast at being alone with one of the opposite sex, one who reminded her far too much of Josiah Bransom. He filled her with dread, yet he had done nothing, nothing except look at her.

"They are lovely," she agreed, her eyes seeking a path to the door by which she had entered.

"I knew your husband well, so well, I feel I must also know you. You're a charming little lady; he was fortunate to have you for a wife, a warm companion in his later years."

"I must get back, Sir Reginald. I've promised to look over Missy's costume before she appears."

"That lovely little sister of yours. She, too, is lucky to have you to perform such tasks. I, alas, am all alone," he sighed. "But, tell me, what role is the lovely Miss Woodard to play?"

"Helen of Troy."

"Delightful! The face that launched a thousand ships, though it was much more than a face which caused such strife in Troy, don't you think?" He laughed at his quip, and as she made no reply, went on, "Is there to be no Godiva?"

"I'm quite sure I don't know."

"Your sister would have been quite exquisite, but I'm sure her future husband would object to such an exhibition."

"Her future husband?"

"Yes. Mr. Edward Bransom informs me they are to marry—but I forgot, it's not yet announced."

"It most certainly is not."

"But that is not my concern. When I'm with one pretty lady it does not do to discuss another, even if that other is her sister."

Penelope found herself retreating from him around the trestle tables on which the plants were set. She had a strong desire to run from him, yet he had done nothing except utter a few foolish words, and she knew how ludicrous such behaviour would appear. Nevertheless, she could not entirely suppress her fear.

As she rounded the end of the long table, she backed into someone and a cry broke from her lips.

"I am so very sorry, Mrs. Bransom. Do please excuse me for startling you." It was Mortimer, who wore a contrite smile. Penelope smiled in return, sighing in relief.

"No, no, it was my fault entirely. Excuse me, you see, I am

in a hurry—I have to look at Missy's dress before she appears."

"And do you always walk backwards when you are in a hurry?"

"Well, no, but I . . . well, you see . . ." She found herself stumbling over her words; she knew her cheeks were flushed, and chided herself for her own stupidity. She had been frightened, like a child, over nothing but innuendo.

Mortimer, looking down the aisle between the rows of plants, caught sight of Sir Reginald's ample figure and said dryly, "I see."

"No, you don't see," Penelope asserted, alarmed at the impression she must have given him. "I must go, excuse me."

No matter what he thought, she was glad to escape; the air of the hothouses, previously exciting and exotic, had become suffocating.

Finding both Missy and Emmeline quite ready, looking lovely as she sincerely assured them, and realizing that she could do little to allay Emmeline's nervousness—which increased as the time for their appearance approached—Penelope decided that her presence in the melee of Greek gods, nymphs and satyrs behind the scenes hindered rather than helped matters. She therefore made her way to the lawn where, on a lace-covered table, were displayed the objects to be auctioned for the cause: a delicate pair of Dresden vases, a magnificent Wedgwood teapot, a lapis lazuli necklace, a miniature of the Prince Regent, and an ancient Book of Hours. The magnificence of most of the pieces took her aback, and she was glad her own small offering was not among them. But she was mistaken, for there, at the end of the table, the gentleman she recognized as Mr. Samuel Trueblood, the connoisseur of art she had met at the Royal Academy, was examining her painting closely through his glass.

"Peculiar," he muttered. "No signature," and catching sight of Penelope he said, "Madam, Mrs. Bransom, isn't it, your eyes are younger than mine, perhaps you can discover who painted this water colour."

"It is unsigned, Mr. Trueblood."

"Ah, so you, too, have looked for it."

"No. You see, I am the artist."

"Indeed!" He looked at her with renewed interest. "Indeed! I had not taken it for the work of a lady. It is exquisite, truly delicate, exact in detail yet never losing sight of the whole. You have, I gather, studied under a master."

"I have been drawing and painting from nature since a child, but I am entirely self-taught."

"Really! That is quite amazing, Mrs. Bransom. Yet I can clearly see you are no dilettante. Has your work not been shown anywhere?"

"Only by a friend of my father's who used it to illustrate his lectures in botany."

"And where was that?"

"At Balliol."

Mr. Trueblood smiled, a wintry smile, but a smile nevertheless.

"I'm a Balliol man myself. You would do me a great favour, Mrs. Bransom, if you would sit with me. The program is about to begin. I cannot be late, for, as you may know, it benefits a society over which I preside."

"And a worthy one. Unwanted, unloved children deserve attention."

"Indeed, and I've no doubt a great deal of money will be raised today. Apart from my own donation, the Dresden vases for which I paid a hefty sum, more than two hundred guineas in point of fact, I shall bid on your painting, and bid handsomely."

"I'm honoured, sir."

As Mr. Trueblood was conducting her to a seat beside his own reserved place in a row near the raised dais, they came upon Lord Mortimer walking hand in hand with two immaculately garbed children, the boy in a white nankeen suit, the girl in pink sprigged muslin, obviously no waifs or strays.

Mr. Trueblood, after acknowledging Mortimer's stiff bow, stopped to pat the children on their heads in the manner of one who was uncomfortable with children and did not particularly like them, a manner which made them cling more tightly to Mortimer, who said gravely, "Mrs. Bransom, would you allow me to present to you my friends, Master Philby Staverton and Miss Cynthia Staverton. Master Staverton is quite the cleverest boy I know; he has just been declining Latin fifth declension nouns for me and remembered that *meridies* is masculine, bravo! As for Miss Staverton, she is not only clever but quite the prettiest young lady of my acquaintance."

Master Staverton bowed and little Miss Staverton curtsied, but neither let go of Mortimer's hand, and, the introduction completed, the little girl asked, "Uncle Charles, may we take our places now?"

"Would you care to sit with us, Mrs. Bransom?"

"Mrs. Bransom is joining me," Mr. Trueblood rasped.

"I see," was the enigmatic response and again, as in the hothouse earlier, Penelope wanted to remind him that he saw nothing at all, but already Mr. Trueblood was guiding her to the seat beside his. She saw Mortimer escort the two children to their places on the other side of the aisle and engage in telling them a story while the children hung on his every word.

Penelope was annoyed to find her seat was immediately in front of Mrs. Plunkett-Gall, who had greeted her with an expansive smile as she sat down. Her strident tones commenting on everyone and everything were to be heard throughout the event.

"Look at Lord Mortimer, how he adores those children."

"How they adore him," said Mrs. Plunkett-Gall's companion.

Mrs. Plunkett-Gall lowered her voice, but only slightly, so that everyone within earshot could clearly hear her comment, "If he hadn't been out of the country at the time of their conception, I'd swear they were his and not Staverton's."

"Oh, I don't know, I think he's just the sort of man who loves children. That's what will make him marry, and it won't be long now, for he's not getting any younger. I've just the young lady who will suit. . . ."

"No, my dear," Mrs. Plunkett-Gall cut in, "I claim that

right. I know exactly what he needs—a nice girl, good family, who'll be happy in the north while he visits his lady in London."

"Such a shame they couldn't have married," her companion sighed.

"Don't be romantic, Maud, it doesn't become you."

Penelope was glad when the pageant began at last with a tableau of Orpheus, a rather stout Orpheus, looking back into the underworld and thus sealing the fate of his wife, Eurydice.

"With a face like that he probably wanted her to stay in Hades," Mrs. Plunkett-Gall remarked, while her companion gave an appreciative snigger.

Similar remarks were made about Pygmalion's Galatea, too fat by far, and Pyramus and Thisbe, who were lucky to have a wall separating them, for everyone knew that, far from being lovers, they fought like demons. Lady Radcliffe's Juno dispatching her messenger Iris to aid Alcyone was complimented, but then Kitty Radcliffe was a friend of Mrs. Plunkett-Gall's. The last tableau, Lady Staverton's Trojan War, outdid all the rest in brilliance, forcing silence from even the pageant's most severe critic. Lady Staverton, assured of her own beauty, had chosen to surround herself by other beauties; Missy was stunningly gorgeous as Helen, saluting a soulful Paris who, without any difficulty, never took his eyes from her. They were surrounded by a bevy of gods and goddesses, among whom was Emmeline, the timidity of her Minerva passing unremarked. But it was Georgina Staverton, with that fascination which comes from a woman aware of her own allure and making full use of it, who drew most of the attention even though her position was at the side of the dais rather than in the centre. Her golden hair was pinioned in Greek fashion in bands of deeper gold, her body swathed in a diaphanous garment of white silk threaded with gold which clung to her body as it fell so as to reveal each curve, each line, so transparent that she seemed quite bare, though it shimmered with light whenever she moved. There was a gasped hush, and Georgina Staverton, clearly aware that every eye was upon her yet without apparent conceit, luxuriated in the wave of admiration which arose from the admiring throng much as a rose opens its petals to receive a summer shower.

Penelope could not prevent herself from turning to watch Mortimer's smile as he saw Lady Staverton before whispering to her children, who reached under their seats to pick up baskets of flowers and ran up to present them to their mother as the audience broke into applause.

The rapture of the moment was clearly borne out in the donations which Lady Staverton came forward to accept, as had the others before her. Guineas, gold pieces of all denomination were placed in the basket she proffered, as much a tribute to her as to the waifs and strays. When she came to Lord Mortimer, rather than reaching into his pocket he took from his neckpiece a diamond pin of exquisite cut and clarity which caused another round of applause. The lady curtsied low, smiling prettily, and said, "The waifs and strays welcome your generosity, sir, but on their behalf I give you my personal thanks."

"With Philby out of the way, undoubtedly we can imagine how she intends to thank him," came Mrs. Plunkett-Gall's strident whisper.

Next began the auction of the articles from the table for which the bidding was brisk, with much good cheer as donors as well as recipients were thanked, Mr. Trueblood's Dresden vases fetching close to one thousand guineas from Lady Radcliffe.

Again and again the gavel fell until at last only Penelope's watercolour remained.

"Vi'lets, lovely vi'lets!" Lord Radcliffe, acting as auctioneer, imitated the flower girl's cry. "What am I bid for these really lovely vi'lets?"

A few desultory calls were made for inconsequential sums until Mr. Trueblood, in self-satisfied tones designed to put an end to the matter, put in a call of fifty pounds—a bid that to Penelope's and everyone else's surprise was immediately doubled by Lord Mortimer.

"Then I'll double your hundred, sir." Mr. Trueblood looked at Mortimer in annoyance.

"Let's make that five, shall we, and guineas rather than pounds."

The crowd, which had begun drifting away to the refreshment tent, returned, enlivened by the exchange. They stood back to watch as the bidding rose higher and higher, the spectators turning from Trueblood, leaning forward in annoyance, to Mortimer, lolling back in his chair, then back to the small watercolour which had just reached the enormous sum of three thousand guineas.

"Whose is it?" was the question on Mrs. Plunkett-Gall's lips, a question echoed in every corner.

Mr. Trueblood rose in high dudgeon. "Damn it, Mortimer, it's yours," he said as he stalked off without a backward glance, leaving Penelope alone.

Mortimer came over, the children hurrying after him.

"Since your companion is gone, perhaps you would like to take tea with us, Mrs. Bransom." He took her arm as he spoke.

They were constantly accosted by members of the party commenting on the painting and the vast sum he had paid for it. To all he gave the bland reply that he was only anxious to contribute to the cause, leaving Penelope to wonder whether he had recognized the painting to be hers or whether his only object had been to annoy Mr. Trueblood.

Lord Radcliffe, freed of his auctioneer's duties, called over, "You certainly dropped a pretty penny this afternoon, Mortimer. Was it art for art's sake or to outdo Trueblood?"

"For the cause, Radcliffe, for the cause, dear boy."

"Ah, to be sure," Radcliffe winked as he spoke.

"Did you really want to annoy Mr. Trueblood?" Penelope asked when Radcliffe was gone.

"To some extent. I dislike him intensely, and I did want to deprive him of something he wanted, but it wasn't just that—I was set on having the painting as soon as I saw it to make a pair with the other I own."

"You knew it was mine then!"

"Of course. And I felt if anyone should own it, it should be me. They were, after all, my violets, were they not?"

11

*There prevails among men of letters an opinion that all
appearance of science is particularly hateful to women.*
        Samuel Johnson
        The Rambler, 12 November 1751

Penelope was alarmed to discover that Meg Watkins had
not returned to Devonshire Place after delivering the costumes for the fete, nor was there any message to explain her
absence.

"What can we do, Henrietta?" she demanded of her
friend the following morning. "It's just not like Meg to disappear without a word. I'm really worried. Something
awful may have happened to her."

"My dear Penelope, you're too naive by half. She's probably off with some young groom she ran into, and by the
time she gets back she'll be in the family way. You'll see.
Servants are such a nuisance."

"I don't believe that, not of Meg. Her constant thanks for
having been saved from the streets, for being allowed to
remain here with us, embarrass me; I always feel she gives
us so much more than she receives. Even if she had found a
lad she liked, that wouldn't be wrong. And even if there had
been some . . . some dalliance, which I doubt, still I am
convinced that she would have returned. What can I do?
Not knowing what's become of her makes me think the very
worst—that perhaps her body may be floating in the river,
or lying in the morgue unclaimed."

Penelope shuddered, and her friend, remarking her worried brow, realized that no matter her own inclination to forget the matter, some effort must be made to find the girl.

"I have it!" she exclaimed. "Samuel Trueblood, he's the man to find her if she's to be found—through that society of his, the Waifs and Strays."

"I don't know." Penelope pursed her lips, remembering Mortimer's dislike of Trueblood, feeling it could not be entirely without cause. "Is he really seriously involved with the society? I've heard it said he's no more than a figurehead."

"I suppose he's a bit of a social climber, but he's not alone in that. I know a lot of people dislike him—Mortimer for one—but he does a lot of good as a patron of the arts. By the way, my dear, that was quite a little spectacle yesterday, the bidding between them for your little painting. It was nice, but my dear, three thousand guineas! Mrs. Plunkett-Gall would wheedle it from me that it was yours, I hope you didn't mind. She did lift her eyebrows when I told her."

"I wish you hadn't."

"Why?"

"Because it was only for the cause."

"Yes, well, I see."

Penelope wished that Lady Halstead wouldn't say "I see" in the same tone as Mortimer had used, but to comment further would only give the matter undue emphasis.

"If Sam Trueblood was willing to bid that high on your little watercolour, Penelope, I've no doubt he'll be willing to put his society to work to find your maid. Must say I wish he would—she really had a way with Emmeline's hair that made her appear quite pretty."

"I'll do as you suggest, Henrietta," Penelope said quietly, not thinking of Emmeline's hair but her poor, dear Meg alone in such a formidable city.

The result of her note was an immediate call by Mr. Trueblood to Devonshire Place and his promise to leave no stone unturned until he discovered Meg's whereabouts and well-being, which elicited grateful thanks from Penelope and an unvoiced decision to paint a floral tribute for his efforts. She found it hard to understand why anyone should dislike him.

Missy shared her sister's concern over Meg, though there was a certain distraction in her air, a distraction that Penelope had observed on the afternoon of Lady Radcliffe's fete and that increased as the days passed, never one without a visit to Devonshire Place of Colonel Bullerton, convincing Penelope that Colonel Bullerton's visits and Missy's distraction were not entirely unrelated.

Indeed, it became obvious even to Lady Halstead, who took it upon herself to examine, with more than usual care, that gentleman's background.

"He has five thousand a year, not wealthy by any means but comfortably off, especially for a younger son; the family's of good English stock, not noble, but no taint of trade about them. Mother's a bit of a harridan, Mrs. Plunkett-Gall tells me, but she resides most of the time on the family estate outside Malmesbury."

"If Mrs. Plunkett-Gall finds her a harridan, she must be one indeed," Penelope commented with some asperity.

"I know you find Mrs. Plunkett-Gall a bit nosy, Penelope, but really if one needs information—and in this case I made it a point to find out about the gentleman since he calls so often—she's the one who knows. She means well, really she does."

"I suppose so," Penelope agreed, though unconvinced. She went on in more thoughtful tones, "Do you think that Missy may be serious about Colonel Bullerton, Henrietta?"

"It's more a case of whether Colonel Bullerton is serious about Missy, isn't it?"

"I've heard he's not one to fall in love indiscriminately."

"Did Mrs. Plunkett-Gall say so?"

"No, it was his friend, Lord Mortimer." Penelope was at a loss to understand why she felt quite so embarrassed at mentioning that gentleman's name.

"Well, *he* should know. Certainly no one can accuse Lord Mortimer of having a similar trait." And sensing Penelope was about to change the subject, she hurriedly interjected, "Confess, Penelope, weren't you surprised when Mortimer paid all that money for your painting? I must say it's aroused a great deal of comment."

"Mrs. Plunkett-Gall's tongue has been busy, I can see."

"Perhaps, though she's not the only one," Henrietta Halstead said defensively.

"And the fact that he donated a diamond worth several times that sum on behalf of Lady Staverton's tableau caused none, I suppose."

"Not none, but that was to be expected."

"Was it not also to be expected that Lord Mortimer would want to thwart a gentleman he detests, for whatever reason?"

"I suppose it was," Lady Halstead agreed, though quite unpersuaded.

Penelope had secured tickets to a lecture on the sciences to be given by Sir Humphry Davy at the Royal Institution on Albemarle Street, a lecture to which she had promised to take Meg. The girl had expressed great interest in the newspaper articles Penelope had read to her of the chemical genius who was sweeping London by storm. Davy was astounding his fashionable audiences by administering, for the delectation of a few among them, something called laughing gas from a silken bag. His lectures, accompanied by the loud noises, bright lights and often pungent smells of his experiments, delighted and enthralled the increasing numbers of ladies and gentlemen who attended. "Fashion and chemistry form an incongruous union," one wag had commented.

Meg had been so thrilled at the prospect of seeing him that Penelope hoped that the occasion might prompt her return, but the day arrived without word from either Meg or Mr. Trueblood. Still, Penelope did not give up hope that Meg might be waiting for her at the hall, and she ventured forth without offering the place to Lady Halstead or Emmeline. She was disappointed, however, on arriving at Albemarle Street—the crowd was enormous, but though she waited until it thinned out, there was no sign of Meg's slight figure. By the time Penelope made her way inside, she was obliged to take a seat at the back from which she was barely able to glimpse the famous chemist, but she could hear him, and his lecture enthralled her with new objects for contemplation as well as amusement. He was keenly interested in the application of chemistry to agriculture, constantly insisting on the utilitarian value of science in forming a beneficent alliance between man and nature.

It was only as Davy finished his lecture with, "We do not look to distant ages—we look for a time that we may reasonably expect—for a bright day of which we already behold the dawn," that Penelope sighted the broad shoulders of a figure some distance in front of her, shoulders belonging to a gentleman immediately called upon to sample the laughing gas.

There was some good-natured badinage between the two men before Lord Mortimer bent over the bag with its long nozzle to take several inhalations.

"That's enough, Mortimer." Sir Humphry laughed. "We can't have you completely inebriated."

"Spoilsport!" Mortimer snorted.

"Well, tell us your sensations."

"Mmmm . . . something like having consumed a whole magnum of champagne all by myself, a little giddy, light-headed, yet no queasiness in the stomach."

"Jolly good."

"But perhaps that's a male reaction, Davy. A lady should try it, she might feel differently."

"Very well, then, choose someone."

Mortimer swiftly scanned the audience.

"Ah, I see someone I know," he said, just as though he did not know half of those in attendance. "Mrs. Bransom— yes, the lady in the back of the hall." He indicated Penelope so that all turned in her direction. "Mrs. Bransom has some outspoken opinions on a number of things."

"Just what we need. Do stand aside to let Mrs. Bransom come up here. I promise it will do you no harm, ma'am."

With all eyes upon her, Penelope could not bear to argue, and she made her way forward to bend over the contraption.

"Don't just breathe, you really must inhale," Mortimer

said, holding the device to her nostrils. "Now inhale deeply, isn't that right, Davy?"

"Yes, that's it."

Penelope breathed in deeply, just once, and then she stood back. Whereas before she had felt timid, even embarrassed by the spectacle she was making of herself, suddenly it was all fun. Slowly a wide smile crossed her features, and the crowd broke into applause.

"There," Mortimer triumphed. "I told you we might rely on Mrs. Bransom for an honest opinion."

The demonstration finished, the hall began to empty, and, bidding good-day to Davy, Mortimer escorted Penelope towards the entrance.

"Well, what did you think of it?"

She was still smiling. "It was really rather delicious. Is that really the effect of champagne?"

"Yes, unless you have too much, which leads to a dry mouth and an unpleasant tummy, often as not a roaring headache. But have you never tried it?"

"Never."

"I begin to think there are many things you have yet to try."

His soft voice, his blue eyes were teasing her, she knew, yet somehow she didn't mind.

"At least now I know what laughing gas is like. In fact I've learned a great deal about science this afternoon. Sir Humphry is impressive in his knowledge."

"He is, and a fine gentleman to boot. Not that I agree with all his ideas, but they give great room for discussion. We've burned out many a candle and emptied many a bottle of port over them."

"Yet to what can you object since it all seems so beneficial?"

"Oh, the unknowns, I suppose. I believe unless these scientific findings are used wisely they may become horned monsters. For my part I prefer to fight more recognizable dragons."

"Yet these discoveries do nothing in and of themselves."

"Just so, if the knowledge is used for the benefit of mankind as a whole and not for the few. All too often, however, these discoveries are converted to personal gain, then there's no telling what harm may result in the wrong hands. The power looms, the new machinery, for instance, good in themselves, but may they not eventually blight England's green hills and dales if money-grubbers seize upon the idea of constructing factory after factory filled with machinery belching smoke and dust everywhere? Davy says that's progress; to some extent I agree, but progress, like everything else, mustn't be allowed to run amuck."

They were, by this time, outside the hall on Albemarle Street, and Mortimer looked around before asking, "You are surely not here alone?"

"Yes, as a matter of fact, I am."

"Really, Mrs. Bransom, I should have thought you'd have learned a lesson from that experience in the park. You could at least have a maid accompany you."

"Well, I couldn't. You see Meg Watkins—the girl I met that day in the park—came to work for us, but I haven't seen her since the day of the fete."

Penelope went on to tell him all about Meg and about her concern. Unlike Lady Halstead, Mortimer did not scoff or pass the matter off lightly.

"London is a cruel place, to be sure, though being London born and bred, the girl is undoubtedly aware of that, so Meg is probably better off than some country wench. Perhaps she may have been homesick."

"I don't believe so. She didn't like her father."

Mortimer had fallen into step beside Penelope, motioning to Glossop, who had awaited him, to follow.

"There is no need," Penelope protested. "Today I know my way."

"We have just been saying what a cruel town this is, and, for a lady, we are in one of its most questionable quarters. Besides, it was stuffy inside. I'm glad of the walk."

As they turned into Bond Street with its loitering dandies and young swells, raking each passing woman with lascivious stares, Penelope understood what he had meant by it being an unsuitable place for a lady. Though protected by her obvious air of respectability emphasized by her mourning dress, she was glad nevertheless to feel Mortimer's hand on her elbow guiding her through the crowded street.

As they came to the corner of Grosvenor Street, Penelope noticed a crowd of raffish bucks taking their sport with a gaudily clad girl of the streets. Sensing her impulse to intervene, Mortimer took her arm more firmly saying, "You really cannot set out to right every wrong in London, Mrs. Bransom. That is the girl's trade."

Penelope might perhaps have obeyed his counsel, had not the young woman turned at the sound of their voices. Seeing her face, Penelope shook herself free of Mortimer's hold and plunged into the unruly circle, flailing at the young men right and left as she did so.

"Leave her alone! Leave her alone! Do you hear, go away! You can't treat her so, she's no more than a child. Go away."

They paid little heed, laughing more heartily, until one of them caught sight of Mortimer at her heels and his taunting died on his lips.

"It's Lord Mortimer," he muttered, and one by one the tormentors dispersed and went on their way.

"Mrs. Bransom. Oh, Mrs. Bransom. You shouldn't, you really shouldn't," Meg cried.

"What are you doing here, Meg?" Penelope looked from her thin child's face with its carelessly rouged cheeks, to the low cut of her bright red chemise. "And dressed like that?"

"Oh, ma'am, I'm that sorry," Meg tried to staunch the flow of her tears. "You must go, reely you must."

"Why? I refuse to until you explain to me exactly what you are doing here looking like a . . . like that."

Meg looked pleadingly at Lord Mortimer, who put in gently, "Surely, Mrs. Bransom, it must be obvious even to you why the girl is here."

Penelope flushed, yet still her eyes searched Meg's face.

"But why, Meg, why? Did I not pay you enough? Didn't you like the work, or being with us? Were you unhappy? Why did you not come back?"

"Oh, mum, I was never more 'appy in me life. It was me ole pot and pan, 'e followed me and made me go back wiv 'im. 'E sold them nice togs wot belonged to Miss Melissa and Miss Emmeline and got 'im some blue ruin and me this 'ere and 'e put me on the street."

"Oh, no!" Penelope shuddered. "But I won't have it. You're to come back, I'll take care of you. And I'll take care of your father too."

"I can't, mum."

"Why not, surely you don't—you don't like such a life?"

"No, it's not that, but you see 'e's took bees and 'oney for me from a gent. I'm to wait 'ere for 'im to come fer me. If I went wiv you, I'd cop it good and proper—when 'e's angry 'e's worse to me than the gents, and they're bad enough."

Penelope looked pleadingly at Mortimer.

"I can't leave her, really I can't. I shall stay here with her and pay the gentleman whatever it was he gave her father for her."

"My dear lady, you've had too much of that potion and you must still be under its influence if you think for a moment I'd leave you here." Mortimer was already motioning Glossop over. "Glossop will see that you both get safely back to Devonshire Place."

"But the gent," Meg protested. " 'E'll be 'ere any minute! Cor lumme, if 'e goes and tells me dad . . ."

"I shall take care of him—and your father too," Mortimer said firmly, helping them into his coach and shutting the door.

As they pulled away, Penelope looked back to see Mortimer approaching a carriage which had just arrived and stopped hesitantly. She couldn't be sure, but the occupant looked very much like a gentleman she had met; perhaps it was only her confusion which made her think it was Sir Reginald Palfry.

She turned to the girl beside her who clung to her hand.

"Don't worry, Meg. Lord Mortimer will take care of everything. I'm sure of it."

12

All men think all men mortal but themselves.
Edward Young
Night Thoughts I, 1742

"**I** don't believe you have any further need to worry about the girl. I had words with . . . with the gentleman involved, but more importantly, I talked to her father. He's a rascal, but I believe the account is settled."

Two days after that awful discovery of Meg on Bond Street, Lord Mortimer had called to speak to Penelope, which had caused instant speculation on the part of Lady Halstead.

"Watkins is, perhaps, no more disreputable than his neighbours," Mortimer went on. "His only interest is in getting enough money, from whatever source, to supply himself with blue ruin—gin. It is a depressing sight to walk through those alleys by the river, to see the glazed stares of people living out their days in a stupor. Makes you wonder about the purpose of life—but I suppose all of us must consider that, whatever our station."

He was an interesting man, Penelope thought, especially when his eyes grew dark and deep, but as though to disperse any seriousness, he laughed. "Enough of that, all of us like to forget at times. You too, I don't doubt, though your garb denies it."

"I do," Penelope agreed quietly. "I can never thank you enough, Lord Mortimer. But I must insist, absolutely insist, upon repaying whatever you found it necessary to pay Watkins, and please don't deny that you paid him to release Meg."

"It was so close to nothing that I refuse to mention it."

"But Meg is my responsibility, not yours. Please, for I feel I have done little enough in the matter."

"Do you call it little enough to take on that band of scoundrels the other day? The way you charged in to come to the girl's aid, I've never seen the like. Pure valour!"

"Coming from Waterloo's hero I should be flattered. It was, as you pointed out, pure laughing gas!" And they both laughed at the remembrance of that experience. "I won't have you changing the subject, sir, and please don't leave it to me to conjecture what I owe you."

"You owe me nothing. I was only too happy to be of service; it is rare that one is able to assist where help is truly needed."

"It would seem you never cease to help, judging from your generous contributions to the waifs and strays at Lady Radcliffe's."

"To be frank, I often feel that such affairs are little more than opportunities for the aggrandizement and pleasure of those sponsoring them. I wonder how many people at that fete actually considered those poor creatures it was ostensibly benefiting. Truly, I felt a far greater sense of accomplishment out of this small matter." Yet seeing Penelope's face was still clouded, Mortimer added, "If it will make you feel any easier, you may sketch or paint something for me— a bridal bouquet, for instance."

"A bridal bouquet?" For some reason, Penelope found herself unaccountably afraid of what his answer might be.

"Yes, for I expect a wedding in the near future. Perhaps it is too early to speak of it, indeed I suppose I should not, but I shall. You see Bully—Colonel Bullerton—intends to set out for Oxfordshire tomorrow. He wishes to talk to your brother."

"To Arthur?"

"Yes. He wants to request his approval to speak to your sister, to ask her to marry him. He has asked me to accompany him, to give him courage, I suppose. I want to emphasize, Mrs. Bransom, that he has said nothing in the matter to Miss Woodard, nor would he should your brother be opposed to the plan."

"Yet surely it is a matter that only concerns my sister, not Arthur," Penelope protested, remembering her brother's outspoken support of Edward Bransom's suit.

"I agree with you, marriage should concern only those most directly concerned, but Bully is, perhaps, the most ethical man of my acquaintance. Sometimes I wonder how he abides me as a friend."

"You are not ethical, Lord Mortimer? That is censure indeed, not entirely justified from my observation."

"You know me little. I do have standards, but they are not always those of the society in which I move. Bully, however, is everything to be desired as a prospective husband. Indeed, were my own sister not married, and happily so, I would wish he might have chosen her as a wife, for he is trustworthy, kind, honest, upright, a thoroughly decent sort of chap. There, you see, already I'm pleading his case."

"And pleading it where it is unnecessary; I am convinced from my own observation that Colonel Bullerton is an admirable gentleman. I only hope you are as successful with Arthur. Certainly, should he ask my advice, I should tell him what I have just told you, but I doubt he will."

"I have a close relationship with my sister, but I know this is not always so in families."

"You mustn't misunderstand. Arthur and I are not estranged in any way, but he does love to dominate, and since I am older than he and not without sense, I find that irksome. But I would do anything I could for him and for his wife, Phyllis, of whom I'm really very fond. Indeed, I'm delighted when they call on my help as each new little Woodard arrives, for I dote on their children. I suppose what I resent is Arthur's opinion that his judgement is superior to mine simply because he is of the male sex."

"I hadn't thought much about it before, but I suppose we males are brought up to believe ourselves superior beings,"

Mortimer reflected. "It's a double-edged sword, however—think what a shock it is for us when we discover we are only mortal."

Yet Penelope, watching the compelling smile that swept across his face, wondered whether he was not, perhaps, superior to others.

"What fools we mortals be—especially when we take ourselves seriously. I try not to, but you, Mrs. Bransom, are always leading me astray."

"I don't intend to." Penelope smiled.

"Alas," Mortimer sighed. "I'm aware you do not."

"When do you and Colonel Bullerton leave?"

"Tomorrow. That is why I am glad to have found you in this morning."

"But you will return to London," she found herself pressing.

"Of course, the season is by no means over. I only hope. . . ."

But Penelope did not discover what it was he hoped. At that moment another visitor arrived, a most inopportune visitor at the sight of whom Mortimer's face assumed a stern, even haughty demeanour.

"Mrs. Bransom, how well you are looking," Mr. Samuel Trueblood greeted her after Mortimer had barely acknowledged his bow. "I called to tell you that so far my search for your maidservant has met with little success, but even though I have scoured the city, I am undeterred. I am convinced I shall succeed, you have my word on it. The matter will be resolved."

"The matter is already resolved, Trueblood," Mortimer drawled. "Mrs. Bransom found the young woman."

"You, Mrs. Bransom! But how is it possible that you succeeded where I have failed?" Samuel Trueblood's sense of the injustice at such a turn of events was apparent, making Penelope hasten to explain, "It was pure chance, Mr. Trueblood. We ran across her by accident. Lord Mortimer resolved matters with Meg's father, who was the one responsible for her disappearance."

"And here I've been spending all my efforts looking for the wench," he replied in aggrieved tones.

"I'm sorry. I should have let you know the minute I found her, but quite truthfully I was so pleased and happy to see her again that I quite forgot."

"And where was it that you ran across her?"

Penelope hesitated, sensing Trueblood would find disfavour with her reply. "It was on Bond Street."

"Bond Street! You mean—was she—my dear lady, how can I put it. . . ."

"Perhaps you should put it as it was; the girl was forced into prostituting herself," Mortimer put in brutally.

"Really, Mortimer," Trueblood protested before turning to Penelope. "My dear Mrs. Bransom, surely you did not take her back into your house after . . . after . . ." His voice faded away as Penelope broke in indignantly, "Of course I did. It wasn't her choice, I daresay it's not the choice of most of the women on the streets."

It was quite clear that Mr. Trueblood found the turn of the conversation distasteful. It was equally clear that Lord Mortimer found the presence of Mr. Trueblood distasteful, for he abruptly made to leave, bowing to Penelope, "I trust I shall see you on my return to London."

"You are on your way to Chenwyth?" Trueblood asked.

"I don't expect to go so far north."

"He is of a taciturn frame of mind," Trueblood said as the door closed behind Mortimer. "I preferred him before all these honours and riches were bestowed upon him. He was a decent enough youngster; indeed, I did all I could to help him, as I did all the family. I don't know what his dear mother would say if she could see his arrogance now."

"She is dead?"

"Both his parents are dead. It was his mother I knew well—a lovely lady. I often think how it might have been if things had turned out differently. She wished to marry me, her children might have been mine, but fate decided otherwise. Mortimer's father consumed far too much wine and gambled money he did not have—he borrowed from me unmercifully, and I gave for her sake."

Penelope saw Trueblood with renewed interest. "And you never married because of her?"

"Never, but she is long since gone—I begin to think that I should—I am not too old to enter that estate."

"No, indeed, I intended no such implication."

Penelope was hard pressed to say nothing of Colonel Bullerton to her sister, particularly when she saw her downcast face at his absence from Devonshire Place in the days that followed. Lady Halstead, however, had no such reticence in her speculations about Lord Mortimer.

"I do believe he has a penchant for you, Penelope, no matter what you may say to the contrary. There was the matter of his purchase of your little watercolour, three thousand, my dear, it's still being talked about. Now he comes calling upon you. I don't wish you to think of me as you do Mrs. Plunkett-Gall, but I must say it leads to conjecture."

"His visit did not concern me." And when she saw her friend's expectant face, Penelope finished rather lamely, "I'm not at liberty to discuss the matter now, but I am sure you will hear of it in a few days."

"Well, Missy, it is still my opinion that your sister has an admirer, a most worthy admirer—but I shall say nothing more in the matter."

Yet in her own heart Penelope began to examine each meeting, each look, each word he had spoken—was it possible that Mortimer had an interest in her? She began, too, to question her own feelings. Why was there a quickening of her senses whenever he approached? Why did she remember how his lips quivered whenever he teased, or how his cobalt eyes grew dark and shadowed at serious matters he might rather forget? Was it possible that she, who had forsworn all men, held a growing attachment for that gentleman? No, she wanted none of them. Yet, as she awaited the return of Colonel Bullerton to discover the outcome of his mission, did she not await with equal expectancy the return of his friend?

Before that time, however, an express arrived from her brother, concerning that visit.

Why did you not warn me? We were quite unprepared to receive such guests. They put up at the George and Dragon, but of course we couldn't allow a gentleman like Lord Mortimer to remain there. I must say he's not difficult, neither of them is, but I had heard Mortimer can be quite arrogant. I saw none of it. He won over Phyllis, and the children simply wouldn't leave him alone—I tried to shoo them off to the nursery, but he would give them rides on his shoulders and tell them stories. Young Arthur wanted to know all about the fighting, but Mortimer seemed to prefer fairy tales, which pleased Beatrice and Stanley, of course. I was truly in a quandary about the purpose of their visit, Colonel Bullerton's offer, for you know that Missy is half-promised to Edward. I was, at first, set on denying him the right to address her, but then Mortimer spoke to me on his friend's behalf—he said if his own sister were not already married he would unhesitatingly welcome Colonel Bullerton, or Bully as he calls him, as a brother-in-law. A man cannot give greater evidence of his faith, yet he said much else of a complimentary nature besides.

Then, the next day, they accompanied us to mattins at St. Anne's where, by the way, your monument to your late husband was remarked upon; I'm sure it is worthy of any London cemetery and is looking particularly fine now the cypresses are growing up around it. Both gentlemen, particularly Mortimer, were the subject of much comment and most well received by all and sundry. Edward himself was all over them, he'd already met them at Devonshire Place, it seems, and he took them around and introduced them as though they were his guests at the Hall rather than ours, which annoyed Phyllis greatly and myself not a little. Of course, he was not aware of the purpose of their visit, nor is he still for I haven't had the heart to mention it. Besides, Missy hasn't accepted Colonel Bullerton—it might be that she prefers Edward and staying in Mayfield as mistress of the Hall. I must say it would make life easier for me if she does; you might tell her that, for Edward is quite set on having her.

With her brother's acceptance of Colonel Bullerton's suit, Penelope sought out her sister and told her all she knew, forewarning her of what was to be expected and showing her Arthur's letter, which Missy finished reading with cheeks flushed, eyes shining.

"I think I should write to him now," she decided.

"To whom, to Colonel Bullerton?"

"No, to Mr. Edward Bransom, to tell him I am marrying Rodney."

"But shouldn't you wait until Colonel Bullerton actually makes his proposal?"

"Oh, I shan't send it until he does, but you see, writing that letter will be the most uncomfortable and unpleasant thing I've ever had to do. Once Rodney is here, I want nothing to mar our happiness."

"Darling, darling Missy!" Penelope hugged her sister. "Nothing shall."

13

Heaven has no rage like love to hatred turned.
William Congreve
The Mourning Bride, 1697

Edward Bransom was furious. He had gone to Kerswell as soon as Missy's letter had been delivered, demanding to know why Arthur Woodard had given his consent. It was a complete misalliance, besides which Missy had been promised to him.

As was often his wont, Arthur had vacillated without actually prevaricating, so that when Edward Bransom accused his uncle's widow of being behind the outrage, Arthur had not strained himself greatly to refute the accusation. After all, he reasoned to himself later, Edward was not entirely wrong.

"That woman! I know she's your sister but I can't help but recall how she has hated me ever since I inherited the estate from my uncle. Am I to blame that she had no child to succeed him? I might have expected she would encourage something to harm me, but I'm surprised you did not step in on my behalf."

Arthur Woodard held out his hands in a helpless gesture.

"You were as kind to Colonel Bullerton as anyone when he came to Mayfield, Edward."

"Well, he had Mortimer with him. I wasn't going to risk his disfavour, nor did I question the reason for their coming here. But you knew it, I'll be bound."

Arthur shrugged weakly. "I did. But I wrote to Penelope telling her I favoured your suit over his. You may ask her when she returns."

"I'll not wait for that. I'm London-bound today, and I shall try to talk some sense into Miss Melissa's charming little head. I shall remind her of what I have to offer. This . . . this Bullerton has nothing by comparison."

But by the time Edward Bransom arrived at Devonshire Place, Missy, accompanied by Meg, had already left for Malmesbury with Colonel Bullerton to meet his redoubtable mother.

"I do hope she'll like me," she had whispered to her sister as she kissed her good-bye.

"Silly old thing, Missy. How could it be otherwise?" Penelope had squeezed her hand, hoping her sister would not notice the tears glistening in her eyes, and, as soon as they were gone, she had gone up to her room and cried. She felt utterly alone. She cried at losing her sister, yet there was another loss she felt—Colonel Bullerton had returned to London alone, Lord Mortimer having gone on to Chenwyth. With Midsummer Day, the quarter day when she had to be in Mayfield to receive her allowance, fast approaching, there was little likelihood she would ever see him again.

Penelope was therefore not altogether sorry to see Edward Bransom in town when he called, for if he was in London he could hardly require her presence in Mayfield on quarter day. But one look at his face, with the fury that surfaced as soon as she explained that Missy was not only well and truly engaged but was already en route to meet her new mother-in-law, made her realize she might expect nothing from him to accommodate her wishes.

"I knew it all along. I told Arthur as much when I saw him. You never wanted your sister to marry me—never. Don't deny it! You never wanted her to be mistress of the Hall in your place," he railed. "It was you who instigated this match. You were responsible for bringing this man into your sister's life, you know that I speak the truth. And I've no doubt you saw to it that she left London before I could reason with her."

Even in the face of his impenetrable anger, Penelope felt for one who might be suffering. "I am sorry, Mr. Bransom, truly sorry, if your feelings for my sister were deep—if you are hurt by her affections being given to another. But it is totally wrong to say that Missy's acceptance of Colonel Bullerton had anything to do with me; it was her decision, hers alone. She loves him, and I have every reason to believe that he loves her. I did talk to Missy when you proposed marriage, only because she asked my advice. I said I thought she should wait and meet other people so that she might be sure of her own mind."

"You see, you admit it. You rejoice, no doubt, that this has made a fool of me in Mayfield. I've talked to the rector; half the village knows."

"That, sir, is your doing, not mine, not Missy's. She had given you no answer, you had no right to speak of it."

"No right. In your eyes I have no right over anything. Do you ever listen to my advice? I was against this jaunt all along, you know that."

"You were, I am aware of it. But I am not convinced that it has been harmful." Seeing his face darken, she hastened to add, "I realize you are hurt now, but don't you see how much better it is to discover, before any formal engagement or hasty marriage, that Missy's affections for you were those of a friend rather than a life partner? I wish it had been possible for no one to be hurt in the matter; Missy does also, and I'm sure she conveyed that in her letter to you. And surely you can see it is better for everyone for her true feelings to be known now rather than later."

"She could have loved me equally well had you not come between us. Nothing you say will ever convince me to the contrary."

"Then I shall say no more."

Mr. Edward Bransom paced the floor, with heavy yet indecisive steps.

He stopped at last, immediately in front of Penelope, shaking his finger in emphasis as he spoke. "I cannot wait to cast the dust of this wicked city from my feet. I shall return to Mayfield tomorrow, and despite my own inclinations,

1 2 6

despite all you have done, I am a gentleman who does not shirk his responsibility. In deference to my uncle's memory, I shall escort you home."

"But I had planned to return with my sister and Meg."

"Your sister has chosen her companion," he replied bitterly. "But who is this Meg?"

"She is the young maid I mentioned to you when last you were here."

"The trollop you picked up off the streets," he sneered.

"Meg is not a trollop," Penelope responded indignantly. "Whatever she may have done she was forced into doing by a good-for-nothing of a father. Now she's in my care, I'll not allow any harm to befall her."

"Knowing how you influence your sister to do your wishes, undoubtedly she'll take care of this Meg for you. I leave early tomorrow. I don't want to keep the horses standing."

Angry words rose to her lips, words that went unspoken. To refuse his offer, hostile though it was, could only cause further acrimony. With as much grace as she could muster, Penelope thanked him and assured him she would indeed be ready early.

14

If die I must, let me die drinking in an inn.
William Mapes
De Nugis Curialium, ca. 1200

"**I** don't see why you are returning to Mayfield before Emmeline and me," Lady Halstead complained the next morning as Penelope's valise was readied in the hall.

"I do have to be there for Midsummer Day."

"I think that's silly, really I do."

"So do I, but it's not the time to argue about it. Mr. Bransom is disgruntled enough as it is."

"But Missy never agreed to marry him."

"I know. Nevertheless, I don't want to irk him any more than he is already. And really, considering our differences, he is kind in escorting me."

Just as Penelope was leaving, a young boy arrived with a note, exceedingly ill-written, a note she did not have an opportunity to study until they had started their journey. Then, to her concern, she discovered it to be from Meg. It was difficult to read and made very little sense, but it was clear that Meg was not with Missy in Malmesbury but at an inn, the Blue Boar at Gerrard's Cross. There was no explanation of how or why she was there, only that she wanted Penelope to come for her.

"Does our way lie near Gerrard's Cross?" she asked Mr. Bransom, who had spoken little.

"We pass nearby."

"I should be most grateful if we could stop at the Blue Boar."

"I do not usually change horses there."

"It's because of this note. It appears, I cannot understand why, that Meg is there. I thought her with . . . I thought her in Malmesbury, but she says she is at the Blue Boar. She asks that I call for her. I cannot understand more, so I cannot explain."

"Meg, your little trollop of a maid?" he sneered.

"Mr. Bransom, I know you think it my fault that Missy has chosen—"

He broke in on her in cold fury. "I think nothing at all, Mrs. Bransom. I am merely escorting you home. I am willing to go out of my way to pick up this trollop of yours, but I do not have to listen to your empty homilies, your attempts at self-justification, all the way. Do I make myself plain?"

"Yes, sir, indeed you do."

In a way it was a relief. She preferred not to converse with him. It was enough that he had agreed to go by way of the Blue Boar, though Penelope was mystified as to why Meg should be there and not with Missy; all sorts of forebodings crossed her mind, but she pushed them aside. Nothing was to be gained by conjecture. She would discover what had happened soon enough. She sat back in the carriage, glad to hold her tongue and watch the passing hedgerows with their profusion of meadowsweet and agrimony. As soon as she was home she would work on her illustrations again; it would take her mind away from Missy's absence—and other things. She remembered the painting she had wanted to do for Mr. Trueblood for his willingness to help her; the larkspur by the Lodge gate should be in bloom and would make a charming study. And Mortimer, she remembered, had asked for a bridal bouquet, baby's breath and cornflowers—cornflowers made her remember the colour of his eyes. She wished he were there, for without knowing why she felt suddenly afraid as Mr. Bransom announced, indicating an elegant establishment of Tudor design, "That's the Blue Boar." As they passed through the low archway into the courtyard, he cautioned, "Now, don't keep the horses waiting."

"I shall try not to."

As she entered, Penelope wished that she were not alone, for she was lost in the bustle of activity inside. Doors to a large dining room were open, and long tables were being set, decorated with regimental flags.

The inn was filled with gentlemen of elegant attire, many of whom resembled the loitering dandies she had seen on Bond Street. They made her uncomfortable by the way their eyes travelled over her, and she drew her shawl closer around, searching for someone to help her find Meg. Though the Blue Boar was clearly a superior hostelry, she felt decidedly uneasy under its roof.

She tried in vain to get the attention of the servants scurrying to and fro. But someone must have noticed her dilemma, for the innkeeper appeared, a solid looking man in worsted and leggings, to enquire politely enough but with evident surprise as he took in her dress of plain mourning, "You here to meet someone, ma'am?"

"Yes," she said in relief. "Meg . . . Meg Watkins. She said I would find her here."

"Meg's a common enough name, but I know of no Meg Watkins."

There was something about the way the innkeeper examined her, about the look in his eye as he did so, that disconcerted her, and she grew increasingly anxious about Meg's presence in such an establishment.

"But she said she would be here. My name is Mrs. Bransom."

"Oh, Mrs. Bransom, why didn't you say so? Yes, of course, come with me."

He conducted her upstairs, through a positive gauntlet of gentlemen eyeing her speculatively. She resolved not to stay a moment longer than was necessary; this was no place for her, or Meg either.

"Here we are, Mrs. Bransom." The innkeeper opened the door to a pleasant and comfortable parlour which appeared to be unoccupied.

"I don't see anyone here," Penelope demurred.

"Oh, they'll be along. You're expected." He smiled at her,

and she thought one of his eyes closed in a familiar way. "I've got to be on my way. We're hard put today with the big dinner and all, so if you'll excuse me."

The room was light and airy with its furnishings of mahogany and gilt-trimmed armchairs. A writing desk stood by the window, and on a low table was a large bowl of yellow roses. Yet, pleasant as it was, it was somehow ominous. There was a door which Penelope opened to find an adjoining bedchamber dwarfed by its enormous curtained bed.

"Meg!" she called, and again, "Meg!"

She was about to open the bed curtains when, with relief, she heard the door of the parlour open.

"Meg!" She ran out—to be confronted by Sir Reginald Palfry.

"Mrs. Bransom, you're here."

"Sir Reginald!" And Penelope remembered the gentleman in Bond Street who had come for Meg; in that glimpse she had had of him he had looked very much like the gentleman before her. Had he and Watkins arranged this? Yet he showed no distress at seeing her there.

"Where is Meg?" she demanded. "Meg Watkins."

"Ah, yes. I just saw the innkeeper, and he told me about Meg. He's a good chap, understanding, discreet."

"Where is she?" Penelope demanded again.

"Where is who?" he asked.

"Meg Watkins," she insisted, thinking him deliberately obtuse.

"I've no idea."

"But you said . . . the innkeeper said. . . ."

"I thought that was your little subterfuge."

"My little subterfuge," Penelope replied faintly.

"Yes, I thought . . ."

There was a gentle tap on the door, which was not opened until Sir Reginald called out, "Come in." Then a maid entered bearing a tray with a wine carafe, glasses and a plate of sweetmeats, which she set on the table beside the roses, quietly, discreetly, without looking directly at either of the room's occupants. As she left, Sir Reginald rubbed his hands together in satisfaction. "There, that's what we need," and he crossed over to pour the wine and hand a glass to Penelope.

"Sir Reginald." She set the glass down firmly without touching the contents. "I should appreciate an explanation."

"An explanation of what?"

"I came here to find Meg Watkins, my maid. Here . . . here's her note, it is no subterfuge."

Sir Reginald glanced down at the scrawled note and handed it back to Penelope without making any attempt to decipher it.

"Very clever, ma'am. It was well to come armed with an explanation, though none is required at the Blue Boar. I thought it clever of you to suggest this place. I am truly flattered. Allow me to drink the health of a very resolute lady."

As he emptied his glass, Penelope stammered, "What are you saying, that *I* suggested this meeting? You must be out of your mind, sir."

The man was mad. It was the only logical explanation for such behaviour. As she hesitated, he pulled a letter from his pocket.

"You don't deny this is yours."

She took it, hoping it might contain some clue to the imbroglio. It was addressed to Sir Reginald; it bore the heading Devonshire Place and yesterday's date. It was, indeed, a note of assignation, specifying that very inn, that very day. It was signed with her name.

"I'm at a loss to say where this came from. I did not write it, but I can understand your misconception. I am beginning to think that we are both victims of a distasteful hoax."

"Come, ma'am, no need for that, I assure you. I understand your reticence in owning to it, but I think no worse of you for taking matters upon yourself. Why, indeed, should there be one law for men and another for women when we all have the same needs, the same desires? Because one is left alone, passions do not die; I'm sure mine did not. As I said before, I am flattered."

"But I did not write this thing; it is not my hand. See, let me show you it is not." Taking the note, she crossed to the writing table, pulled out a piece of paper and hurriedly copied the words in her own hand. "There, compare it for yourself. The styles of writing are not at all the same; you can see for yourself."

Sir Reginald examined the two letters and agreed, "The hand is quite different. I cannot understand it."

"Nor can I, but I hope I shall find out. Good-day to you, Sir Reginald."

In the courtyard another rude shock awaited her. There was no sign of the Bransom coach. The stable boy was insolent in replying to her queries.

" 'Ow should I know, there's 'undreds come and go every day."

"But it's not half an hour since we arrived. You took care of the horses. I went inside, and the gentleman remained behind."

The boy scratched his head. "Oh, yus. The gent 'e went inside, then 'e come out and told the coachman to drive on."

"Drive on! Did he say where to?"

"Coachman told me 'e were from Oxford way—s'pose that's where."

The innkeeper was of little help. He didn't remember speaking to Mr. Bransom. No, he had nothing available. He might be able to get a post-chaise from the next village but it wouldn't come cheap and he would require cash on the nail, five guineas, even ten. Penelope hadn't five shillings on her, let alone five guineas, and she knew of only one person to whom to turn. Perhaps, as her husband's friend, Sir Reginald might be willing to assist her.

Sir Reginald was sitting in the armchair where she had left him, the carafe of wine almost gone, looking decidedly glum. He listened to her tale and offered to take her back to London, in fact, wherever she wished to go, and she sighed in relief.

"London will be admirable. Thank you, thank you, you are most kind."

"You won't mind if I dine; I've had nothing since breakfast. I doubt you have either, Mrs. Bransom. We could both use a bite, and the food here is excellent, if they haven't expended all their effort on the dinner being given below, some reunion or other. Let's see what they have to offer, shall we?"

He was in such a genial mood, she could scarcely refuse though all she wanted was to leave. She hoped they would eat below, but he said it wouldn't do for her to be seen in the taproom. He ordered carefully, mutton broth, turbot, beef ribs, collared eel, potted partridge, some green peas, ale with the meal and port to follow.

"All right with you, my dear?"

"I'm really not hungry."

"Well, you will be by the time it gets here."

"Will there be time enough to return to town, would you not sooner dine there?" she pressed.

"I couldn't wait that long to eat, wouldn't survive, I'm afraid."

He filled her glass, ordered another carafe of madeira, and a desultory conversation ensued until at last the maid arrived to set the table and bring on the first courses.

Though Penelope had little appetite, Sir Reginald consumed everything with relish, speaking little as he ate, sighing in satisfaction as he munched on fish, meat, and poultry, and not leaning back until the last plate had been well sampled, whereupon he belched loudly and apologized.

"Sorry, Mrs. Bransom. I suppose we gentlemen enjoy our sustenance more than you ladies, you scarcely ate a thing. Considering your fair form, I suppose. I remember your husband as a man who enjoyed his food, though his girth never showed it as mine does; still, I like a man to have a substantial figure. I knew Josiah well. He spoke to me of you, told me a great deal, man to man, of course. He was quite naturally disappointed in your inability to bear him a child. Still, not your fault, is it, if you can't?"

Penelope disliked his look, his conversation, and the lateness of the hour. She got up.

"Now you have had your repast, Sir Reginald, we must leave."

"A meal is never finished without a taste of port; Josiah used to say that."

Penelope considered he had had quite enough wine, but the table was cleared and the wine brought up over her protestations.

"Yes." Sir Reginald stretched his ample form in his armchair. "Yes, Josiah told me a lot about you, a lot." He examined her intently as he sipped his port. "A slim body, he said, but well-formed with skin firm, smooth to the touch."

"That is enough, quite enough. You are drunk, sir; if not drunk, then you have consumed quite as much as is good for you. You promised to take me back to London. I have waited for you to eat and I have waited for you to have your port. Now it is time to go."

"Hold on." He smiled. "Hold on, there, Mrs. Bransom, or could I call you Penelope, for we are old friends in a manner of speaking. Let's look at things as they are. We're both here for whatever reason, no fault of ours, but here we are. We're both grown ups, we've been married, we know what things are about, and there's no chance of you getting caught, if you know what I mean. Now it may not have been planned, but the fact is I've been interested in you from the start. There's no reason this might not lead to something more permanent, for I'm not opposed to settling down. Oh, I know you've not your sister's beauty, but you have a certain charm. Truth to tell, widows have a singular attraction for me; there's something about a youngish woman in mourning that's appealing—a sort of forbidden quality that makes her irresistible."

He moved with unexpected alacrity, pulling her to him, silencing her cry by pressing his lips on hers—lips still moist and greasy from the foods he had consumed, lips so heavy they muffled all sound, lips which devoured her as they had the meal, lips which revolted her as much as his hands, which roved her body, pressing her to him with a horrible intensity. His bulk was so great that no amount of struggle was of any avail, and when at last she ceased to resist, her strength spent, he eased the intensity of his hold and sighed in satisfaction without releasing her.

"There," he breathed at last. "Let's go into the next room, shall we, and get comfortable."

She lashed out at him. "You disgust me, a liar as well as a scoundrel. You had no intention of taking me back to London, did you? I should have known any friend of his would be a rotter."

"What's this, maligning your husband while you wear his mourning? You're no better than I, you little hypocrite! No matter, a pennyworth of love is worth a pound of jaw."

Before he could catch hold of her again, she flung open the door and was relieved to see two young men passing by in the corridor, simpering fops though they were, pink complected with glazed eyes indicating their state was less than sober. They were not, however, too befuddled to notice a female form.

"Ah, goddess of the night, we are at your service. Allow us to show you the delights of the Boar." The shorter of the two spoke, then hiccupped violently. They both bowed low, bumping into one another and almost losing their balance as they did so, sending them off into paroxysms of laughter. They made to seize Penelope, either for support or to enforce their invitation, when one of the young dandies noticed the solid form of Sir Reginald in the room behind her.

"Oh," the young man hiccupped again, more violently. "Sorry, thought you were looking for company. Come on, old chap."

He motioned to his friend, who lingered until he, too, caught sight of Sir Reginald, at which they both lurched down the hallway muttering, "Find someone else . . . Remember that little French maid was here last time, the one with the red hair. . . ."

"And the bowed legs," his friend quipped.

"Bowed with good reason!" Again they both went into spasms of mirth, punctuated by hiccups, as they turned towards the staircase.

"That's your choice if you leave," Sir Reginald flung at her. "Drunken dandies or that riotous bunch of soldiers downstairs. Better the devil you know."

"I'll take my chances with the devil I don't."

15

Do not make me kiss, and you will not make me sin.
英語の proverb

英語 proverb

The corridor was dim once the door was shut. Looking along the hallway, Penelope saw the two inebriated young gentlemen hesitating at the head of the stairs, waiting for the outcome of the exchange they had been watching. She hastily turned in the opposite direction, with no idea of where she might be going but terrified they might come after her.

As she sped along the hallway, the door of one of the rooms unexpectedly opened, and she fell headlong into the arms of a tall figure resplendent in regimentals on his way, no doubt, to the dinner below.

"I beg your pardon, ma'am," he apologized.

Never had she known such relief. "Oh, Lord Mortimer, it's you! Thank God it's you!"

"Mrs. Bransom! What in the name of heaven are you doing in a place like this? What has happened to you? Tell me!"

For the first time Penelope realized her dishevelled state, bereft of bonnet or shawl, her hair loose about her face.

"I . . . it's difficult to explain."

"I dare say it is. The Blue Boar is hardly the sort of place to find a lady such as yourself. Has someone mistreated you? May I be of service to you?"

Another door opened, and he took her arm.

"You had best come inside. It is my bedchamber, yet safer than standing in the hallway for all to see."

"What can I do for you?" he asked again, once inside. Then, seeing her face in the brighter candlelight he poured her a glass of brandy. "Here, drink this."

"No . . . no thank you, I don't want . . ."

"I didn't ask if you wanted it. Drink it, you need it."

He stood watching her, arms folded across his chest, immaculate in white pantaloons and tall Hessians, which made him look taller than ever. The scarlet lacing across his black jacket with its high collar of matching scarlet emphasized the authority of his words.

She drank the fiery liquid that burned her tongue but gradually loosened her taut muscles and soothed her pounding heartbeat.

"Thank you, I feel much improved," she began, but he held up his finger to his lips to silence her. There were footsteps in the hallway and the sound of loud conversation, followed by a sharp rap on the door.

"Come along, Mortimer, we want to get started," a hearty voice called out.

"Go on down. I shan't be long," he replied quickly without opening the door.

"Was that a lady I heard in there with you? Hope not, or we'll see nothing of you unless you care to bring her along so we may share her company."

"I never share my ladies, Weston," Mortimer joked. "In this case you're wrong, though—I'm just getting my boots on. Go along, I'll be down."

"Make it soon; I'm famished and you know the dinner won't start without you."

Mortimer turned back to Penelope as the sound of footsteps and voices retreated towards the staircase.

"Now, how can I be of help?"

"I should explain, though I'm not sure I understand. . . ."

"It's not important, you need explain nothing to me. All I want is to be of service to you."

"All I need is a carriage, any sort of conveyance, to take me home."

"It's late. It will be dangerous to travel through the night."

"But I can't stay here."

"No, that's true."

There were more voices in the hall and another rap at the door. "I'll be there in a moment, go on down," Mortimer called. Then, when they were gone, he said, "Look Mrs. Bransom, there's a regimental reunion of the Fifteenth downstairs. I have to be there to give a bit of a speech, but I shall come back as soon as I can break away. In the meantime I'll have Glossop bring you something to eat."

Penelope shuddered, the sight of Palfry consuming all that food filling her mind. "No, nothing to eat, thank you."

"Well, some tea at least. And you may use anything of mine you wish to. I'll have him bring some water so you may wash."

"Thank you. You're very kind," and Penelope smiled for the first time that day.

"I've done nothing. Do rest. Glossop will see to it that no one disturbs you. In the meantime, I'll think what's best to be done. Somehow it will be possible to slip away later, for the drinking will be long and steady tonight. Whatever happens, though, you must not be found here."

By the time Mortimer returned, Penelope was rested and refreshed, comforted by that confidence which comes of having protection and support at hand. She had washed her face and hands and combed her hair and tied it back, for she had no bonnet with which to cover it.

"My chaise is at the side door, Mrs. Bransom. Glossop will stay to ward off any questions while I am gone; it's so riotous below I doubt I'll be missed. But wait, you can't leave like that." He took his long travelling cloak and wrapped it around her, fastening it at the neck as though she were a child and tucking her hair under its high collar. "There, that's better. Take my arm and remember, stay close and keep a tight hold on me. Should we meet anyone just lean your head into my shoulder so they won't recognize your face. All right, are you ready?"

He smiled down at her, and she knew, as they sped along the hallway, her light footsteps keeping pace with his long strides, that she wasn't afraid of anything at that moment, not even as they passed the door to Palfry's room.

As they descended the stairs, she again saw the inebriated

pair of young gentlemen who focussed bleary eyes on her but averted them as Mortimer put his arm protectively around her.

They had to pass the taproom to gain the entryway, and as they did so Sir Reginald Palfry came out wearing a decidedly ill-humoured look. He bowed to Mortimer, who did little to return his greeting, except to draw Penelope's head closer against his shoulder murmuring, "Come along, darling, it's getting late. The wind is changing direction and that may mean rain."

The next encounter did not come until they were outside in the courtyard making their way to the waiting chaise when a loud halloo called after them.

"Mortimer, hey Mortimer, where are you off to? The party's only just beginning—Baring's promised to consume five gallons of ale and they're laying odds." It was Weston's voice and Mortimer muttered, "Oh, damn!"

"Hello, hello, who's that with you—there, I was right, I knew you weren't alone upstairs."

Weston was joined by someone else who called over, "Why Mortimer, that sly dog, if that don't take the cake. I swear that's the little widow he has on his arm, the friend of Lady Halstead."

As though he had not heard them, without reply, without turning back, Mortimer put his arms around Penelope and put his head down to hers to kiss her fully on the lips. Though his act was completely unexpected, she made no attempt to resist him; indeed her response was as different as could possibly be from her response to another kiss earlier that day. Rather than struggling to free herself, she clung to him, forgetting the onlookers behind them who had prompted the embrace, barely hearing Weston's disconsolate comment, "That's no little widow he has with him—there's only one woman he would kiss that way, and we all know who that is. We might as well leave him; there's little chance of retrieving him from that lady's arms tonight."

Their steps receded. The door to the inn opened and closed behind them, and the courtyard was quiet. Yet Mortimer did not immediately release her from his hold or take his lips from hers, and when at last he did, Penelope felt an unexpected reluctance to part from him, a reluctance made even more embarrassing by his whispered, "I beg pardon for my action, but I had to give the lie to their suspicions. I hope you did not misunderstand."

In the darkness she could see only the outline of his face, and she felt oddly rejected by his apology. Nothing more was said as he helped her into his chaise and climbed up beside her to take the reins, setting the horses off at a fast clip. In silence they rode on, the chaise swaying as they rounded bends in the road, Penelope holding on firmly to her seat so she might not be thrown against the driver of the vehicle to whom she felt she should make some explanation even though he asked for none.

Before many miles rain began to fall, turning to a steady drizzle and then a pelting shower. Mortimer reached over to draw up a rug across her knees despite her protests. "You should have it—I already have your cloak and you must be getting drenched. Your uniform will be quite ruined, not to mention the fact that you may catch your death of cold."

"I hate to admit it in an age when Byron's melancholy is still all the rage, but I am disgustingly hardy. As for the uniform, I no longer need it except for evenings such as this when we dress up and swap war stories, boasting and bragging and drinking far more than is good for us. Perhaps the end of the uniform may make an end of my passing my time in such silly affairs."

"In favour of other affairs." Penelope commented, wishing as soon as the words were spoken that she had not.

"Perhaps," he agreed quietly.

"I'm sorry, it's none of my business. Do you suppose we may reach Oxfordshire tonight?"

"I had hoped we would, but this bloody rain is making the going difficult. Oh, sorry, my pardon, Mrs. Bransom. When I get back among my cohorts my language reverts very quickly to the field, I'm afraid."

They were passing a farmhouse set back from the road. The flicker of candlelight behind curtained windows, the smell of smoke from a burning fire coming from the chimney was cosy and enticing on such a night. Penelope turned back to watch it, the only light on a black and dreary night, visible until they rounded a curve when again the vehicle swayed, this time more sharply and then skidded wildly in water and mud as the horses plunged and reared. Penelope was sure they would overturn, but miraculously Mortimer controlled the team, bringing them to a halt but not before the chaise had plunged into a ditch.

Mortimer got down to examine the damage.

"Is it bad?" Penelope called after him in the dark.

"Stuck in more than a foot of mud by the look of it," Mortimer's voice grew louder as he came back.

"Is there much damage?"

"I don't really know, but we're going to need help to get it out. This team's already spent their best force tonight. I believe I saw some light not far back; let's see if they can help."

Together they trudged through the mud and slush towards the flickering light that beckoned them on. As they were making their way across the farmyard to the thatched house, a figure in mackintosh and heavy boots, holding high a lantern, approached from the direction of the barn.

"Good evening, if I may call such an evening good," Mortimer called out. "My carriage is stuck out on the road. I wonder whether someone here could give me some help."

In the light of the lantern, lifted even higher at the sound of Mortimer's voice, the ruddy face of the young man carrying it became wreathed in a big grin.

"Colonel Mortimer, sir, is it really you?"

"By God, Rooke, I might have known you'd turn up at a time like this, always there when needed, no matter the place or hour."

"Well, Colonel, yon elm wood's not the Soigne, nor's Topplescroft Farm Hougoumont, and Wintersglade's hardly Waterloo, but by the Lord it's raining now like it rained then. Come on in, we've comfort to offer we never got that night. Father's inside, me mum's still up too. She'll take care of your lady, have both of you to rights in a trivet, she will."

As the young man opened the door he called out, "Dad, mum, you'll never believe who's here!"

Drenched and mud-covered, they stood in the hall as Mrs. Rooke came out, intent at first on berating her son for not using the back entrance, then immediately flustered at the sight of such visitors in whom, despite their state, she recognized quality.

"It's him, mum, Colonel Mortimer, you remember, I told you about him."

"Good Lord have mercy! How many hundred times you did, Stan—not without good reason," she hastened to add. "Come in, sir, you too, me lady. Bert, Bert! Come, see who's here. You're never going to believe it."

Mr. Rooke appeared from the parlour, taking the pipe from his mouth.

"Well, I'll be . . . if it isn't Lord Mortimer."

"You have the advantage of me, sir, but you must be Rooke's father. I must confess to being surprised that you recognize me, particularly in this state."

"I'd know you anywhere, me lord. Read all about you, besides all Stan told us when he got back, all you done for him and all. Never thought the day would come when we'd see you in the flesh and blood so to speak, and under our very own roof, did we, mother? We always wanted to thank you for what you done for our boy, we might never have seen him again else. He's a good lad is our Stan. I often wanted to write to thank you but never was one for putting pen to paper, but if you'd allow me, sir, I'd like to shake you by the hand."

Mr. Rooke extended a warm, calloused palm to Mortimer's firm but exceedingly damp hand while that gentleman hastened to disclaim, "I owe my own life every bit as much to your son and others like him as they owe theirs to me. You're absolutely right about your boy, an excellent young man. You have nothing to thank me for, Mr. Rooke, but I want you to know how it gladdens our hearts to find ourselves under such a hospitable roof on a night like this. Our carriage is damaged—a skid, the wheel stuck in a ditch—your light was a welcome sign, for it was difficult to estimate any damage beyond the obvious."

"We'll take care of all that, me lord. Just you and your lady come in and warm yourselves by the fire. Who'd ever have thought to see such rain in June—a soft drizzle, yes, that I wouldn't've minded, but my corn don't need this drenching, nor do you."

Inside, the parlour was every bit as cosy as Penelope had imagined it to be when passing on the road. A pair of high-backed armchairs stood on either side of a roaring fire before which a large and lazy sheepdog dozed.

"Move over there, Mortar," Mr. Rooke commanded. "There's those who need that fire a sight more than you," and half apologetically he turned back to Mortimer, "I hope you don't mind, me lord, but Stan give him that name when he come back, said it was the name they give to you on the field, said you held 'em all together—given in great affection, I need not tell you that. I never heard him speak of anyone the way he talked of you, and that includes the Iron Duke hisself."

Mortimer, embarrassed by such copious yet honest effusions, bent down to pat Mortar as the dog reluctantly relinquished his place.

"It's an honour to share the name with such a noble beast," he said as Mrs. Rooke bustled in.

"I've got the maidservant to set a fire agoing up above, me lady. If you'd come with me, there's warm water for you to wash in and dry clothes you can change into."

"I thank you indeed, Mrs. Rooke, you're very kind, but I believe I should tell you . . ." Penelope began in confusion at their obvious misunderstanding of her status.

But Mortimer cut in and, rather than correcting the Rookes' misconception, confirmed it with, "My wife wants you to know how grateful we are for your hospitality to us, we know we're putting you to a great deal of trouble. I'm glad that you thought of the matter of dry clothes, Mrs. Rooke, for I've been worried about her catching a chill ever since the rain began."

"You're on the road late, me lord," Mr. Rooke said.

"Yes. We're on our way to meet with family friends in Oxfordshire. We'd have got much further but for this downpour."

"It's an ill wind blows no one any good, me lord. We're delighted to have this opportunity to be of help, aren't we, mother?"

"Indeed we are, Bert. Come on upstairs, Lady Mortimer."

With one last imploring look at Mortimer—who seemed impervious to her embarrassment—Penelope followed Mrs. Rooke, who kept up a steady stream of chatter as they mounted the narrow staircase.

"You must forgive the room, me lady, it's so small. If I'd known, Bert and me would've moved and given you ours. But it's clean, and the bed's right comfortable. Milly's getting sheets and bed clothes ready and night things for the two of you. For now I've pulled out something of mine I think will fit you. I used to be much thinner than I am now; my frame was not so different from your ladyship's when I married and I had this frock made then, so you see it's ancient but still good. Fact is that it was so good that even when I could no longer wear it—six children changes the shape of a woman so—even then I couldn't bring myself to make it over for children's things like I done with my others. Someday it'll find good use, I said to meself and, you see, I was right. Suppose it's outdated now and nothing of the sort you're used to, but I was that proud of it, and I'm proud that the lady of my son's commander will wear it."

She held up an azure marquisette overdress with frilled petticoat of matching hue and an elaborate Egyptian lace fichu fitted around the lowered neckline.

"Oh, it's beautiful, Mrs. Rooke, far more beautiful than anything I own," Penelope said impulsively.

"Now, now, Lady Mortimer, I know that can't be so, but I'm glad you like it just the same. Milly's here for anything you need, but I'll have to go down to get something on the table. You'll be starved, both of you, after being out in such weather."

By the time Penelope came down, clad in Mrs. Rooke's blue dress, her brown hair still damp but combed back and tied with a matching blue ribbon supplied by Milly, it was to find Mortimer, jacket removed, wearing an open-necked shirt, tankard in hand, deep in discussion of the problems of supplying an army with food.

"I suppose there were times when I hated Boney as much as the next man, but there's no denying that the man on St. Helena's a genius and not only a military genius, though he gave our brightest strategists ample proof of that. He was a brilliant administrator, he knew what was needed and how and where to get it. He recognized the truth of that old saw—an army marches on its stomach—and he paid more than lip service to it. He discovered a certain Nicholas Appert who had invented a process of preserving food so it would last for years by filling up stout glass bottles, firmly stoppering them, and then immersing them in boiling water in a bain-marie where he'd boil the deuce out of them. He preserved fruit, vegetables, meat, even milk that way, and the Little Corporal recognized the benefit for his ever moving army. It wouldn't have to spend time foraging, cut down on sickness, not to mention reducing the chances of scurvy in men at sea. Monsieur Appert wrote a book on the subject—*L'Art de Conserver pendant Plusiers Années Toutes les Substances Animales et Vegetales,* How to Preserve Meat and Vegetables for Years, or something of the sort—and Napoleon awarded him a prize of twelve thousand francs for his simple but ingenious idea. For all the evils of war, it acts as a muse to sharpen men's minds and produce their best as well as their most diabolical inventions. I've no doubt we'll hear a great deal more of Monsieur Appert's preservation process, Mr. Rooke. In fact, I've been thinking if metal containers were used instead of glass bottles, it would be an improvement, for they'd be unbreakable and could be thoroughly sealed, and make a good use for our Cornish tin."

"Excellent, Lord Mortimer, excellent. Stan always said you found ways to do things when others couldn't."

"Mostly wouldn't." Mortimer laughed and then caught sight of Penelope, who had been sitting quietly listening to him. "There you are, dry again and quite, quite lovely." The way his eyes dwelt upon her as he spoke made Penelope flush.

"It's Mrs. Rooke's dress," she said lamely.

"I remember when Mabel had that made. It cost a pretty penny, but when I saw her in it I knew it was worth every one. Stan was born nine months to the day after she first wore it. I often joked that it turned into a more costly venture than I'd anticipated, not that he didn't turn out to be a good lad."

"I'd be proud to have such a one for a son of mine," Mortimer agreed, his eyes still on Penelope.

"You have children, me lord?"

"No, not yet."

Mr. Rooke raised his tankard. "I'd like, if I may, to drink to a bonny lad born to your good lady nine months hence."

Mrs. Rooke, entering at that moment and noticing Penelope's confusion, intervened, "That's quite enough, Bert. There's food on the table and these gentlefolk must be tired. Did you know it's close to eleven?"

Yet it was well past midnight before they rose from the farm table that had positively groaned with meats, cheeses, fresh breads, butter, jams and jellies.

"You're an excellent cook, Mrs. Rooke," Mortimer said as they were shown upstairs.

"Wait till breakfast, me lord, we'll have some fresh trout for you—mother's got a way of cooking it over oak wood that makes my mouth water just to think on it."

As they climbed the stairs, Mrs. Rooke fussed, "I think there's everything in there. The fire's been re-stocked, but there's plenty of coal in the scuttle—on a damp night like this you may need it to keep the chill from the air."

"Now, Mabel, I'm quite sure Lord Mortimer needs no instruction in how to keep a bedroom warm," the farmer chuckled.

"Bert, mind your tongue, you shouldn't talk so to quality, really you shouldn't," his wife scolded.

"Lord Mortimer's not offended by my calling him a man, I'm sure of that," her husband retorted.

"Perhaps if we'd had you as well as your lad over there with us, Rooke, we'd have finished that business even quicker," Mortimer, sensing Penelope's confusion at the farmer's good-humored but suggestive remarks, put in hastily.

"I'm sure I'd've gone if I'd known you. Oh, the stories Stan told us."

"Time for that tomorrow," Mrs. Rooke cautioned. "They must be dead tired."

"We thank you for everything. No one could possibly have shown us greater kindness; isn't that so, Penelope?"

She nodded her agreement, unable to find anything to say as they approached the room that was to be theirs for the night. Yet it was only when the door was firmly closed, leaving them alone together without the safety of Mr. Rooke's blustering voice and Mrs. Rooke's fussing that the complete intimacy of the situation descended on Penelope. She stood still in the middle of the tiny room overwhelmed by its huge four-poster bed.

"How could you go along with their misunderstanding," she whispered in exasperation.

"How could I explain something I myself don't understand? Even if I did, these good farm folk live in a different world."

"You were thinking of your reputation," she threw at him.

"As a matter of fact, I was thinking of yours. Farmer Rooke would have winked an eye and thought me a good fellow; even Mrs. Rooke would have little to say to me, but to you, no matter how innocent you were, she would have said a great deal or silently made your position intolerable. You've nothing to be afraid of, not from me at least. Here." He held up the nightgown carefully laid out on the bed. "Put this on. You've no need to worry, I won't look."

He turned his back to her and opened the window shutters to stare out at the dark, drenching night, his tall frame leaning against the low window casement.

"Young Rooke went to look at the carriage. He's sure we can have it out of there in the morning. He says he's always up with the lark—he'll get a couple of their best men on it right away. We'll be able to leave after breakfast, none the worse for any of this."

"You may turn around now." Penelope stood, enveloped in the voluminous nightgown, about to fasten a nightcap on her head.

Mortimer took it from her, saying, "You'll be asking for trouble going to bed with your hair still damp. Didn't your mother tell you that? Sit down. I'll brush it dry for you."

She sat still, lulled by the rhythmic movement of the brush on her hair, feeling a sense of enchantment at the motion, yet aware that such enchantment was perilous, that she must guard against it.

"You're an expert with the hairbrush," she said to break the spell fast falling upon her.

"So would you be if you had an elder sister who was firmly convinced that her crowning glory was her hair."

"You mentioned your sister, but I didn't realize she was older than you."

"Only by two years, but enough to make her bossy." He laughed. "Don't misunderstand, we've very fond of one another. She's married now and, like you, a dutiful wife, utterly devoted to her husband. God forbid that anything should happen to John, but if it did I would hope she wouldn't worship him beyond the grave."

"You refer to the dark clothes I wear."

"In part. You know, you looked beautiful in Mrs. Rooke's dress tonight. If you consider those sombre things of yours a mark of respect, I should point out that the shade of blue you wore tonight is considered in places like Armenia to signify the celestial heavens where, it is hoped, the loved one rests. In China they mourn in white for purity; in Egypt they use the colour of leaves in autumn; it is only in our own western countries that we wear dismal black to signal an absence of life. If you must mourn on ad nauseam for this husband of yours, why not do it with some flair?"

"But you don't understand, you don't know . . ." and Penelope broke off, afraid to speak, afraid to say too much.

"I know a great deal. I saw that enormous monument you set up in his memory while I was in Mayfield with Bully. A prince could not have desired more; indeed while there I heard nothing but good of him, so you are probably justified in mourning his loss, but you must think of yourself as well as of his memory. You are far prettier than you would have others believe, and I believe my sister would envy this thick and lustrous hair."

"It's perfectly straight," Penelope put in.

"No, that's not so." His hand paused in its brushing, resting lightly on her shoulder. "You have a most charming curl. Look."

He took hold of her fingertips to guide them over what was, to be sure, a definite curl at the nape of her neck before bending down to touch that curl gently with his lips. At that touch, Penelope turned to take the hairbrush from him. "I think my hair is quite dry now."

His eyes caught and held hers as he agreed, "I think you may be right. I'm sorry, I hadn't meant to do that, I couldn't resist the impulse. Though you've said nothing, I suspect that someone did try to take advantage of you today—no, you've no need to tell me, it's none of my business, but I want you to know you have nothing to fear from me. I know the blameless life you have led; I know how carefully you guard yourself and your good name. I understand, therefore, how very difficult and embarrassing this situation must be for you, and I want to assure you that it's not my way to take advantage of women, particularly helpless women. I've seen enough of that in my time—it's horribly degrading to the attacker as well as the victim. I've never made love to any woman who hasn't indicated that she desired me also—I should get no pleasure from a conquest by force. Nothing shall pass between us tonight, unless it were of your choosing and that," he said, taking up a rug folded at the foot of the bed, "is hardly likely to be the case. You may be assured that no word of this incident will ever come from me."

He lay the rug on the floor and stretched out on it, folding his arms across his chest and, when she made no move, he urged, "Do get to bed, it's late."

"I feel selfish; the floor is so hard and uncomfortable."

"It's far better than I've had on many a night. Now hush, say nothing more for we shouldn't want to disillusion the good farmer should he overhear the argument. Goodnight."

Penelope lay in the huge bed, watching the light of the fire dancing on the low ceiling after the candles had been doused. She was sure she would never be able to sleep under such strange circumstances. She listened to the rain pounding against the window, the crackle of the fire in the hearth, her companion's even breathing, and presently her eyelids closed and the world of reality slipped away.

16

One hour of downright love is worth an hour of dully living on.

Aphra Behn
The Rover, 1681

Later she supposed it had been because Reginald Palfry's conduct at the Blue Boar had reminded her so much of her late husband, though it might have been the oddity of finding herself sharing the same bedroom, if not the same bed, with a virtual stranger. Whatever the reason, her nightmare, her dream of forced submission, recurred. As always, she wasn't sure whether she dreamed or was awake; she was shaking, covered with perspiration, the bedclothes in a turmoil, and there were arms about her holding her fast, though they seemed unusually comforting rather than restraining.

"You're all right, Penelope, you're all right," someone was repeating over and over. "Listen, listen to me, please. No one is going to hurt you, do you understand? Don't be frightened. I'm here, but I promised to do you no harm, nor shall I, so don't cry. Was it me you were afraid of? You mustn't be." It was Mortimer, smoothing her hair away from her damp brow with firm, sure fingers. He was real; the other was a dream. "You are safe, do you understand? I shall do nothing to harm you, nothing, nor shall I allow anyone else to. Do you believe me?"

"Yes," she whispered. "Yes. I'm so sorry—it was a dream, just an old dream. I cried out, I suppose, and woke you. Truly I'm sorry."

"I sleep lightly, especially in unfamiliar surroundings. As for our host, I'm sure you didn't disturb him; even through the thickness of these cottage walls I can hear his snores. There, listen!"

And Penelope heard a snort from the next room and laughed softly.

"Well, that's a relief. I'm all right, really I am."

Yet though she was fully awake, she made no objection when he continued to sit on the bed beside her, holding her close; in fact, she clung to him like a child, comforted by his presence.

"What was it about, that dream of yours?" he asked at last.

"It was nothing, a nightmare, a silly nightmare."

"Do you often have them?"

"Yes."

"Had it anything to do with your husband?"

"Yes," she said quietly. "Yes, it had."

She couldn't see his face, only the outline of the shoulder on which her cheek rested, and in the background the glow from the fire's dying embers—the shoulder, the fire, both gave her comfort.

"You know, Penelope," Mortimer said gently, "living as you do in the past is enough to cause nightmares. Your dark clothes, the way you seclude yourself and live on memories can only serve as a constant reminder of what once was and is no more nor can ever be again."

"You're right," she said and later he was to wonder at the relief in her voice. "You're right, it can never be again."

"It's not healthy to live in the past."

"I'm foolish to dwell upon it."

"Perhaps you might learn to live now, in the present moment."

"I think the present frightens me."

"Why?"

"I . . . I don't understand it."

"And the past you think you do?"

"No, not entirely."

"It seems to me you're no different from most of us; we don't really know what living is about, but we do the best we can with it. I know for my part I much prefer the present to what went before, and I hope the future is going to be even better."

"You're very wise."

"No, I'm selfish, that's all, but many times it was rather forcibly brought home to me that if I didn't take advantage of the present moment there might not be another."

"Perhaps the present is less frightening than the past."

"You're an enigma, do you know that? When first I met you I took you for a benevolent provincial lady, very proper, horribly respectable, older than you turned out to be but perhaps that was because of your dress, and there you were behaving as no other woman of my acquaintance would dare, striking at that burly rapscallion in defence of a child. A brave and charitable lady, I thought, a worthy soul. Then, when next I saw you, I thought you were in league with that awful Plunkett-Gall woman, and I took you for one of her ilk and believed I had been mistaken in thinking you sensible and decent. As a consequence, I behaved quite outrageously towards you; I've long owed you an apology for my conduct, though I won't say that there were not moments that evening that I enjoyed—but then, as a boy, I always found stolen apples to be sweetest. And now here's yet another Penelope Bransom, a terrified little girl, afraid of nothing more than ghosts. They can't harm you."

"I wonder."

"You are still afraid, then?"

"In a way I am, Lord Mortimer, and in a way I'm not."

"Don't you think that under these circumstances you might bring yourself to call me Charles?" he asked, to which she responded gravely, "I suppose I might."

"Then say it."

"Charles."

"There, you see, that wasn't so difficult, was it?"

"No."

"I'm glad. Otherwise, I should have had to revert to calling you Mrs. Bransom and I much prefer Penelope. Let's see, she was the beautiful wife of Ulysses, king of Ithaca, wasn't she?"

"I believe in fable she was noted for her modesty rather than her beauty."

"I remember the story now; her husband went off to fight in the Trojan wars, and even though he was believed dead and she was besieged by suitors, she scorned them all and sat spinning her life away."

"No, she was weaving a robe for Laertes, her father-in-law."

"And each night she undid her work so that it might never be done, for she had promised to make her choice from among her suitors once the robe was completed." He paused, "She never did re-marry. You are well-named."

"You didn't finish. Ulysses did return but was not recognized by anyone except his old dog, and there was a trial of strength in progress to see who might win Penelope's hand, and he was the only one who could bend the great bow, and then all knew who he was. It ended happily ever after."

"In a great blood bath, as I remember, for he killed all the importunate suitors. Not an especially good bedtime story, was it? People don't come back from the dead the way Ulysses did."

"No, they don't," she agreed in relief.

"I suppose I should be glad of that, for my presence here beside you would surely be misunderstood. Tell me when you're ready to go back to sleep."

"I don't suppose I shall. I don't usually, not after I've had that dream."

"What do you do, then?"

"Just lie and think."

"About what?"

"Oh, I don't know. Things."

"Well, if you're not going to go back to sleep, perhaps I should stay here to ward off any demons—you've no need to fear, I shall stay atop the bedcovers while you're safe beneath them."

Under the warmth of the covers, Penelope realized by the cool, damp air on her face that the fire had died.

"Do you think we should re-light it?" she asked.

"To be honest, getting a fire going has never been one of my strong points. It smokes and smoulders and I fume and curse; like as not I'd awaken the good farmer and his wife with my futile efforts."

"Then do cover yourself up."

"No, it's not necessary. I'm all right."

She felt his hand. "But you're cold, you're awfully cold."

"My hand may be, but that's all. I'm entirely human, Penelope, and quite as close to you as the warmth of my blood will allow, without . . ."

"Without what?"

"Without that something happening which you don't desire and to which I would be hard put not to succumb, yet would greatly regret if I did."

In the silence that followed she scarcely dared move, scarcely dared breathe. Why did her heart pound at those words? Why did her blood course through her veins at the touch of her hand on his? Why did she tremble inside at the close proximity of their bodies? And why, almost involuntarily, did she move to press her lips against those neck muscles so ill-portrayed in the Royal Academy bronze, until he took her chin to raise her face to his?

"If you would kiss me, I would that you do so on the lips," he murmured.

And what force was it that led her to put her arms around his neck and draw his face to hers, to put her lips upon his and to kiss him, softly, sweetly, then with wild abandon? Was her impetuosity only because he returned her kiss with a passion she had earlier tasted yet not fully known? Then, when she wished it might never end, he stopped and released his hold of her.

"Penelope, if you wish to remain untouched, you must tell me to go now and I shall." He waited before adding, "But I hope you will tell me you want me as I want you."

The voice that replied must have been hers, though it seemed to come from a stranger—it was low and soft, yet the words which came from it were clear and unequivocal.

"Stay with me, Charles. I want you to."

17

It was a lover and his lass,
With a hey, and a ho, and a hey nonino,
That o'er the green cornfield did pass . . .

Shakespeare
As You Like It, 1599

How was it possible to awaken in the morning so completely satisfied, so utterly unashamed? There must be some wanton streak in her, Penelope thought as the sunlight filtering through the half-opened shutters fell upon her eyelids to bring her back from that netherworld into which she had drifted after—after all that had been.

She was loath to open her eyes for fear it had been a dream. She had dreams, but never one like that. She stretched in contentment; she had touched a height of happiness that she had never before known to exist. She had thought she knew all about that; after all, she had been married to a man her father had called virile, yet she had discovered she knew nothing, nothing at all. It had been as though she had never before been touched.

When she had asked him to stay with her, she thought she knew how it would be, yet she had invited him knowing he wanted to make love to her, being willing that he should more as a gesture of giving pleasure than of receiving it. His kiss, it was true, had aroused unusually pleasant sensations; she had felt as much that first time when he had kissed her on the Lambournes' terrace; but that was only a kiss. She knew what must follow; she allowed it without expecting anything different except that the act would be performed by one who had been kind to her rather than one she despised. She had lain there, waiting with a sense of dread for it to happen as it had so often happened before, the brutal seizure, the lust of possession.

It had happened, but nothing, she discovered, was the same. She might have been a virgin on her wedding night, so little did she know of the store of ecstasy Mortimer unlocked in her that night.

They had kissed, many times they had kissed, and while they had kissed his fingertips had travelled across her skin—oh so lightly like butterflies on a summer day— lighting here and there on a path to those unknown regions . . . a path followed again and again with caresses each time more decisive, each time more insistent. Those fingers were butterflies no longer but eagles' wings taking her on a frenzied course until she cried out in anguished desire—she cried his name until she reached that terrible, wonderful pinnacle that she had never before known. She should be ashamed; she was sure she should be ashamed. Women were not supposed to feel such urges, her father had told her so. Women were to lie still, to submit, while men enjoyed such vile pleasures. She should be ashamed to have experienced such complete depravity, such utter delight. She should be ashamed . . . but she was not.

And it had been no dream, for she opened her eyes and there beside her on the pillow lay his head, his dark hair tousled, his eyes closed, his fine features unusually soft in repose. A bare arm lay across her in a gesture of possession but not dominance, rather as though he could not bear to part from her even in sleep. Softly she touched his hand, running her fingers along those fingers which had wrought such havoc and caused such delight.

Gently she raised her head, the better to watch him as he slept, to be privy to something vulnerable and unknown about him. As she watched, her heart filled with joy and longing and desire and the sinful knowledge that she wanted everything to happen again just as it had happened before. She was sure it must be sinful for her to desire him so, the sin lying not so much in the fact they were not man and wife but in her aroused passion. That was unnatural in a woman; she had often been told she was unnatural before, but never for such reasons.

She could not resist leaning forward to touch those lips with her own, and immediately his eyes opened and his hold upon her tightened.

"Darling wanton hussy," he murmured, his voice still muffled with sleep.

"That's no more than I've been telling myself ever since I awoke."

"How dare you be so beautifully depraved?"

"I don't know."

"So horribly loving?"

"I don't know, though was the fault entirely mine?"

"Mmmm." His lips were tracing a path across her neck and shoulder. "Not entirely, perhaps, only ninety-nine percent."

"Oh, Charles," she protested, repeating his name again more softly, then more softly still, for his fingers were on those secret places. "Oh, Charles!"

It was almost noon before they next awoke; the sun had been high, the skies showing blue through the casement window, the song of the birds under the eaves falling for hours on deaf ears.

"I suppose we should go down," she murmured without moving.

"I suppose we should," he agreed.

But it was not until much later that they descended to dine on Mrs. Rooke's fine fresh trout which entirely justified the praise it had been given. While at the Blue Boar Penelope had been unable to eat anything, yet at Topplescroft Farm she found herself ravenously hungry, enjoying food as she had not enjoyed it since a child. She blamed her appetite on the country air and Mrs. Rooke's superior cooking, deliberately ignoring Mortimer's innuendo that her prodigious store of energy needed replenishment.

The meal finished, Mortimer went off to see to the carriage that had been hauled out of the ditch while they slept, and he returned with the news that the wheel rim was very likely cracked.

"I told young Rooke it would be wise to get the smithy to look at it, but the man's awfully busy at this time of year. I instructed him not to put the blacksmith out on our account, that we would not object to staying on for a day or so; that is, if it is all right with you?"

"Quite," Penelope agreed, afraid to look at him for fear her eyes would betray her eager wish they might never have to leave.

"Good then, that's settled."

She looked up to see his smile and she smiled back at him. "Yes, that's quite settled."

"Let's go for a walk, shall we, see if we can find Stan and the men out in the cornfields."

They set out across the farmyard and along the lane leading to the cornfields beyond, saying little, though occasionally Penelope would pause to point out wild marjoram and goldenrod already in bloom or to remark on the fine crop of blackberries to be expected that year. They walked, hand in hand, close to one another, so close that Mrs. Rooke, wiping her hands on her apron, watching them from the parlour window as they went, remarked to her husband, "Love birds, real love birds, they are. Half the day spent in the bedroom."

"Well, it's a comfy enough bed—besides, quality don't get up with the lark like us do. Probably get up that time every day."

"Stan said he was usually up afore the men over there. Look at them, Bert, the way they walk so close, like they can't stand for a breath of air to come between 'em."

Mr. Rooke stared out over his wife's shoulder.

"That Lord Mortimer's a fine figure of a man, he is," he said.

"She's not so bad either. Funny, last night when they came, I thought she was a plain little thing. Fancy him choosing her, I thought to meself, but today she looks positively radiant. I suppose the rest did her good."

"Rest or whatever."

"What do you mean, Bert?"

"Well, I don't suppose they slept all the time, do you?"

Mrs. Rooke turned to her husband and laughed. "You are a one and no mistake." Then she looked back, but the pair were disappearing as the lane wound up the hill. "Wonder how long they've been married," she mused. "She just wears a plain gold ring, no diamond or gemstone, and her clothes was plain, almost dowdy; she's a down to earth sort of person, really." As she watched they reappeared at the crest of the hill, two figures melding into one. "I think they're kissing. Isn't it nice to see the flame still burning so bright?"

"I can show you a bright flame still burning after four and twenty years in harness, Mabel, if you care to step upstairs."

"For goodness' sake, Bert, and me in the middle of making puff pastry for the pie tonight—that needs cool hands or it's no good."

"In that case we'd better wait."

"We better had."

Days at Topplescroft Farm passed one by one in perfect harmony, filled with good food, fresh air, pleasant companionship and nights in the big bed under the eaves with the room lit only by the fire flickering in the hearth—intimate nights, ardent nights.

Paper and charcoal were found for Penelope, and Mortimer lay beside her as she sketched the weeping willows down by the stream where the livestock were watered.

"It eludes me, always it eludes me." She held her head on one side, critically studying her work. "It's not right. The willow is deceptively regular and simple, yet essentially fluid, and my reproduction is always stiff and unnatural."

He looked up at her, studying her as she worked. "I love to watch you when you concentrate. You draw your brows together and fix your eyes with such determination on their object—I know you're seeing something entirely different from what I see—a green tree with drooping branches and a few brown and white cows around it."

"Well, it's not just the tree," she explained, "but the space around the branches, the shapes of the other trees, the beeches and poplars, then there are the planes of the cornfields beyond and the sky above, the quality, the depth of the shadows."

He looked at her work. "You may be dissatisfied, but I think you have great talent. I must admit to a twinge of jealousy at the way your art absorbs you."

"That's praise indeed, coming from England's hero."

"I didn't do anything for England; what I did was for foolish, selfish reasons. I'm a hypocrite for taking the honours I was given."

"I suppose we're all hypocrites in some way."

"Perhaps so, if not of virtues then of vices. None of us are entirely as we seem."

"But there is no dispute about why you went away to the army, you made no pretence."

"So you've heard it all, from what source I wonder," he quizzed.

"It doesn't matter. And it doesn't matter why you went; the point is that you did and you served with great valour."

"Only because I didn't care, I had nothing to lose. And I've done nothing since except play the fool a great deal too much."

"Nothing! Why you're probably the most active and open-minded person I've ever met, always willing to listen, to absorb new ideas. I heard you talking the other night about the feasibility of preserving food in metal containers; that's an imaginative leap of thought that would never occur to others. And just think, if it were possible, what a difference it could make to have fruit, vegetables and meat available year round, at the pole or the equator. Look too at the carriage of your own design, the way you thought out construction of an indestructible wheel . . ." She broke off abruptly, flushing, and he grinned.

"You saw through my ruse then, you remembered. You knew all along there was nothing wrong with the wheel of the carriage, that I just made that up so you would stay."

"Yes, I knew all along."

"Come here." He took the pad from her hands and gently pulled her down beside him. "If we might find a way to join your intuition and sense perception with my practical and intellectual knowledge, what wonders might result."

He kissed her. "I'm most horribly enamoured of you, but I suppose you know that too. Do you remember the first time I kissed you on the terrace at the Lambournes'? You said hell would freeze over before you'd ever allow me to do that again, or words to that effect."

"How wretched of you to remind me of that."

"Do you want me to stop?" he asked after kissing her again.

"Hell, I believe, is freezing over."

She never wanted it to end. She never wanted to leave Topplescroft Farm. She never wanted to be separated from Mortimer, yet she knew it could not last forever.

She completely lost track of time, but one morning she rose early to open the window shutters and find a scene of unusual activity and bustle in the farmyard.

"I wonder what's going on."

"It's probably quarter day, Midsummer Day. It's a busy day for farms and estates, accounts being settled, all that sort of thing."

"No, it can't be, not Midsummer Day already."

"Why, is it important to you?"

"Yes. I must be in Mayfield today, I really must."

"But we were going to picnic by the old Abbey. You were looking forward to it."

"I know, but I had no idea so much time had passed— that it was Midsummer Day already. I must go, really I must."

"Then if you must, you shall." His voice was cool, distant. "I shall take you this morning."

It crossed her mind that she should tell him, tell him everything about her husband, about his illegitimate children who depended upon her for their support; about Edward Bransom, who would give her her allowance only if she were there to receive it. She considered it, but she thought also that in all their hours of intimacy he had never once spoken of the future. Until he did, she should not speak of those things.

"I must go back alone."

"Of course. It would hardly do for you to ride in to Mayfield on my arm." Was it irony in his voice, or did he merely want to protect her name?

"You will come to me, won't you?" she pleaded.

There was no irony as he replied, "Nothing and no one could keep me away."

18

Nought treads so silent as the foot of time.
                    Edward Young
                    Love of Fame, 1728

"Where on earth were you, Pen?" Arthur complained. "It's close to a week since Edward returned from London; we were sure you would be with him. I heard you arrived in a hired chaise this morning, but if the rector hadn't seen you, I doubt I should know even now that you were back. It was foolish not to have come with Edward, even though you may not get on particularly well with him. You should not have travelled alone, anything might have happened. Of course, I understand that it must be awkward because of this business of Missy marrying Bullerton—not that I object to him personally, mind, for he's a nice enough chap and I admit I gave him leave to speak—but all along I hoped she would refuse him, for she was half promised to Edward and I can't blame him for feeling put out, really I can't. There are times when I wish I hadn't done so, for Edward's been most difficult ever since. His prospects are so much better, what with the Hall and the estate and should anything happen to you, Pen, though God forbid, all of your income will revert to him, too. Had Mortimer not been there, I should most certainly have denied Bullerton the privilege of speaking, but there, it's done. I wish, however, you had advised her; you know what an influence you've always been in her life."

"Missy made up her own mind, Arthur, and that's as it should be. Anyway, I happen to have great respect for Colonel Bullerton."

"I trust you're not implying that you have none for Edward. I should remind you that, despite everything, he is still my friend."

Penelope avoided the issue. "Look, Arthur, I've really had a very busy day, it being quarter day, and I still have many things to do. I must send this draft off to replenish my dwindling account and I haven't yet set things to rights here at the Lodge. It seems I've been gone for an age. I appreciate your coming, I don't really mean to hurry you, but unless there is anything I can specifically do for you just now, I should appreciate being left alone. Tell Phyllis I shall be with her as soon as I can tomorrow. I've no need to remind you that I shall, of course, oversee matters at Kerswell and care for the children while she is confined. But she knows she can count on me as always."

Yet when her brother at last took his leave, still grumbling, Penelope sat at her desk, pen in hand, idly following the progress of a pale blue dragonfly as it darted over the lawn and around the yew hedges; it was of exactly the shade of blue of the dress of Mrs. Rooke's that she had worn at Topplescroft Farm. Celestial blue, Mortimer had said it was, a colour used for mourning in some strange country, Armenia, wasn't it? It seemed so long ago, yet it had been only that morning she had resumed her own dark attire, which had dampened her spirits, but not as much as the parting that followed. When would she see him again? He had said he would wait upon her as soon as he could. It could not be too soon, for she missed him terribly. Perhaps he would be there at the end of the week; she looked across the lawn, imagining his tall figure striding across it and felt she could scarcely live without him.

Unseeingly, she continued to watch the dragonfly's progress, her eyes soft with memories. Mortimer, next to her at the table, watching her sketch, his face on the pillow beside hers—and quite suddenly a deep pink suffused her cheeks at remembered intimacies.

It had happened so, earlier in the day when immediately

following her return to Mayfield she had made her way up to the Hall. It had been a dour-faced Edward Bransom who had blustered his greeting, prepared for a wrathful reproach which never came. Its absence puzzled him, as did the unexpected radiance in Penelope's aspect, the luminous glow in her eyes. His own had narrowed in suspicion. Where had she been those past days since he had driven away from the Blue Boar? Not with Palfry, as he had schemed, for he'd returned there the next morning, hoping to expose Penelope Bransom as a lascivious woman unfaithful to his uncle's memory, only to be confronted by that jaded, disgruntled gentleman bedded down with some slattern. The scene had disgusted Bransom, causing him to wonder once again how his uncle could have befriended such a lecher. But, oh, that it might have been the widow under those bedcovers! What an opportunity to get even with her after she had ruined his chances with her sister. She'd been there, he knew, for he'd found the note he had written copied in her hand and had pocketed it. It might, one day, be useful.

He'd gone on to London to discover she wasn't at Devonshire Place either; nor had she preceded him to Mayfield. Where had she been? he wondered yet again. And why did she, usually so outspoken, say nothing, no rebuke, no recrimination? All of his schemes to even the score, to break his uncle's will, had come to nought. He was particularly bewildered because, far from appearing angry or downcast by what had occurred, she seemed positively serene. He wanted to question her, to force from her where those intervening days, and more importantly, those intervening nights, had been spent and with whom, yet to do so must incriminate himself.

When she was about to leave without mentioning anything, he could restrain himself no longer.

"What happened to you at the Blue Boar? You said you would only be gone for a minute, and I waited and waited. When I finally went in search of you, the innkeeper was most insolent and unhelpful. I could see nothing for it but to leave."

She had looked at him unflinchingly. "I came out and you

were gone, but I took care of myself. It turned out quite well."

There had been that look in her eyes; he'd never seen it there before—it was a man who made a woman look like that, he was sure of it, but it had not been Palfry, that was certain. He would find out in time. Perhaps he might get even with her after all.

Not all Bransom's deceit, or Arthur's ill humour, or Phyllis's petulance as the day for her delivery approached, could put Penelope out of countenance. She waited for Mortimer to come; nothing else mattered.

Daily she went to Kerswell and took the children walking with her in the meadows among the daisies and buttercups. She provided them with paper and charcoal so they might sketch with her, instructing them on the anatomy of the plants they drew, praising Beatrice who, though youngest, took her work most seriously. Yet all the time her mind was filled with him, and the joy she usually brought to such a task was diminished by her distraction. She would find herself daydreaming of those hours at Topplescroft, only to be brought back to reality by the children's squabbles or demands for assistance with their drawings, assistance she supplied with her usual patience but with such detachment that even the children became aware that she was different.

"What's happened to Auntie Penny?" they asked one another.

"Perhaps she's sick," Stanley said.

"Or perhaps she's in love," Beatrice mused.

"Just like a girl to say a silly thing like that."

Yet it was not until Arthur demanded of her whether she was going to mope around forever now that she was home that Penelope became aware that the change in her was noticeable.

"I'm not moping," she protested.

"You know very well you are and have been ever since you got back from London. I suppose it's because Missy's not here."

"Yes, that's it," Penelope agreed hastily, feeling guilty as she did, for she realized she had scarcely thought of her sister.

"Well, don't come to me for sympathy on that score. If you'd followed my advice instead of flying off to town, we'd all be a sight better off—Missy would be mistress up at the Hall, Edward would be a sight more affable than he is, and you wouldn't be moping. Aren't you sorry now that you insisted upon this London visit against both Edward's and my own wishes?"

Was she sorry? she wondered. Suppose she had never met Mortimer, suppose she had not run into him that night at the Blue Boar, suppose those days at Topplescroft Farm had never happened, suppose . . . but she wouldn't suppose. For the first time in her life she had known what it was to live; she would have nothing changed, nothing.

"No, Arthur, I'm not at all sorry."

"Then you must live with the results."

She would gladly, yet she wanted more than memories; she wanted him to come as he had promised. She waited as day followed day to become a week, and one week followed another with no sign, no word from him. As she walked back and forth to Kerswell, her eyes scanning the road for a sign of his coach, Penelope's elation gave way to consideration.

She remembered Mrs. Plunkett-Gall's comments on Mortimer's relationship with Georgina Staverton. Could he have returned to London, to that lady, and forgotten all about her? She remembered his own words at the Royal Academy showing that he lived only for what the moment offered him. Was that all it had been to him, an episode?

Her consideration gave way to despondency, yet hope refused to die. He would come, he would. He must have been delayed; some matter of business must have prevented his coming, but he would come, he would.

Yet instead of Mortimer it was Missy who came to Mayfield, Missy and Meg, both changed, both more self-assured. Meg was comfortable in her position and she acted with responsibility as she settled into life at the Lodge. Nor was Missy the girl who had left; she too had become a young woman embarked on her course in life. As lovely as ever— no, thought Penelope, watching her busily preparing her trousseau—she was even lovelier, content and serene. And

Penelope, who had never considered her own looks, found herself searching her looking glass for redeeming features in her own face. She was ordinary, she decided, quite ordinary. Brown eyes, brown hair perfectly straight; even if there were a curl at the nape of the neck, it was not visible except . . . no, she refused to think of the circumstances under which she had discovered the existence of that curl.

Phyllis at last delivered her baby, a boy, and she had so wanted another girl, she mourned. And Penelope remembered all the other deliveries; whatever the sex of the baby, it always seemed Phyllis wanted the opposite.

"He's healthy and strong," Penelope said, holding him. She would never hold a baby of her own, that was not possible. And she remembered Mortimer's love of children. When he at last settled it would be because he wanted children; she had heard that more than once. He would never want a woman who was defective, barren. Her inability to conceive was a shameful thing; it was something she could never confess to anyone, never. He had not come; it was as well that he had not, for she had no right to the expectations his coming might have caused.

She divided her time between Kerswell and the children and the Lodge and Missy's trousseau; she was not only helping Missy with her clothes but she was also sewing a dress for herself, since Missy had asked her to be her matron of honour. It would be blue, celestial blue; she refused to spoil Missy's wedding by wearing black, let Edward Bransom make of it what he would. It was as they were sewing one day that Missy mentioned Mortimer's name.

"Rodney has written that he has seen Mortimer, and he has gladly accepted to be at our wedding."

"Indeed?" Much as she would, Penelope could not keep the interest from her voice. "He saw him in London?"

"Yes, at Lady Staverton's."

"I see," Penelope said, her eyes fixed on the seam she was sewing.

"Rodney extended the invitation to Georgina Staverton as well, more because she is a particular friend of Mortimer's than anything else. From what Rodney says, I gather he does not altogether approve of their friendship, but he can never bring himself to criticize Mortimer."

"She is coming then?"

"Yes," Missy nodded. "She indicated that she would very much like to."

So he had gone from her arms to those of Lady Staverton. She might have known, Penelope thought bitterly. She couldn't help but pursue the matter, though. "Has Colonel Bullerton seen much of Lord Mortimer in these past weeks?"

"No, I rather think not. Rodney said Mortimer appeared very distracted over something—he had just returned from Southampton and was leaving almost immediately for Bristol, I'm not sure of the reason. But Rodney said that he most particularly asked after you and sent his warmest regards to all here at Mayfield."

"How very gracious," Penelope's voice was as cold as her heart.

19

There is scarce any condition in the mind which does not produce a suitable agitation in the fan, insomuch that if I only see the fan of a disciplined lady, I know whether she laughs, frowns or blushes. I have seen a fan so angry that it would have been dangerous for the absent lover who pro-voked it to have come within wind of it; and at other times so languishing that I have been glad for the lady's sake that the lover was at a certain distance from it.

Joseph Addison
The Spectator, 27 June 1711

Sometimes a light surprises
The Christian while he sings;
It is the Lord who rises
With healing in his wings:
When comforts are declining,
He grants the soul again
A season of clear shining,
To cheer it after rain.

Blue and red reflections from the stained glass of the window commemorating her husband danced across Penelope's hymnal as, in the Bransom pew on that seventh Sunday after Trinity, she joined in singing Cowper's words. Her mind wandered from the hymn to the illustrations she was making for a collection of Cowper's poems; she had been surprised and not a little delighted when a London publisher had written saying he had heard of her work from Samuel Trueblood and asking whether she would agree to perform the work. He had even insisted upon paying her for doing something that was, for her, a great pleasure.

Set free from present sorrow,
We cheerfully can say
Let the unknown to-morrow
Bring with it what it may.

She stood between Missy, whose glow increased daily as her wedding approached, and Edward Bransom, whose ill humour increased at a similar pace. Surprisingly, Penelope found herself unaffected by a situation far from pleasant for her, for Bransom clearly regarded her as the instigator of his misfortune, possibly supported in that opinion by Arthur Woodard, who was anxious to find favour again with his friend. Penelope did nothing to disavow Bransom's beliefs; in any case, to do so would have been without avail. Nor did she blame her brother, who would forever live in Mayfield alongside Bransom, for not supporting her. She had not expected that he would. Though Arthur was weak, he was not a bad man; she could not say the same thing for Bransom, who, she was sure, was behind the unsavoury meeting she had had with Palfry at the Blue Boar.

Perhaps it was because she was busy with her painting, with the children at Kerswell, with Missy's wardrobe; perhaps, too, it was because it was an exceptionally warm summer that she found herself unusually fatigued by her round of duties. What little leisure remained to her she preferred not to spend worrying about Edward Bransom and his peculiarities, and she tried to think as little as possible about Charles Mortimer, hoping that eventually the memory of him might fade. He would be at Missy's wedding; she would prepare herself to see him then, and that would be an end to the matter.

A stir could be heard at the back of the church, a hum of voices, heads turned. Beside her, Edward Bransom looked back to discover the cause of the disturbance, ready to rebuke any worshipper showing lack of respect. Abruptly, with an air of great importance, he left the pew to return minutes later, his face wreathed in obsequious smiles, ushering into the Bransom pew the one person most able to disturb Penelope's peace of mind. Their eyes met as he held out his hand to share her hymnal, to which she firmly returned her gaze as together they finished the last verse:

> *Though vine nor fig-tree neither*
> *Their wonted fruit should bear*
> *Though all the fields should wither,*
> *Nor flocks nor herds be there;*
> *Yet, God the same abiding,*
> *His praise shall tune my voice;*
> *For, while in him confiding,*
> *I cannot but rejoice.*

Thereafter, Penelope remembered not a word of the sermon, usually interminable, particularly on a hot day, but this time passing all too soon. She sat beside Mortimer in confusion. She would have to speak to him, to speak in front of others as though nothing had passed between them. Why had he come, just as she was beginning to put the incident in proper perspective? That was all it had been, an incident; she was foolish to have thought otherwise. It could not possibly be more than that.

All too quickly, the service ended. They left the church, Bransom deep in conversation with Mortimer, to be joined by Arthur and Phyllis, then Mr. Osborn, the rector, then his wife, while Penelope stood very slightly apart. Arthur's children surrounded Mortimer; it seemed he would have preferred to talk with them until Phyllis ordered the nursemaid to take them home.

"My dear Lord Mortimer," Bransom intoned, "had we but known you would be here today the sermon would have been in your honour, would it not, Mr. Osborn?"

"Indeed, it would." Mr. Osborn beamed. "I should have been delighted to devote my little homily to your gallantry in ridding our country of that monster who threatened the peace of us all. . . ."

"Sir, please! If you wish to honour anyone, let it be the

common soldier, that unsung hero who endures so much for so little."

"Ah," Edward Bransom put in, "you are too modest. Where would that soldier be without men such as yourself to lead him?"

"Our dear Duke has said that Waterloo was won on the playing fields of Eton," Mr. Osborn purred.

"I'm a Harrow man myself."

"I beg pardon, my lord, no offense meant, I'm sure."

"And none taken."

"But to what do we owe this unexpected pleasure?" Edward Bransom asked. The obsequious smile on his countenance flickered as Mortimer answered, "I've come regarding the wedding of my friend, Colonel Bullerton. He has asked me to act as his best man, and in that capacity there are certain matters I should discuss with the rector."

"We shall look for you at Kerswell for dinner," Arthur Woodard put in, determined not to be outdone; after all, Mortimer was to stand up at the wedding of *his* sister, not Bransom's. Arthur began to think that there were advantages to the match after all, and that Bransom was the one who should wish to sustain their friendship.

But the failure of his overture was greeted by a supercilious smirk from Bransom as Mortimer replied, "I'm sorry, Woodard, I'm on my way north. Another time, perhaps."

Mortimer turned to Missy, though his eyes were on Penelope as he spoke, "I should like to call in at the Lodge on my way—I have a message from Colonel Bullerton. Will you be at home?"

"I believe we shall, shall we not, Penelope?" Missy also looked enquiringly at her sister who agreed unwillingly, "I expect that we shall."

"Good, in an hour, then."

He was about to turn away and Penelope sighed in relief. She had not had to speak to him publicly after all. But then he turned back to ask, "Are you quite well, Mrs. Bransom?"

"Quite."

"It is a long time since we have met."

"I believe it may be."

1 7 3

"I have a fan—a sandalwood fan—that was discovered at the Lambournes', thought possibly to be yours. I shall bring it."

The exchange was nothing but commonplace, yet Edward Bransom's eyes narrowed. Was it possible, he wondered, before immediately dismissing the idea, that his uncle's plain widow might have the hero of Waterloo for an admirer?

From her bedroom window Penelope saw him coming, his tall figure striding across the front garden, just as she had always imagined. She had always thought she would run to him, throwing caution to the winds, not caring who might see. But she did not move, except when she saw his eyes look up, and then she shrank back.

Why had he come now? Was she merely another conquest? She couldn't face him. Missy sent upstairs twice for her, and at last she plucked up courage to descend. Even then, she stood in the hallway, unable to go into the room because her heart was pounding so.

As she reached out to grasp the door handle, the door opened and Missy came out.

"There you are, Pen!"

"But where are you going?"

"Do please go in and keep Lord Mortimer company. I shan't be long, I promise."

He stood with his back to her as she entered; he was examining the illustration of a bedewed rose on which she had been working. But as soon as he heard her step, he turned.

"Penelope!"

His voice, low, rich in pronouncing her name was just as she remembered it, and his eyes clear and blue as they searched her face.

"Penelope, my dear Penelope!"

She grasped the back of a chair, foolishly delighted at seeing him, yet afraid, afraid he would come too near, afraid she would give in to him, even though she knew he couldn't care as she cared. If he did, he would have come to Mayfield long since as he had promised.

1 7 4

"What is your opinion of the rose?" she asked in an attempt to prevent anything intimate from passing between them."

"The rose?"

She nodded in the direction of the easel. "It's an illustration for Cowper's poem 'The Rose,' for the part that goes 'The plentiful moisture encumbered the rose, And weighed down its beautiful head,' or something like that. I've been having difficulty with the dew on the petals, it seems too heavy, too solid." She knew she was talking too much, but if she talked then he could say nothing to divert the conversation. "I feel fortunate in having a commission to illustrate a new edition of Cowper's collected works. A publisher wrote to ask if I would do it; my name had been suggested by Samuel Trueblood."

She saw a cloud cross his face at the mention of that name, and stopped.

"How very clever of him to think of it," Mortimer said sharply.

"I thought it kind." She looked towards the door. "Missy is not back yet?"

"She is writing a letter to Bully for me to deliver. I think she will be engaged at her task for some time—at least I hope so." He looked at her earnestly. "How are you, Penelope?"

"As I told you, I am well, quite well. And you?"

"I've missed you."

"That I gather." She was unable to keep the irony from her voice.

"I'm sorry—I couldn't come before. I've had matters to attend to, matters still unresolved; I must leave again almost immediately, in fact. I wanted to let you know, but I couldn't write to you for obvious reasons."

"It concerns Lady Staverton, I suppose."

"Ah, you know of it then."

"Missy mentioned that Colonel Bullerton had said something of seeing you there," Penelope said coldly. "I quite understand that you could not get away."

"Your tone indicates you do not completely understand."

"My tone merely indicates that the matter does not concern me."

"That is true, it does not. Nevertheless, I thought you might wonder that I did not come after the time we spent together. . . ."

"That time was madness," she broke in.

"If madness, then a glorious madness."

"Only madness. I don't know why you came." Penelope felt herself close to tears. "I wish you had not."

"Do you *really* wish I had not?" He began to cross the room towards her, causing her to grip the chair back even more tightly.

"Please . . . don't touch me." All the urgency she felt inside was conveyed in her hushed cry. If he touched her, she could not resist him though he had visited a thousand Lady Stavertons instead of coming to her as he had promised.

He stopped short. "No, I shouldn't dream of doing anything you wouldn't welcome. But I'm at a loss to understand. Is this the same Penelope who wore the blue dress, who laughed with me, who walked with me, who slept beside me under the eaves. . . ."

"Please, I beg you, say no more."

"I'm not to touch you, not to talk to you . . . why?" he demanded.

"Because, as I said, it was madness."

"So." His face was cold, his voice angry. "So, this is what happens when once again you fall under the spell of the man buried in that mausoleum—I saw the stand of fresh lilies on his shrine, I saw you had once again donned your mourning costume. Had this been India, undoubtedly you would have climbed upon that saint of a husband's funeral pyre and committed suttee! When are you going to give it up, Penelope, when will you relinquish the role of the inconsolable widow? You're still young, vital, you deserve more than this, this . . . this living death."

"I am quite satisfied with my life, at least I was until . . ."

"Until when?"

"Until you came into it, if you must know. You have confused me."

"I have awakened you, Penelope; don't go back to sleep," he pleaded.

"Lord Mortimer, I don't tell you or Lady Staverton or anyone else how to run their lives. Please don't tell me what to do with mine."

His eyes narrowed. "Is it because I went to Georgina's side that you are angry? But you must realize I have known her for a long time—she needed me."

"Of course she needed you, I know that."

"Then since you know, you must understand."

"I do understand."

"Very well then."

But it was not very well, they both knew that it was anything but very well.

"I came here on a fool's errand today," he said bitterly.

"A fool's errand?" she questioned.

"I thought you would run to me, I thought it would be the same as when we were together at Topplescroft Farm. I was foolish enough to think that I might persuade you to give up this morbid worship at the master's grave, that you might put aside these hideous widow's weeds in favour of gay, vibrant colour—that you might, in fact, give up death with him for life with me."

"Life with you?" she repeated, not altogether comprehending. As though to convince her of his sincerity, his voice broke as he murmured, "I've missed you so, Penelope. Have you in any way missed me?"

Her look must have told him, for she dare not speak, she dare not say what was in her heart, though the pressure on the chairback she still held increased until the knuckles of her hand whitened.

"You did!" he triumphed. "You may not own to it, but you did. Oh, Penelope, we can have such a wonderful life together, a life filled with art, and science, and love, and lots and lots of children. . . ."

But the smile that had crossed her face to light her eyes and curl the corners of her mouth, suddenly froze, the joy of hope that had swept over her died.

"No, no it can never be," her guttural cry broke in.

"Why not? Why can't it be?" he demanded.

Even as she stood there, longing to fling aside the chair she was holding, to throw herself into his arms, it was Josiah Bransom's voice that echoed in her ears, "You're barren, madam, barren. Do you understand the word? God did not make you as he made other women." As if to drown out that voice she cried aloud, "I can't!"

"You mean you won't," he responded tersely.

"Can't, won't, is there so much difference?"

"There's a great deal of difference, Penelope, and you know it."

If only he hadn't come—if only he would go. Her voice trembled as she said, "The picture you paint, it can never be."

"Because you won't allow it to be, isn't that it? Because you've been dead for so many years, you're afraid to live, isn't that it, Penelope? Damn it, I shall make you live whether you want to or not!"

He strode across the room and tore the chair from her hands, and instinctively she held her hands over her face, knowing if he touched her, she must give in, she must tell him everything, she must listen for the scorn in his voice that he would undoubtedly attempt to obliterate under the guise of kindness.

"That's not important," he would probably say, but she would know that it was, that he loved children, and that she would be forever robbing him of having his own.

But he didn't touch her. He flung the chair aside, then crossed the room to look out of the window.

"I'm sorry, Mrs. Bransom. You must excuse me. I had no intention of frightening you. I most heartily beg your pardon for all I've said that has, apparently, upset you so." Then he turned back to demand quietly, "I must ask, though—are you sure there is no reason why we *should* not marry?"

"Should not marry?" she repeated uncomprehendingly.

"You are quite sure you are not . . . not with child?"

"Quite sure." Would that she might have been! Her eyes filled with tears as slowly she shook her head.

"Then it is over."

"It is over." Her whispered response was barely audible as the door opened to admit a smiling Missy with her letter in hand.

"Meg says she will bring the tea tray at four. Would you rather it were served here or in the garden?"

"I'm sorry, I can't stay," Mortimer announced. "I am on my way to Chenwyth and must go on to Liverpool immediately after. But I shall see that your letter reaches Bully, Miss Woodard. I look forward to the August wedding, a joyous occasion for us all."

But Missy, handing him her letter, thought he seemed less joyous than ever before, and Penelope barely spoke when he paid his adieus. She sensed something had happened between them and waited for her sister to speak of it, but Penelope took up her brush and started to paint again. Suddenly she dashed it across the work, ruining it.

"Oh, Pen, what is it, what is wrong?"

"It's no good, Missy, it's just no good. Nothing's any good."

"One good thing is that Lord Mortimer found Mama's fan, he said you'd left it on the terrace at the Lambournes'—remember the night you had to chaperone us, and how you hated it? As soon as I saw the mother-of-pearl trim on the sandalwood, I assured him it was yours—I told him how pleased you would be to have it back."

Missy handed her the sandalwood fan, which Penelope opened unwarily to find written thereon:

> *Since he loves now who scarce did love before,*
> *Let she who has loved now love all the more.*
> *M*

Her eyes welled with tears. Why had she not been made as other women were made? Why was she defective, incomplete, barren? How differently she might have responded when he spoke of a life together, no matter for what reason he had delayed coming. But then, immediately, he had spoken of children—lots and lots of children—that impediment she had forgotten in her momentary jubilance at his offer. It was that which had crushed the joyous response that burst to her lips.

Suppose she had been honest, suppose she had confessed her infertility, what would he have said? That it made no difference, that he loved her anyway? But if he had, she would not have believed him. He worshipped children, she had seen him with Arthur's, she had watched Lady Staverton's children, the way they had clung to him. To be unable to have any of his own would always have been a cause of deep disappointment, she was sure, whether he owned to it or not. For a time, perhaps, they might have been happy, but later would he not have come to think she had robbed him of something precious in life? Might he not even think of her as flawed, defective? His unspoken disillusion, for she was sure he would never speak of it, she could not have borne. It was better to allow him to believe she worshipped the dead than to confess the shame of her infertility. But oh, if only she were formed as other women, complete, able to conceive . . . how differently that day might have ended.

20

*What is easy to understand we despise; we need prodigies
and miracles.*

> Synesius
> *Egyptian Tales,* ca. 400

She repeated those words written across her fan again and
again; the phrase never left her even when she slept.

> *Since he loves now who scarce did love before,*
> *Let she who has loved now love all the more.*

Was it possible that she, a woman of neither great charm
nor great beauty, had inspired love in a man sought by so
many? Was it possible that she had at last been offered the
glass slipper by the prince and she had refused to put it on?
Did he love her enough that it would not have mattered to
him that she could never—no! She stopped herself short,
refusing to allow that path of conjecture that could only
lead to hopeless fantasy. She must face life as she had always
done, with frankness and honesty.

As if to remind her that she had acted rightly, Mortimer's
fondness for children was always being remarked upon. "I
only wish Arthur would pay half as much attention to his
family as Lord Mortimer did when he was here," Phyllis
complained. "He treated them with . . . do take your fingers
out of the jam, Stanley . . . with such kindness, and they
were so good. Now look what he's done, smeared jam on my

favourite chairseat. It will be back to the nursery with you, young man."

The young Woodards were equally fond of him. "I'm going to the Army to be a hero like Lord Mortimer," Stanley affirmed stoutly.

"Lord Mortimer does not smear jam all over my best chairs. Go and wash your hands instantly or I shall send for nanny and she'll stand for no nonsense."

"Is Lord Mortimer coming to Auntie Melissa's wedding, Auntie Penny?" Beatrice asked shyly as Stanley, spurred by the thought of an irate nanny, hurried away to wash.

"He is to be best man to Colonel Bullerton, the gentleman your aunt is marrying."

"I hope he likes my dress."

"You and Sally will be perfect little flower girls," her mother purred.

"Perhaps, but I hope he thinks I'm prettier than Sally."

"He's likely to find you a sight more conceited, especially if you press him for compliments all the time like you did when he stayed here," her older sister complained.

"I did not," Beatrice wailed. "He said I was pretty."

"Well, you liked it, and you wouldn't leave him alone. You know you did."

"Children, children!" their mother interposed sharply. "Go away, all of you. Give your Auntie Penny and me some peace, do. You're lucky, Pen, not to have any children. I daresay Lord Mortimer only dotes upon them because he has none of his own."

"Perhaps," Penelope agreed without conviction.

"You know, you're not looking at all well, is anything wrong?" her sister-in-law asked.

"Nothing. I'm a bit tired, that's all."

"Not doing too much for Missy's wedding are you? You shouldn't have to, with the wedding breakfast here at Kerswell—I know I have cook complaining already. Anyone would think we were having large parties every week to hear her go on so."

"No, I'm not over-taxed on that account."

"Well, I don't know what it is then, but even Arthur remarked that you're not at all yourself, and I'm sure he never notices anything. If I didn't know better, I'd swear you were in the family way—in those first months I'm good for nothing; I look just like you do now—dark circles under my eyes, tired all the time, off my food, irritable . . ." She stopped short. "Lord forbid, Pen, I'm not suggesting that is the cause with you, don't misunderstand. Just don't wear yourself out because your sister is marrying. Is there anything I can do for you?"

"There is one thing that must be done, Phyllis, something I am loath to do."

"And what is that?"

"Would you explain the facts to Missy?"

"Facts?"

"Yes, the facts about . . . about being married, a woman's role, you know what I mean."

"Of course," Phyllis agreed matter-of-factly. "I shall be glad to, though I dare say she knows everything already. Young girls seem to nowadays, though I'm sure I don't know how, whispering and giggling, it's quite disgusting. I'm sure I didn't."

"Nor I. That's a great relief to me, Phyllis, I do appreciate it."

"Well, if that's all that was troubling you, perhaps now you'll feel better."

"I daresay I shall."

But she didn't. She who was always active and energetic, an early riser, stayed abed until eight or nine in the morning. She ate little, her nerves were on edge, and even her painting, her greatest solace, did little to ease her mind— she became convinced her work was no good. Missy began to insist upon her taking breakfast in bed and afternoon naps.

"Anyone would think you were my mother instead of my little sister," Penelope complained, though secretly glad of the rest.

"I'm not a little girl anymore, Pen."

"I know you're not. I should stop calling you Missy and give you your proper name."

"Don't, I love your nickname for me, even though I won't be a Miss any more."

Something in her sister's face made Penelope ask, "Has Phyllis spoken to you?"

"Yes." Missy busied herself with Penelope's breakfast tray. "But I wish you had instead."

"I'm sorry. I should have, except . . ." Penelope stopped, knowing full well why she had not.

"Except what, Pen? You and your husband were so happy that that part must have been happy too, wasn't it?"

Penelope had for a long time had an urge to tell her sister the truth about her marriage to Josiah Bransom, for the deceit, particularly toward one she loved, weighed heavily upon her. But though she was resolved one day to tell Missy everything, to do so on the eve of her wedding would be thoughtless, unkind.

Yet it was not Josiah Bransom of whom Penelope thought as she replied, "I assure you that it can be quite, quite wonderful. With someone you love, it can bring the greatest happiness to a woman. I only asked Phyllis to speak to you of it because she knows about childbearing—I know nothing of that—I never shall."

"I wish that you had had a child, Pen, for then I wouldn't feel as I do about leaving you. I'm sure I've never felt more unhappy than now that Mr. Bransom was . . ." she broke off abruptly.

"Was what?" Penelope prompted.

"Unable to father a child—at least that's what they say in the village. I know you're going to berate me for listening to such gossip."

"I'm going to berate you because it isn't so—I mean, the making of a child is between a man and a woman. I could be the one at fault."

"How like you to accept the blame."

"It is probably so."

"Well, it can never be known, so it is no use to conjecture. I'm just sorry to be leaving you alone."

"I'm scarcely alone with Arthur, Phyllis and all their family. And I have Meg, too, don't forget."

"And she is a treasure, Pen. You should see what a fine stitch she sews. Rodney's mother wanted to know where I had found her, and I had to admit Meg's finding was none of my doing. She is quite an exceptional girl, especially when I remember how much she has learned in the short time she has been with us."

"Perhaps Meg should be with you, especially when you begin housekeeping."

"No, she will be a comfort for you here at the Lodge."

"I admit I am very fond of her, but we shall see. You may need help later."

"Perhaps . . . when we begin a family." Missy flushed at the thought.

"Yes, Meg would be wonderful then, for you need someone you know at that time, not a stranger. Of course, I shall come to you whenever you want, you know that."

"I do, Pen." Her sister grew pensive. "I wonder whether Phyllis realizes how lucky she is having you always there. I'm afraid she and Arthur make use of you—Rodney and I would never want to do that. What would they have done if you'd had a family of your own to care for?"

"As you said yourself, it is useless to conjecture about something that can never be. Now, no more of this lying abed. Apart from anything else, I really must finish that first set of illustrations and get them off to London so that I shall know whether they are satisfactory."

Penelope did finish them and send them off, and though not entirely satisfied with the results herself, she awaited word from the publisher of his opinion. Perhaps by the time she heard, she would be recovered from her fatigue caused, no doubt, by the recent turmoil in her life.

Phyllis came to tea one afternoon for the purpose of pronouncing judgement on Missy's wardrobe.

"I do think you were foolish to promise to wear your mother-in-law's dress for the ceremony. It's a nice, sentimental touch, but it will be horribly outdated; it's probably a quarter of a century since she married."

"Thirty-four years, to be precise, but it's beautiful," Missy insisted. "I shall try it on and you may see for yourself."

"Arthur and I have decided that you should see a doctor," Phyllis began as soon as Missy left the room. "I've asked Mr. Wisham to call."

"Oh, Phyllis, really! I'm just a little tired, that's all."

"But you've never been tired, not like this, not for so long. The children noticed it, they said you don't play games with them as you usually do. And Beatrice said you told her you'd rather take a nap than go in the woods with her and sketch—that was when Arthur decided we should call Mr. Wisham. He said he'd noticed you weren't up to snuff and, my dear, when Arthur notices anything it must be bad. I'm sure he never bothers about me, though I'm utterly debilitated at the beginning of each new addition to our family. Of course, after that dreary course is underway and I adapt to my changed condition, then I feel all right again, occasionally quite glowing. But those first three months, my dear, I tell you—but I suppose I shouldn't really—though you've been married and know about the other business, you've never been through this. Take my word for it, Penelope, you've not missed anything. I shan't be sorry when my childbearing days are over, and that's a fact."

"What's it like exactly, Phyllis?" Penelope questioned.

"Giving birth—do you want the lecture I gave Missy?"

"No, no! I just wondered what you meant about becoming debilitated at the beginning . . . in those first months?"

"Oh, that. Well, I get terribly fatigued. I usually want to stay in bed the whole time, but since I don't look enlarged then I get little sympathy. In fact, I only know for sure when my domestic affliction doesn't come. And you know how I enjoy my food, but at that time, just when I need enough for two, I don't care to eat. Speaking of food, this is a fine caraway cake, but you've barely touched yours, Pen. Do give me the recipe, and I'll have cook try it."

"I shall."

"Of course, I have cook trained now; as soon as she sees me becoming poorly, she makes me up a calf's-foot jelly that simply works wonders. I shall send some over to you tomorrow. Even though your complaint cannot possibly have a like cause, it will probably do you a world of good along with Mr. Wisham's aperient—I shall tell him to give you that rather than his black draught which, apart from tasting vile, never does me the least bit of good. I must say I believe you're paler now than when I arrived."

"It's probably the thought of Mr. Wisham's black draught." Penelope laughed, though inwardly stunned, for as Phyllis had been speaking she had been trying to remember the last time she had had her monthly course. Not since the end of May had she washed out her flannel menstrual rags—almost three months ago. It wasn't possible; it simply wasn't possible, yet all of the symptoms Phyllis described were there, all of them. It had happened once before, of course, after her marriage; that had been from fear, the doctor had told her. He had said she must relax in both mind and body to conceive; she must have all willingness to receive the seed. It was something she had never been able to do with Josiah Bransom; she had always become frozen at his touch. But it had not been so with Charles Mortimer. Was it possible that she was not, after all, barren? Was it possible that she was now bearing his child?

As if to prove it was so, when Penelope took the calf's-foot jelly sent over from Kerswell she felt a great deal better, so that when Mr. Wisham arrived to give her a cursory examination and prescribe his aperient, he pronounced her in good health.

"There, you see," Phyllis announced in triumph. "That calf's-foot jelly is good for everything."

"It is indeed." Penelope laughed, her cheeks flushed, her eyes shining.

"Now you're positively glowing."

"I feel very well and very happy."

"Well, we were silly to be so concerned, I suppose. But it would have quite spoiled the wedding."

"It's going to be a wonderful wedding—I'm better, really I am."

"That I can see. You know, I've been thinking about Missy's dress. I feel that the train should be shorter, not much, only a few inches, but it will make all the difference. You said that Lady Staverton will attend—I was surprised at her coming all this way to a country wedding—she's a real fashion plate and mark my words, she will notice."

Penelope, who had given no thought to that lady, experienced a momentary pang. But then she remembered that *she,* as attendant upon the bride, would be standing next to Mortimer before the altar. She would have the opportunity to be alone with him and to tell him. No matter that he might once have had a passion for Georgina Staverton—"scarce had loved," he had written on her fan—it was over. The lady was, besides, very definitely married. There could be no future with her. No mention of that lady could destroy Penelope's peace of mind now that she, who would have been grateful to have a child by a man she detested, was to have one by a man she loved. She rejoiced; life had been too good, too kind.

"Emmeline has written that they will be here in plenty of time. I didn't mention it to her, but I sent an invitation to Mr. Wendling. I believe he likes her, and I think she likes him."

"Missy," her sister accused, catching the speculative gleam in her eye, "you can't become a matchmaker before your own wedding."

"Of course I wouldn't do any such thing; you know I wouldn't. However, if two people like one another and happen to find themselves in one another's company, it's up to them whatever happens."

"I suppose it is."

"I must admit that I always hoped that something might happen between you and Lord Mortimer. Rodney said he noticed that Mortimer treated you quite differently from others."

"Really! How?"

"Well, he didn't flirt with you, for one thing."

"That would seem to indicate he cared less." Penelope felt a flash of disappointment.

"Rodney thought otherwise, and I must say that I noticed his expression softened whenever you were near."

"Did it? Did it really?"

Missy, who had expected a caustic reply for daring such

speculation, said no more but felt infinitely happier. Perhaps Rodney had been right. If only it could be so. Mortimer would be there at the wedding with Rodney; surely everything would be conducive to furthering any interest that already existed. Her heart lightened, for she had so dreaded to leave her sister alone. While Missy was quite sure that she was the happiest woman in the world, Penelope, for different reasons, was of like opinion.

Lady Halstead arrived with Emmeline.

"I couldn't resist bringing this Alençon lace Clark and Debenham were displaying, just right for a wedding, I thought, though I suppose you have everything finished by now."

"Beautiful, just beautiful, but I wonder—would you mind if Penelope used it on her dress? It would be perfect."

"Well." Lady Halstead's face fell. "I hardly intended it for the sort of thing Penelope wears."

"But wait, you must see it first." And Missy sent Meg to fetch Penelope's pale blue dress.

"Oh my dear, at last! I began to think she would wear those dreadful things until the end of her days."

"I did, too, but I'm really hopeful of something else now."

"What is that?"

"I know I shouldn't say anything, but you see, Lord Mortimer is to be Rodney's best man, and Penelope is my matron of honour."

"Yes?" Lady Halstead raised her eyebrows, waiting for Missy to continue.

"Well, what I mean is that I think that he has some partiality to Pen, Rodney thinks so too, and when he sees her in that blue—she looks heavenly in it, really she does, and with that Alençon trim, well, what I mean is . . ."

"I know what you mean—I must admit I had entertained similar thoughts, but there's no chance for that now."

"No chance, but why?"

"Well, haven't you heard? It's been in the newspaper. . . ."

"Henrietta!" Penelope entering greeted her friend with a kiss. "And look who else has just arrived on his way north to Shropshire."

"Surely not!" Lady Halstead began. "Oh, I thought you meant . . . Mr. Trueblood, how nice to see you again."

"Mr. Trueblood has arranged for me to illustrate a collection of Cowper's poems. He stopped to see what progress I was making, and I have persuaded him to stay and attend the wedding."

"How nice."

"But what piece of news were you imparting as I entered? Don't let us spoil your story."

"It concerns Georgina Staverton," Lady Halstead began, but clearly she had lost her zest for the topic and it might have been left to rest had not Mr. Trueblood shook his head sadly,

"Ah, that poor dear lady. I'm sure our hearts go out to her."

"But what is wrong? Is she ill?" Penelope demanded sharply with an odd sense of foreboding.

"No, it's her husband. The ship on which he was returning to England has been long overdue. Lord Mortimer, on Lady Staverton's behalf, has been travelling back and forth to all the main ports seeking information from incoming vessels that travel the Atlantic sea route. He's quite worn himself out in the search." Lady Halstead lowered her voice infinitesimally, "There's been speculation at all his zeal, of course, for everyone knows how he feels about her. Anyway, it seems he has found out what he wanted to know. There was a terrible storm in the Atlantic, and it was thought, at first, that the ship Philby Staverton had taken might have turned back or sought harbour elsewhere, but now they have learned that it went down, and all aboard have been lost."

"Oh, no!"

Lady Halstead was surprised by the anguish in Penelope's cry. "Awful, of course, but I hadn't realized that you knew him, Penelope."

"I knew him . . . by sight." She knew, too, that his death left Lady Staverton free—was it to assure that fact that Mortimer had so diligently searched the ports?

"Lady Staverton, of course, has donned the deepest

mourning—though she still insists she will attend Missy's wedding since she had promised to do so, but mainly, in my opinion, because Mortimer will be there. Frankly all of London realizes that now she can have what she has so long wanted."

Lady Halstead shot a sidelong glance at Mr. Trueblood, who concurred with disgruntlement. "Mortimer, you mean. That's been no secret."

"Well, he's helped her through the whole awful business, but as Mrs. Plunkett-Gall says, fate will have its way, and they were intended for one another. She was disappointed, for I think she had chosen some young lady she was certain would please him, but that's out of the question with Lady Staverton free. She's the only one he ever really wanted, the reason he went off to fight in the wars."

"I heard something of the sort," Penelope agreed faintly, aware that some comment was required. She felt quite cold and lifeless.

"You know, Penelope, I think you were right about that woman."

"Lady Staverton?"

"No, Mrs. Plunkett-Gall. She's going all over town calling it a love match made in heaven. I do find it rather tasteless with Sir Philby hardly cold—or damp—well, you know what I mean."

"Mrs. Bransom, are you quite well?" Mr. Trueblood asked, noticing her pallor.

"I think I need some air, that's all."

"Perhaps this may help." Mr. Trueblood picked up a sandalwood fan from the corner table and opened it, but though Penelope snatched it from his hand, closing it swiftly, it was not before he glimpsed the words written across it with that scrawled initial M.

21

Before the altar where she had repeated her own vows, Penelope found her mood not entirely different from when she herself had been a bride. Then she had felt removed from the ceremony in which she was participating, and that same shroud of impassivity again descended upon her to carry her through a difficult day.

Though she stood beside him, she had barely looked at Mortimer since greeting him on his arrival, that greeting cool, even distant. Yet though she did not look at him, she was acutely conscious of his presence. She was perhaps even more acutely aware of that elegant figure in deepest mourning who never stirred far from his side.

Lady Staverton had never been more gracious to Penelope. "We are both widows now," she sighed, "and I am better able to understand your grief, though you, I see, have set aside your mourning while I have just adopted mine. Life is too short, time too swift—I'm sure I don't mind wearing black for a year. Besides providing a mark of respect, I find it quite elegant and it does set off one's jewellery famously. I must admit, however, that that shade of blue is far preferable for your complexion."

"It is a shade of mourning in certain parts of the world, or so it is said," Mortimer put in. It had been an answer Penelope had given to Edward Bransom earlier in the day at his obvious disfavour of her setting aside her black.

His reply had been less approving than Lady Staverton's, "How interesting. Perhaps I should adopt it later, not quite yet, of course, but eventually black, however elegant, may become tiresome."

"You might consider yellow, Georgina. I understand that was the colour adopted by Anne Boleyn on the death of Catherine of Aragon." Turning to Penelope, Mortimer went on in similarly caustic tone, "You, Mrs. Bransom, seem not to have found disfavour with the darker shades until now—though perhaps you may have worn that particular blue before."

Penelope's flush and lack of response were evident, though Lady Staverton, as usual busy with her own concerns, was already launched into another topic.

"You should have told me what a charming part of the country this was, Charles. Quite, quite lovely, yet you hardly mentioned it."

And Penelope, feeling she had been remiss in not having conveyed her sympathy earlier, put in, "You must allow me to express my sorrow at your bereavement, Lady Staverton. It is always a difficult time, no matter how . . . no matter how much support one has from friends. Missy was honoured that you agreed to put aside your grief for a moment to be witness to her own moment of joy."

"My dear, I had promised Charles that I would come—I could not disappoint him, or your sister. How my friends have rallied around me at this moment." She lifted a lace-trimmed, snowy-white handkerchief to a dry eye. "I thank God for Charles, he has been an angel, a veritable angel. Without him I might not have survived these past few weeks. No disclaimers, Charles, I'll not have them, for I speak no more than the truth."

Obviously discomforted by her praise, he put in coldly, "I did no more than is to be expected from one's friends."

"Why, you spent every moment from the time I first told

you Philby was missing, soon after your regimental reunion it was." She turned to Penelope. "I was so anxious to see him; he completely disappeared for a few days, though I knew he had been at the dinner, for Colonel Weston told me so, but I couldn't find him. He wasn't at Chenwyth, for I immediately sent an express to him there. At last I discovered him in London; he was such a tease, he wouldn't tell me where he'd been, but as soon as I told him what had happened he took matters into his own hands, simply scouring all the ports in search of news. Indeed, it was all I could do to prevent him from setting out for Jamaica himself, and where should I have been without him? I'm quite sure he would have gone, though, had it not been for the captain of the *Argonaut,* who was able to furnish some first-hand evidence of the wreck."

"I believe it is almost time to go in," Mortimer reminded sharply.

"How sweet the bride looks, how happy! Indeed, I well remember the day I married, but every woman does. I am quite sure that you do, Mrs. Bransom. At such times I suppose it is quite natural for a woman to reflect upon the past; women are so very sentimental, more so than the opposite sex. Undoubtedly you were married from this very altar, Mrs. Bransom."

"Yes."

"A charming little church. I love these old parish churches, nothing like the splendour of our London places of worship, of course, but they have a certain *je ne sais quoi.* What is the parish church like at Wrexford, Charles?"

"Before I get started with a dissertation on gothic churches of the perpendicular period in general and St. Oswald's in particular, I really think it would be wise for you to take your place, that is if you wish to witness the ceremony." His reply, abrupt as it was, forced an end to the conversation.

Since Penelope had learned of Philby Staverton's death, she knew she could never tell Charles Mortimer of her condition. That he would propose marriage to her once told of her condition, she had no doubt, but that the proposal would be freely, willingly extended when he knew that

Georgina Staverton was at liberty to remarry was questionable. Even though she wanted and loved him—in fact because she did want and love him—she could not bear to marry him convinced that he desired another.

She resolved to say nothing, but her situation was difficult, even precarious. Fleetingly she thought of mixing an infusion of aqua composita—Gascoigne wine, galingale, camomile, cinnamon, nutmeg, cloves and anise, said to induce bleeding—but that was only a fleeting thought. All her life she had longed for a child; now that her wish had at last and quite miraculously been granted, she could not cast it aside. Yet she needed time to seek a solution, and her eye fell upon an advertisement in the *World of Fashion* that promised an answer to her need to disguise her condition. It read:

> The Corset Elyvatone, ingeniously designed by Mrs. Bell, corset maker to HRH the Duchess of Kent, for pregnant ladies to prevent flatulence, reduce protuberance, support the stomach, bowels and relieve dropsical symptoms.
>
> The Bandage Corset, with its regenerating and sleeping ceinture, is indispensable to ladies before and after accouchement. By means of a spring, these elegant corsets may be loosened at pleasure, if too tight, without damaging the dress, or the viability of the lace knotting, or the delicate skin tortured by tags harshly coming in contact. A second spring affords the facility of completely and instantaneously unlacing the corset, by which the body may be indulged by reclining in a recumbent position, without the smallest inconvenience. Swoonings, vapours, oppressions, and spasms are relieved by this corset; and as a Bathing Corset it is equally invaluable for the rapidity with which it can be taken off and put on.
>
> The Corset Elyvatone is made only in London under the superintendence of Mrs. Bell at her establishment on Charlotte Street, and all orders are directed there. Ladies are respectfully cautioned against Pretenders. Only ladies giving their real names and addresses are to be shown. No one connected with trade will be served.

Though Mrs. Bell's discrimination of her customers sounded almost as formidable as her corsets, Penelope took measurements and directed an order to Charlotte Street. It had been delivered with all speed. She was, in fact, wearing it, though it was proving less comfortable than the advertisement had indicated. Nevertheless she had been able to retain her waistline at its usual nineteen inches.

She had followed the service only spasmodically, finding it bitter irony to have to listen to those words at Mortimer's side. What was he thinking? she wondered, as the rector concluded. Was it of their days together; did he ever think of those, or only of Georgina Staverton? Their future together seemed bright, her own difficult and uncertain—she had been right, after all, in believing that she was never destined to reign as queen of the May or wear a glass slipper. But, come what may, she would survive.

"Forasmuch as Rodney and Melissa have consented together in holy wedlock, and have witnessed the same before God and this company, and thereto have given and pledged their troth, each to the other, and have declared the same by giving and receiving a ring and by joining hands, I pronounce that they are Man and Wife, in the Name of the Father, and of the Son, and of the Holy Ghost."

As Mr. Osborn's voice died away, and the bridal pair turned, there was an audible sigh from the congregation, a sigh that became a murmur at the sight of Missy's radiant face. At that moment Penelope was equally filled with happiness for Missy and agony at the thought that she would have to share the ride to Kerswell with Mortimer. She was relieved when Lady Staverton attached herself to them outside the church and even more so when, as they climbed into Mortimer's coach, Lady Staverton motioned to Samuel Trueblood to join them. Thus they rode, the ladies together, the gentlemen opposite with their backs to the horses.

As soon as they set off, Lady Staverton began, "A lovely wedding, simple but entirely satisfactory, with a church small but spacious enough to accommodate those attending. I do believe I prefer that to a vast throng. Thirty or forty well-chosen guests, and perhaps to have them stay for a period to celebrate the nuptials. And these charming rib-

bons with which we were supplied as souvenirs of the occasion"—she held up a nosegay of pastel coloured ribbons
given to each lady attending—"such a nice touch, altogether
quaint and charming. I must remember it. And your dear
little nieces who distributed them, enchanting. How sweet
little Cynthia would be in such a role."

"There's nothing like a country wedding to put one in a
marrying frame of mind, is there, Lady Staverton?" Trueblood bantered wryly.

"Really, Samuel, I should take exception to that, you are
naughty to speak so. Don't you think him naughty,
Charles?"

"Positively Machiavellian," Mortimer replied without a
hint of humour.

"Come now, that's a bit harsh. But if Samuel is Machiavellian, what pray, am I, or do I take my life in my hands in
putting the question to you when you are in such a petulant
frame of mind?"

"For the moment, my dear, you remind me of nothing so
much as la Veuve Cliquot."

"But that is champagne."

"Exactly, Georgina, you're bubbling."

"Now you are being naughty, Charles. I really don't know
why you gentlemen tease me so, and to dear Mrs. Bransom
not a word. Now to whom would you liken Mrs. Bransom?"

"With Mrs. Bransom I fear I am not very inventive.
There is only one person who comes to mind, Penelope for
her constancy, and that, if I am not mistaken, is her Christian name."

"What a charming name, madam," Mr. Trueblood put in.
"Penelope has long been a particular favourite of mine,
along with Rosalind."

"Rosalind," Lady Staverton mused. "Nice, a little flowery
for my taste, however. I believe that was your mother's
name, Charles, wasn't it?"

Mortimer, whose eyes had turned to the window as soon
as Trueblood began to speak, appeared not to hear the
question, so Lady Staverton turned to her companion to
comment, "Bully tells me he's taken a place in Surrey near

Brook Hill for six months until they decide where to settle. Undoubtedly you'll visit them there."

"Undoubtedly I shall. Though Missy is a number of years younger than I, we have been very close to one another for a long time."

"You'll miss her then."

"I shall. But to see her so very happy makes it no sacrifice to lose her to Colonel Bullerton."

"He's charming. You know I introduced Bully to Brook Hill, for he visited me there at our country place, Staverton Park, and he was so enchanted with Wotton Common and the beauty of the Weald that, for Bully at least, he grew almost poetic on the subject."

"Then I shall greatly look forward to seeing it."

"And when you do, if I am at Staverton Park, you must promise to visit me. Charles is very fond of the area, though he insists he prefers his native Shropshire."

But Mortimer, for whom the remark was intended, continued to watch the passing countryside without comment, causing Lady Staverton to remark that she was finding him most taciturn.

"I suppose it comes of losing your best friend to matrimony, but you, Charles, were among the first to promote the match. I can better understand Mrs. Bransom's lack of cheer than I can yours, for the loss of her sister's company must be far more deeply felt, especially here in the country with nothing whatsoever to do. But there's no reason why you should not spend your time in town now, Mrs. Bransom. It's true that the better part of the season is finished, but there is still plenty to do."

And Lady Staverton, with copious detail, began to list London's amusements. Penelope, who had felt distinctly ill at ease throughout the ceremony and even more so during the ride—suffering a discomfort both of mind, caused by her situation and proximity to Mortimer, and of body, induced in no small part by Mrs. Bell's Corset Elyvatone, which, ingeniously designed though it might be, in no way relieved her—was distinctly of the opinion that she would swoon before they reached Kerswell. She clenched her gloved hands tightly together and leaned her head back against the seat, breathing deeply, glad that Mr. Trueblood had taken up Lady Staverton's conversation and that Mortimer continued to look out of the window. Oh, that the day would end!

Taking pains to be unobtrusive, she sat, waiting only for the ride to be over, terrified she would succumb to the faintness fast enveloping her. She was surprised when, quite suddenly, Mortimer ordered the coachman to pull over and opened the door.

"A little air, I think, may help, Mrs. Bransom," he said quietly.

"Thank you," was all she could bring herself to whisper, but her eyes, before she closed them, conveyed her gratitude.

"What is it, Charles, why are we stopping? What's the matter?"

"Nothing that a little peace and fresh air won't settle, I'm sure."

"You're an observant man, Mortimer. I do believe Mrs. Bransom is on the verge of fainting." Mr. Trueblood's voice, in fact all the voices, seemed distant.

"I think she's been doing too much, preparing for the wedding," Lady Staverton said.

"It's the heat, ma'am. I myself find it exceptionally warm today, don't you, Mortimer?"

"I must say I noticed nothing," Lady Staverton interjected. "I don't know how you did, Charles, for you've paid no attention to anything or anyone since the ride began."

Penelope felt an arm about her shoulders and a flask at her lips. "Just a sip, it's brandy. It will help, really," Mortimer was saying. She took the sip, and the fiery liquid brought the blood back to her head.

She opened her eyes. "Sorry, silly of me, really it was."

"It's the heat, Mrs. Bransom," Trueblood commiserated.

"You've been overdoing things, I expect," Lady Staverton put in.

"Are you sure you're all right? Would you like to get out for a bit? Or shall we take you home?" Mortimer asked.

"No, no, please. I want nothing to spoil Missy's day. Promise to say nothing. I'm quite all right, I assure you. It's just the heat and the excitement."

Despite her disclaimers, Mortimer insisted on taking her down with great care and keeping a firm hold of her arm on their arrival at Kerswell. Yet his touch served only to discompose her further, and she was glad when Phyllis called for her assistance with the iced compote, which had been put out too soon and needed remolding and perhaps some additional Curaçao.

"Mrs. Bransom is not . . ." Mortimer began, but Penelope threw him an imploring look to silence him before hurrying to assist her sister-in-law, glad to escape.

Being occupied, she felt better. The wedding feast, with its prescribed gaiety and traditional humour, was underway, as important a ritual as the solemnization of vows they had witnessed in the church. Mr. Bransom had insisted upon attending because, he said, his position demanded it though his heart was not in the spirit of the event. He made up for his misery by partaking freely of haunch of venison, leveret pie, stewed pigeons, grouse, saddle of mutton, greengage tart and the iced compote, remolded and recongealed. Colonel Bullerton's quite formidable mother was taken in hand by Mortimer and entertained so completely that she was unable to interfere, and wherever Mortimer was, there too was that elegant mourning figure.

At last the cake was cut, and Mortimer was called upon to toast the bridal pair. "Today we have all witnessed these two delightful people—one of whom I have long known and greatly respected, the other who, though known by me for a shorter period, holds an equally high place in my estimation—make five grave declarations and two supreme promises to one another: one to love and cherish, the other to love, honour, and obey. These promises are binding, yet freely and willingly entered into; they are promises that convert duty into trust. There is more true happiness in the folly of love than all the wisdom of philosophy, but I do not intend to expound on either, for these two people must be, as I should be in their stead, anxious to depart and enjoy one another in shared and mutual solitude and bliss. I shall detain them no longer than to say that their joy is my joy, or, since I am sure I speak for all gathered here, our joy." He raised high his goblet, "To Melissa and Rodney. Let those love now who never loved before, let those who always loved now love the more."

As he spoke, his eyes met Penelope's for an instant with a look of profound solemnity, a look intercepted and long reflected upon by Samuel Trueblood.

Then all was over. The bridal pair at last climbed into the carriage, and as it was about to pull away, Missy leaned out to toss her bridal bouquet quite deliberately into her sister's arms.

Mr. Osborn laughed. "Dear me, that won't do, Mrs. Bransom. The bouquet is intended for the next bride."

"Perhaps Mrs. Bransom is to be the next bride," Lady Staverton replied sharply. "Widows do remarry."

Penelope passed the bouquet to Emmeline saying, "Missy intended it for you. I'm afraid I stood in your way."

Soon after she made her escape, glad it was over. Everything was over, though her difficulties were perhaps just beginning.

22

The instances that second marriage move
Are base respects of thrift, but none of love.

Shakespeare
Hamlet, 1601

Her first illustrations accepted, Penelope worked on the next set, aware of the publisher's wish to have the entire project in hand as soon as possible. She too, was anxious to complete the work, for the money, which originally had mattered little to her, might provide a mainstay in light of her uncertain future.

She worked hard, too hard, yet her concentration was diffused by her ever-present worries, and she was aware, when at last she dispatched them, that their quality was uneven.

She was not surprised, therefore, to receive a letter indicating less than complete satisfaction with the results. She was surprised, however, to find that letter signed by Samuel Trueblood, who would soon be journeying back to Shropshire from London and would stop in Mayfield to discuss the matter.

He came on an afternoon when she was in a state of despondency. Nothing she had done since receiving his letter seemed right. Just when she had thought it might be possible to make a living from her work, she felt devoid of ability or talent. She would have a child in the spring, a child she would under no circumstances give up, but a child that would give Edward Bransom every right to deny her her widow's portion. Apart from herself, there were those other poor souls who relied upon her for support and would be denied the livelihood on which they had come to depend. Just as trying too hard with her work made it less successful, so trying not to think about Bransom's illegitimate children made her dwell upon them all the more. And thinking of them made her more conscious of the difficulties her own child would have to face and firmed her resolve to do everything within her power to ease that lot. Her resolve did not, however, extend to approaching Mortimer in the matter. She had heard nothing from him since the wedding, nor had she expected to. Now that fate had allowed him what he had most wanted in life, she refused to step in and make claims upon him to ease her position, or even to protect the future of another. Aware of Samuel Trueblood's philanthropic bent, she determined to enquire of him whether it might be possible to find other assignments to do illustrations in the future.

He came at last, and though she did not know him well, she felt unaccountably glad at seeing his long, narrow face, his older, wiser aspect. It being a warm afternoon in early autumn, she asked Meg to bring their tea out into the garden.

He began immediately with the object of his journey, producing those illustrations which had proven unsatisfactory.

"These pinks you did for *The Winter Nosegay*, they are perfect in every detail, yet you have been so caught up in detail that you have not paid attention to the whole. They should move into the snow in the background, not stand out apart from it. I have much the same criticism for those illustrations you have done for *The Task*. I expected much more from you in those Winter Walk episodes; these scenes are disappointing. None of them lives up to the quality of the dew-covered fallen rose you sent earlier.

"Were these not from you but from one of lesser ability, there would be no question of accepting them as they are. But as soon as I saw them, I felt they could only serve to spoil your rising reputation. I set great store by your ability, an ability I believe I have discovered. I have staked my own reputation in recommending you for this task, and quite selfishly I do not wish to be proven wrong."

"I should never wish to disappoint anyone who puts their faith in me, least of all you. I appreciate your attention, and I shall, of course, re-do these with your comments in mind."

Penelope handed him his tea and a slice of simnel cake. After carefully sipping his tea and setting the cup in the saucer with equal care, so that the handle was at right angles to the spoon, he asked, as though it had long been on his mind, "Tell me, since those illustrations completed before your sister's wedding were so superior to these, is it the loss of her company that is causing you distress? You must forgive my asking, but I sense you are unhappy."

Penelope answered him in all honesty, "You are right, I am not happy. But dearly as I love my sister, much as I miss her, to resent her present happiness with a fit of the doldrums would be unworthy of me."

"Then, if it is not because of your sister, what is it?" And when she said nothing, he pressed further. "I sense it is a love affair, an unhappy love affair. You need say nothing. But I want you to know I am your friend."

He leaned across and patted her hand awkwardly. Penelope who, until then, had believed herself entirely alone, felt tears come to her eyes, at the sight of which he brought out a large handkerchief and handed it to her.

"Please, I can't stand to see a woman cry." It was that last, sounding as it did stiff but very much like her father, that produced a veritable torrent.

He said nothing, allowing her to go on, sitting back until she finished crying.

"There, do you feel better now?"

"Yes."

"Is there anything I can do to be of help?"

"Yes, that is—could you help me to find some other employment, similar to the Cowper work, something to provide an income?"

"You need money, then?"

"Yes," she replied almost unwillingly.

"I see. I had thought that your husband left you well provided for."

"He did, but there were conditions. I fear I may lose that allowance."

"Lose it?" Trueblood questioned sharply.

"As I said, there were conditions."

He grew thoughtful. "In such cases the widow is often precluded from re-marrying. Is that so in your case?"

"Yes."

"And you wish to re-marry, is that it?"

She had never meant to tell him; she had never meant to say a word until she was forced to. She had no idea why she did, perhaps because of his paternal attitude, his kindness. Whatever it was, she found herself blurting out, "I am with child."

His expression changed sharply from one of consideration to shocked anger. "Mrs. Bransom, you of all people! I had taken you for a good, a fine woman even, a woman of moral principle."

He continued at some length on her want of propriety, and though Penelope had hoped for sympathy, she felt he had every right to be harsh in his judgement.

"If you tell me because you want my advice, all I can do is suggest you throw yourself on the mercy of the blackguard, whoever he is, and demand that he marry you. Who is he?" he urged, and when she made no reply, he went on, "I take it you know who it was; you surely don't fall into bed with every Tom, Dick and Harry who comes along."

Penelope rose. "That, sir, is quite enough. I should not have told you, but having done so, I have nothing more to say on the subject."

His eyes narrowed suddenly. "It's Mortimer, isn't it, Charles Mortimer?"

She gasped. "How could you possibly know!" Then she remembered. "You saw my sandalwood fan."

"Not only that, but I noticed the way you behaved when you were with him on your sister's wedding day. You were not at all . . . well, you were quite unlike yourself. Have you told him?"

"No, and I don't intend to."

"Why not? If he knows it to be his, he will marry you, arrogant, insolent philanderer though he is. He vaunts his

205

honour and his valour; I'm sick to death of hearing of his heroism. He wouldn't want it voiced abroad that he'd ruined a respectable woman. He'll marry you."

"That is probably true, but for my own reasons I have no intention of telling him, nor do I wish you to do so. In fact, I would like your word in the matter that you will not."

"Has it something to do with Lady Staverton now being a widow, and you don't wish to spoil that?" he guessed shrewdly. When she made no reply he muttered, half to himself, "All these heroics. But still, there's to be a Mortimer child, and he doesn't know it." Abruptly he turned to Penelope. "As long as the child you are carrying is his, I believe I may have the solution to your problem."

"The solution? I'll not try to rid myself of it, if that's . . ."

"No, no, of course not."

"Then you will help me to find employment."

"My dear lady, the occupation of a professional illustrator is precarious at best; that would not do. No, I think it best that you marry me. I shall give you a home, and Mortimer's child shall bear my name."

"Mr. Trueblood!" Penelope was completely taken aback, not only by his suggestion but by the change in his attitude, which once more was kindly and paternal.

"You have nothing to fear from me. I think only of your well-being. I shall take good care of you and the child. I shall encourage you in your art. And I shall be a good father to Mortimer's child."

It was, she felt, that last thought that was uppermost in Trueblood's mind.

"Why is it you want Mortimer's child?" she asked.

"My dear," he leaned over to pat her hand with his own— dry, cold and somehow lifeless. "It may be hard for you to understand, but I have long been the one behind the reputation of the Mortimers. I have taken care of the family, though little enough thanks I've earned for my pains. Rosalind, his mother, would have married me had not that good-for-nothing father of his come between us. But I held no grudge that she chose him over me; she was forced to do so. I've rescued all of them at one time or another—to Mortimer I freely gave the money for his commission. Where would he have been without it, yet he has not a good word to say for me. I'll give his son a name, not for the sake of reward, but for the sake of his dear mother."

Could it be so? Penelope wondered. Could this man that Charles Mortimer hated really be kind and benevolent? She felt unsure, yet he presented the only solution to her hopeless quandary. While she had little enthusiasm for his offer, it presented a way out. What right had she to refuse him?

Trueblood waited for her acceptance, lips set in a firm line of determination, his eyes never leaving her face. Mortimer despised him; she knew that, yet he was a philanthropic, principled man. Her choice lay in accepting the offer or telling Mortimer: the latter she would never do.

"Thank you, sir, I appreciate your offering a solution to my problem. But I feel it only fair to say that I do not care for you in the way that a wife should care for a husband."

"As you cared for that first husband of yours? The one to whom you erected that dreadful mausoleum—I should have expected you to have found something in better taste. . . ."

"My late husband chose that himself, before his death."

"A wise precaution, perhaps, but believe me, I shall show greater discrimination. Certainly you show great respect for the dead, up until this unfortunate occurrence, that is, and I daresay it was not entirely your fault; for some reason Mortimer exerts a strong influence over your sex, though now Georgina Staverton's free I've no doubt she'll bring him to book."

"I daresay she will."

"Well, madam, what is it to be? You must realize there is no time to delay."

"Then I accept, Mr. Trueblood. You have my gratitude for your kindness."

"I am a just man, not necessarily kind. You may expect honesty from me, just as I expect as much from you. It is arranged, then. We shall marry from Belfriars, my home in Wrexford. I am on my way there now. I shall arrange for the banns to be read. I shall communicate to you any necessary details. So, unless there is anything else, I take my leave of you. Good-day, Mrs. Bransom."

He bowed, then shook her hand as though to seal the agreement, much in the manner she supposed he sealed his business transactions. She was relieved he made no show of affection; the arrangement would, perhaps, prove quite satisfactory.

23

Samuel Trueblood had left; the matter was resolved. She no longer had need to worry, yet there was no sense of elation at the resolution of her difficulty. She would tell Arthur and Phyllis, but not yet, in the morning. She only wanted to rest, not to think of anything. She would live in Shropshire, it was where *he* lived. She never wished to see him again, but she supposed their paths would cross, living in the same village; Wrexford must be a small place. What if he and the child were to recognize their bond one day? But that was the stuff of novels; such things didn't happen in life.

She was suddenly tired, very tired; she wandered upstairs to her room to lie down but when there found she had no desire to sleep. Instead she just lay watching the fluttering of the chintz curtains as the afternoon breeze wafted through the open dormer window.

Idly she wondered how Missy was doing with her Rodney; she remembered the way they had looked at one another at the altar, so very much in love. She would never look at a man in that way, not at the altar anyway. In her mind's eye she saw her first and her future husband's faces side by side, then the images blended into one composite whole. She shuddered, the breeze perhaps. She drew her shawl closer around her shoulders.

She would be free once and for all from Edward Bransom; that was a consolation, free from the memories of the Hall, from those awful reminders at the church, from all the hypocrisy she had been forced to endure in order to support those loveless children Josiah Bransom had brought into the world. She had no doubt Trueblood would take care of them; after all, he presided over that society for orphans and strays, and what were they if not that? It would perhaps be a delicate matter to speak of, but it would be done. Everything was resolved.

She closed her eyes and tried to sleep, but almost as soon as she did so the door opened, and Meg stood at her bedside, murmuring apologetically, "I'm sorry to disturb you, Mrs. Bransom, really I am."

"What is it? What's the matter?" Penelope sat up. She knew Meg wouldn't have disturbed her without serious reason.

"I'm sorry, I didn't want to come, really I didn't—I told 'im you was resting, but 'e insisted on waiting, says 'e won't go till you come." Tears rose to the girl's eyes as she spoke.

"He?" Penelope caught her breath, feeling the colour rushing from her cheeks. He had come. By some unfathomable means he had found out, and he had come.

"I shall be down immediately. You were quite right to disturb me."

"I didn't want to, but like I said 'e wouldn't go, so I said I would just come up to see if you was awake."

"Well, you see, I am awake. Tell him I shall be down immediately. I must comb my hair. He is in the parlour, I presume."

"I told 'im to wait in the 'all."

"Well, go down immediately and see him into the parlour and bring some refreshments. I suppose he has come from London."

"Yes ma'am, 'e 'as."

Still the girl stood there until Penelope said, "Do go along, Meg. I shall be there in a minute."

"Yes, Mrs. Bransom."

She combed her hair and put on a freshly-starched cap. For a moment she thought of changing into the blue dress she had worn on Missy's wedding day, but she decided that would take too long. With a deep breath to steady her nerves, she descended the stairs and entered the parlour.

"Ah, mum. Nice of you to come, but I tole my little girl you would though she got quite cheeky with me, she did, till I tole 'er I wouldn't 'ave no more of 'er lip."

"Mr. Watkins!" Penelope said faintly, and quite abruptly sat down in an armchair.

"She tole you I come, didn't she?"

"Yes, she did."

Meg arrived with a tray of lemonade, biscuits and cheese which she set down, then handed one of the glasses to her father.

"Got 'er trained, I see. It's a long way from Jim Brown, though I 'adn't expected nuffink. Your good 'ealth, mum." He took a swallow and was clearly disappointed, mumbling as he wiped his mouth on the back of his sleeve, "Thought it was a 'od of mortar, or Charlie Freer, still . . ." He threw back his head and quaffed the rest of the lemonade, then took a handful of biscuits and several pieces of cheese, crammed as much as he could into his mouth and slowly munched the contents while Meg looked on, undecided whether to remain or leave, until Penelope motioned her to go.

"You said you came to see Jim Brown, or was it Charlie Freer?" Penelope prompted when she was gone.

He guffawed. "Charlie Freer, I thought it was beer. Jim Brown's town, mum, I come all the way from town."

"You came all the way from town to see me?"

"I did, mum, purposely from London for that."

"Then it concerns Meg, I presume."

"Me dear little soap and water," he said soulfully.

"Mr. Watkins, if we are to understand one another, I would appreciate it if you would refrain from using that odd . . . that odd manner of speech and come directly to the point. I understood that Lord Mortimer had settled matters with you when you had that despicable scheme for Meg. He told me that he had paid you a considerable sum, and that for that sum you had agreed to leave your daughter alone, that she was at liberty to come here to Mayfield to live with me. Is that correct?"

"That's the ticket, mum." Ostentatiously he lifted his glass to drain the dregs; just as pointedly Penelope made no effort to refill it, and, with a sigh, he put the glass aside and took another piece of cheese. "Leastways, it's mostly right. A soap and . . . I mean a daughter's supposed to 'elp 'er aged parent, it's 'er duty, I'm sure you would agree."

"Not in the way you proposed, I would not agree at all."

"Times is 'ard wiv me, mum, very 'ard indeed, specially since the girl left me."

"Look, Mr. Watkins, neither Meg nor I owe you anything. If you have come to beg money, I'm afraid you have made a fruitless journey."

"Oo, I don't know."

"Well, I do. Meg has what I pay her, which is not a great deal. Neither do I have much, but what I do have to spare is spent on those charities I consider worthy." Her tone left no doubt that she did not consider Mr. Watkins at all a worthy cause, but it seemed lost upon its object.

"It's like this, Mrs. B, I think when you 'ear what I got to say it's you who'll be pressing the old bees and 'oney on me so I won't rabbit about wot I know. I seen a few things in this 'ere village, I seen that 'uge stone you 'ad put up for Mr. B, I 'ave, and I've 'ad a pint or two at the George and Dragon. I know some things, things you wouldn't want others 'ere in Mayfield to know. I know 'ow to keep me mouth shut, but not for nuffink."

Penelope clenched her hands together. Was it possible, could this man, this awful man, know her secret? But no one knew, no one, except Mr. Trueblood, and under the circumstances surely he would have said nothing, least of all to Watkins.

"What is this thing you know?" she asked slowly, deliberately.

"That's more like it, that is. I'll tell you what I know, and

I'll tell you what I want. It's about 'im, the one what lies in the graveyard."

"My husband! Mr. Bransom!"

"The very same. I din't know why when I first 'eard the name Bransom, but it rung a bell like. Then I 'eard you was from Mayfield, still I didn't know till someone said it was in Oxford, and that's when the old penny-come-quick clicked. That's where she come from, me old worry and strife, dear old Bessie, God rest 'er soul. She was good in 'er own way, thought the world of me, she did, would 'ave done anything for me, but she passed on soon as this one come into the world, God rest 'er soul." He bowed his head dolefully.

"I'm sorry, truly sorry, Mr. Watkins, that you lost your wife in childbirth, sorrier still that Meg lost her mother, but I fail to understand what you are trying to tell me."

"The worry and strife, she come from Shepleigh—that mean anything to you, mum?"

"Shepleigh." Penelope remembered the village well, with its wretched hovel on the outskirts where Mr. Bransom had taken her that day to display his offspring.

"I can see from your mince pies you know summat of it."

"I know it's a neighbouring village."

"A village where there's a bawdy cat and mouse where gents gets their frying pans on poor ivory pearls like my Bess."

"Just what is it you are trying to tell me, Mr. Watkins?"

"What I come to say is that when the cow and kisses—the missus—come to London she already 'ad a bun in the oven—Meg. I give 'er my name out of the goodness of my 'eart, I did."

"That was commendable, indeed, a fine action."

"Bleedin' fine, indeed. Finer than the one what Friar Tuck'd 'er, the one whose name she give me at the end." He paused triumphantly, waiting for Penelope to prompt him, before demanding, "Well, don't you want to know who it was, the man what puffed and darted it, the name of Meg's real father?"

"I imagine it was my late husband, Josiah Bransom," Penelope replied calmly.

"Cor 'struth!" If the ground had suddenly opened under his feet, or if the heavens had opened up to rain fire upon him, Mr. Watkins' face could not have expressed greater amazement. He stood, open-mouthed, spluttering, just spluttering for several seconds.

"And you have come all the way from London to tell me that Meg is closer to me than I had realized. My response is one of delight. I thank you, Mr. Watkins."

"You knew . . . you knew all along," he accused.

"No, I knew nothing. I find it the strangest coincidence that Meg should be one of my late husband's illegitimate children, for I thought I knew all of them."

"All of them!" he spluttered helplessly.

"To my knowledge my late husband produced twelve off-spring by various women. I now find that number to be thirteen, an unlucky number some say, but the thirteenth moon, the blue moon, is a lucky moon, an auspicious sign, completing the year's cycle. I have a double cause to rejoice that Meg is the thirteenth."

Watkins face was a brown study. "You knew, and still you put up that bloody stone to 'is memory. They said down at the George and Dragon you worshipped 'im."

"I have no illusions about my late husband, none what-soever, nor had I while he was living. He behaved un-scrupulously, and I have made it my business to search out those children he fathered, to take care of them, at least until they are old enough to take care of themselves. I felt it only right, for his conduct was reprehensible. I had not heard of your Bessie; I knew nothing of Meg, no doubt because Bessie ran off to London without telling anyone. I am sincerely sorry for that, sorry, too, that she died bring-ing into the world a child he had fathered. But I'm glad, very glad, to learn the truth now. I thank you for telling me. I shall give you a guinea to defray the cost of your journey."

"A bleedin' guinea!" Watkins exploded.

"You expected more?"

"A bleedin' sight more! You may know your old pot and pan weren't no Robin 'Ood, but the rest 'ere bloody well don't. You wouldn't want this rabbitted up and down the 'igh street, and roast porked in the George and Dragon, now would you!"

"If you feel you must speak of it, Mr. Watkins, there's nothing I can do."

"A pony now'll keep me tongue still, some bees and 'oney sent regular and I won't jaw, no one's the wiser, bob's your uncle. Don't want Meg knowing she's a tisket, do we?"

"I shall tell Meg myself. If you choose to tell others here, I regret it, but really it doesn't matter. We shall be going away soon, so it's of no great moment. As for ruining my late husband's name, I have long wished that would be done, but I knew I would never dare do so myself. It is no more than he deserved all along."

"Why din't you Noah's ark on 'im, then?" the enraged man spluttered.

"Each of us has our price, I fear. My silence was bought and paid for, not entirely for selfish reasons, his illegitimate children—his tiskets, as you call them—benefitted by that silence. Now it's no longer important. I'm going to re-marry, and my settlement will automatically be discontinued at that time. So, you see, it really doesn't matter who knows."

"And you're going to send me off 'earts of oak?"

"I offered you a guinea."

"I'll do better than that—what I know's worth bees and 'oney to someone."

"That's up to you. Good-bye, Mr. Watkins."

He stomped from the room, and almost immediately Meg came in, crying.

"'E's not taking me, is 'e, Mrs. Bransom?"

"No, Meg, he's not. In fact he brought good news, the very best in the world. I don't believe he'll trouble you again, or try to take you away."

"But 'e's me dad."

"No, Meg, he's not your dad."

And slowly, carefully, trying to hide her own dislike of the man who really was Meg's father, Penelope explained what she had learned.

"But it's not possible!"

"I think that it is, and truly I'm delighted. It makes yet another reason for keeping you close to me, and, by his own admission, since he's not your father I don't believe Watkins will interfere in your life anymore."

"Oh, Mrs. Bransom!" As the tears continued to roll down Meg's cheeks, Penelope put her arms around her.

"Meg, I'm going to tell you something no one else knows, at least not yet. I am going to be married."

"Mrs. Bransom, I am 'appy. Is it that 'andsome gentleman that you was with that day you found me on Bond Street? 'E's so nice, so kind."

Penelope shook her head. "I'm marrying Mr. Trueblood, the gentleman who called this afternoon. When I do, I shall go to live at his home in Shropshire. I want you to come with me. I want you to go to school and then decide what you would like to do. What do you think of that?"

"All I want to do is to be with you."

Penelope hugged her, hiding her face in the girl's shoulder. "Oh Meg, Meg! I need you possibly more than you need me."

24

*Always leave something to wish for; otherwise you will be
miserable from your very happiness.*
Baltasar Graciàn
The Art of Worldly Wisdom, 1647

"What do you mean by sending that dreadful person to
see me!"

Penelope had not expected yet another visitor that day.
She was emotionally drained and completely exhausted
when Mr. Edward Bransom had been announced. She
would gladly have refused to see him, but knowing she
would soon be parted from him forever, she considered it
better to create no further acrimony and, with as much
grace as she could muster, asked that he be shown in.

"He said he had seen you. How dare you allow him to say
such lies about that saintly gentleman, my uncle," Bransom
continued to rage. "Infamous, utterly infamous. I had him
thrown out on his ear."

"That may have been a mistake," Penelope replied
calmly. "Watkins has a garrulous tongue and will not be
loath to use it in the village."

"Malicious slander; no one except a silly woman would
listen to his filth."

"Mayfield thrives on gossip, and slander, after all, is only
gossip with a touch of virulence. You might have done better to treat the man with greater tact if you don't want his
tales voiced abroad."

"Disgusting! How can you, my uncle's widow, sit there

completely unperturbed in the face of such loathsome, vile accusations?" Bransom's face, flushed with fury, emphasized the family resemblance between uncle and nephew to such an extent that Penelope was convinced her misgivings about him as a husband for Missy were entirely justified.

"I sit here, sir, unperturbed as you put it, for I have long since had done with crying and gnashing my teeth over your uncle's behaviour. Watkins' visit this afternoon was, in many ways, a relief and a blessing. His accusations were no lie. Josiah Bransom's misdeeds have been long known to me; I have borne that knowledge on my own. I need no longer do that. Now you may shoulder the burden and protect his good name if you will. I am finished with the task, free of it, thank God."

"Protect his name. How dare you! His name has no need of protection. Everyone knows the kind of gentleman he was."

"Everyone knows the gentleman he showed to the world. I came to know another Josiah Bransom, totally different from that gentleman. I wish I could say that I kept my knowledge to myself willingly, or from a sense of honour—I regret that is not so. I only did so to protect my living and that of others. I had promised I would tell no one. I obeyed to the letter the terms of that will of his so that I might not jeopardize my portion. You have always harangued me about what became of the money you so carefully handed out to me each quarter; now I am free to tell you. Apart from that amount necessary for my own and my sister's maintenance here at the Lodge, every penny went to the upkeep of your uncle's illegitimate children, twelve of them—now thirteen with Meg. He told me his secret to prove to me his . . . his virility. Having brought these children into the world, he thought no more of them, he abandoned them. I could not, in all honesty, live on his money, knowing they starved. That is where my allowance has been dispensed each quarter."

Edward Bransom's face grew pale as she spoke, and he replied in some agitation, "I don't believe you. My uncle was a pious gentleman. He would never lower himself to consorting with . . . with loose women and prostitutes."

"Not all of them were prostitutes. Meg's mother, I believe, was a simple country girl."

"You have only the word of that blackguard Watkins that it is so."

"Mr. Bransom, if you care to, I can take you, as your uncle once took me, to see some of these offspring of his. They may have been born on the wrong side of the blanket, but once you laid eyes upon them you would be convinced, as I was, that they have your blood in their veins." Penelope could see that Bransom was now clearly shaken and, despite her dislike of him, she pitied him. She went on in a softer voice, "None of us likes to discover he has worshipped an idol with feet of clay, Mr. Bransom. I have overcome my disgust of your uncle by caring for his progeny. Perhaps now that you know everything, you may wish to take on the responsibility."

"Me—pay good money to a bunch of bastards—I should say not! More fool you if that's how you've been wasting good, hard cash. They can have no legal claim on the estate."

"No legal claim, sir, a moral one only. I sought them out; I have paid them without any mention of your uncle through my solicitor. You need have no fear of retribution from those poor souls. However, once the matter is known, they may put two and two together, for the one stipulation I made in giving their allowance was that part of it go for at least the rudiments of an education, that, presumably, would include arithmetic."

"Let them go hang. No one will listen to a bunch of bastards over the owner of Greystone Hall."

"Perhaps, perhaps not."

"How you can just sit there like that I can't understand. You're his widow, you wear his weeds."

"And you, above all people, know why I wear those weeds. And you know who ordered the installation of those ghastly funerary monstrosities, who arranged every detail of his funeral, who made an enduring symbol of his own name, and who bought my silence, my acquiescence all these years. I'm not proud of the role I've played. Had it been for myself alone, I should long since have broken the terms of that will and allowed my portion to revert to you. That is what you have always wanted; well, now you have your wish."

"How do you mean? Watkins' accusations will not serve that purpose," said Bransom, his eyes narrowed in speculation.

"No, sir, Watkins would have provided a valuable witness for my own side had I chosen to fight those terms. Now that is of no consequence."

"What do you mean?"

"I am to marry again, very soon. Then my settlement automatically becomes yours."

"But you said you would never re-marry. I thought you never would of your own free will."

"So did I, but things have changed."

"And who is the lucky gentleman, might I ask?" Bransom sneered, but he faltered at Penelope's swift response, "It is not Reginald Palfry."

"Whoever said it was?" he bluffed.

"Play the innocent if you wish."

"It is you who play the innocent. You side with scoundrels who would blacken my uncle's name, but I am of finer mettle. For some time now I have had it in my power to put you out without a penny to your name, to break my uncle's will. I took pity on you and chose not to do so."

"What do you mean?"

"I hold in my possession an incriminating letter from you to Palfry, a letter written in your own hand appointing an assignation with that gentleman."

"A fine gentleman, indeed—no wonder he and your uncle were bosom friends. As for that letter, it was forged, as was the one I received directing me to go to the Blue Boar. You, more than anyone, know all about those letters, which were part of one of your crude schemes, a scheme that didn't go as planned, as crude and ugly as your imitation of my hand."

"Such a fertile and distorted imagination you have in your attempt to circumvent the truth. The note I hold is yours, in your own hand; any court of law would uphold that."

"Ah, so you got from Palfry the copy I made, the copy that proved your note to be false. I had forgotten about it, but it doesn't matter. You have no need to use it; in fact you have no need to scheme any further, for your wish has been granted. The estate is yours now in its entirety; I shall no longer take any part of it. Very soon I shall move from Mayfield to Shropshire. I trust our paths may never again cross."

"Shropshire! Why, isn't that where Mortimer is from? Surely you can't be—"

Penelope broke in sharply, angrily, "No more of your speculations, Mr. Bransom. I am marrying Mr. Samuel Trueblood."

"Of course it couldn't be Mortimer. He'd never have you and your taste runs true to older men. I had thought when you disappeared from the Blue Boar that perhaps some younger swain had succumbed to your well-preserved charms."

Penelope was aware that her cheeks flushed as she replied quickly, too quickly, "That is quite enough of your insolence, Mr. Bransom."

Edward Bransom's eyes narrowed, aware, though not sure how, that he had gained a point.

"Though our relationship has never been good, let us try to part on cordial terms." Penelope held out her hand, a hand he refused to take.

"You came between your sister and me. I shall never feel well disposed towards you."

"I deny that as I have before, but I shall not deny that I was happy when Missy made her own choice freely, and now I am glad that that choice fell elsewhere. I find too many of your uncle's traits in you for me to believe she would have found happiness as your wife. You have my money; that is all you ever wanted from me. I see no point in prolonging this conversation."

"Nor I, madam. I do not wish you good-night nor good-bye."

He swept from the room, slamming the door behind him, pushing aside the maidservant who hurried to open the front door for him.

That she had always known he was after her settlement, that he had allowed himself to be so obvious, infuriated him. She was right, of course; now he had what he wanted, yet somehow the money wasn't enough. What right had she to leave with her head held high, uncowed, unbroken? Somehow she had gained the upper hand—he wouldn't have that. He would break her! Only then would he truly feel he had succeeded.

He ruminated as he spurred his horse on towards the Hall. She would suffer, but how? Then he remembered Watkins; perhaps that blackguard could yet serve a purpose. He'd lay ten to one odds Watkins, who would gladly do anything for a few guineas, had not gone further than the taproom at the inn. Dismissing the groom who came out to stable his horse, Bransom hurried in to retrieve the note Penelope had written, the one he had found in Palfry's room after that debacle at the Blue Boar. Then he set off at full gallop for Mayfield's George and Dragon.

25

It is not good to be too free
It is not good to have everything one wants.

Blaise Pascal
Pensées, 1670

At last Georgina Staverton, the woman Mortimer had always desired, the woman for want of whom he had been willing to give up his life, was his, and yet he was not happy. All the way to Chenwyth Mortimer had reflected upon life's irony.

He had seen Georgina back to Brook Street after Bully's wedding. During that journey she had been seized by a sudden determination that they should turn the horses towards Gretna and secretly marry. Where was the harm, when everyone knew they would marry eventually? He, who all his life had acted impetuously, had found himself pointing out the folly of such a madcap scheme, noting the importance society placed on a proper period of mourning. It would be viewed as a lack of respect for the dead; her children would suffer, and she would jeopardize her position in London society. To run off just as though they had something to hide, as though there were some secret pressing reason for it, could only provoke gossip and, in the end, do harm. He had pleaded patience; they had waited so long, what did a few months more matter to them? Reluctantly, she had acquiesced, but only after a secret engagement had been entered into, with the date of the wedding set to follow immediately upon her dispensing with black crepe.

As he travelled north, Mortimer had occasion to reflect on the young man once so desperately in love he'd have stopped at nothing to keep that lady at his side, society be damned. Did he care what the Plunkett-Galls thought—never! What had become of him? Why had he pleaded caution when Georgina had said words he had always wanted to hear come from her lips? Why had he, who cared nothing for propriety, been so anxious to observe society's strictures, while Georgina, usually so quick to uphold the rules of conduct, would so willingly have set them aside?

When she had told him that her husband was missing, he had searched frantically for news of his whereabouts, not, as others thought, to ascertain for certain that he was dead, but hoping against hope that he was alive. With Staverton gone, all impediments to marriage with Georgina, the marriage that had once been his only wish, were gone—yet now the thought of such a marriage made him utterly miserable. What had gone wrong? He was at a loss to understand himself. He knew he had to be alone, to think.

He had left London almost immediately, to settle urgent estate matters he had told Georgina, relieved she had not pressed him to explain what those urgent matters were. When he arrived, he had done nothing, wandering disconsolately from room to room. He rode north, towards the Wrekin—that wooded, whaleboned ridge that rose abruptly from the surrounding countryside—crossing the rich clover fields where the plovers cried and wheeled, galloping between hedgerows aflame with hedge-maple, to where the Severn separated the southern hills from the northern plains, that place he used to go as a boy to search for the city it was said Hadrian had built there.

Then he knew what was troubling him. She was everywhere, in the cry of the birds overhead, in the surrounding blaze of the turning leaves, in the ripple of the water at his feet. She had awakened him to that world of hers. He had always known that world, but he had never seen it before as he now did and always would . . . and always she would be there. He had gone to her, wanting her, and she had spurned him for a life of memories. Her rejection had hurt him far more deeply than had Georgina's long ago. Then he had been young and passionate, his pride had been hurt. Now he was older, wiser, and something more than his pride suffered: he was left with the emptiness of having lost something precious, something irreplaceable.

Was it possible, though, that he wanted only what he could not have? He thought back on those few days they had spent together, days of ecstasy, to be sure, yet what he remembered most about them was a deep contentment, a serenity never before known. He was a different man from the soldier who had gone to the wars, different too from the victor who had returned vowing to live for pleasure. Pleasure alone was not enough, there was more to life than pleasure.

His mind returned to Georgina; how would their life together be? Women, women! He would put all of them from his mind.

He threw himself into the task of designing a metal container capable of storing food, perhaps spurred by Penelope's enthusiasm for the plan when he had mentioned it. He experimented with sheets of Cornish tinplate with a base of wrought iron refined with charcoal, forming the sheets into cylinders with notched lock seams. All his concentration and energy were placed in the task. It went well, yet, feeling utterly unsociable, he decided to prepare supplies for a decade and leave for the northernmost Hebrides or darkest Africa.

He was disturbed in his work by yet another woman in his life. His sister, Eunice, arrived unexpectedly one afternoon.

"You didn't tell me you were coming, Charles. Had I known, I would have seen that everything was in readiness for your return. You know how the servants let things go when you're away. Mr. Trueblood has often mentioned the trouble he has, being away from Belfriars so often; he says he makes it a policy never to let the servants know exactly when to expect him, but if everything is not completely in order, if so much as a speck of dust is found anywhere, they know to expect instant dismissal. He may be a bit harsh but, on the other hand, you're far too lenient. Look at those windows; I doubt they've been cleaned since summer. How long have you been back, close to a week, and nothing's been done about them. Disgraceful!"

"My dear Eunice, I really hadn't noticed, but if they bother you I suggest we take our tea outside where there are no windows."

"How like you, Charles. You never were very good at managing these things. You need a woman to take care of them for you."

"The last thing I need at the moment is a woman!" he exploded.

"Dear me! Touchy, aren't we? Are you in love again, Charles?"

"No, I am not."

"Well, apparently Mr. Trueblood is, for he's getting married."

"Samuel Trueblood getting married! By God, I never thought I'd see that day. He doesn't know what love is. If he's marrying it's for something other than that; he's got a reason for everything he does."

"You are caustic today, Charles. What's wrong?"

"Nothing, nothing at all."

"'Nothing' in that tone of voice very definitely means something, but I won't press the point," his sister said.

"Tell me, who is the brave lady who has taken on the onerous task of becoming Mrs. Trueblood and seeing to it that there's not a speck of dust on the armoire in the event her lord and master might arrive without warning?"

"I really don't know, no one I'd ever heard of. I can't for the life of me remember the name, though the vicar mentioned it to me this morning. He's to begin calling the banns on Sunday; you'll find out then."

"It's not important. Let's discuss something else; you know how I detest that man."

"I never really understand why you're so bitter. Had it not been for him Chenwyth would be long since gone when Daddy squandered everything—and don't forget he gave you the money so you could go to the Army. Look at everything that came out of that—not that you didn't earn it."

"He didn't give anything, Eunice; I borrowed and repaid with a pretty penny of interest. Not that I care about that; I'm only saying he does nothing from the goodness of his heart, he exploits everyone."

"Well, John thinks he's done a great deal for Wrexford. Belfriars was nothing, and he's made it into quite a show-place; a well-maintained estate is good for the neighbour-hood. And he's charitably-minded, a good man to have in the parish, the vicar says, a guiding light in that society for the orphans, and a supporter of the arts. I can't understand why you dislike him so."

"Because he's a hypocrite, that's why, and if there's any-thing I can't abide it's a hypocrite. Give me an outright villain any day. And speaking of outright villains, how's that husband of yours?"

"Charles, you're incorrigible! John's an angel and you know it."

"Well, tell him to come over and bring his foxhounds; we'll give them a run before hunting begins and while we're at it I'll see if I can't knock some of those angelic qualities out of him."

"I'll tell him." Eunice's eyes suddenly lit up. "I have it! I know why you're out of sorts—it's because Rodney tied the knot and you feel left out. That's it!"

Her brother decided against deflating her triumph by arguing the point. Besides, in some ways Bully's wedding was at the root of his ill-humour.

Mortimer liked his brother-in-law, who, while not the angel that Eunice would have him, was nevertheless a very sensible gentleman. Mortimer might perhaps consider him a trifle lacking in humour, while he occasionally found Mor-timer rather flippant, but the two men made allowances for these faults and on other matters found solid meeting ground.

They rode hard all the following afternoon, the hounds baying at their heels, and as they were returning, passing close to Belfriars, they saw Trueblood's carriage approach-ing on the main road.

"The illustrious patron of the arts is about to be in residence, I see," Mortimer remarked. "Makes me want to race across the park and warn the servants."

"Believe me, you don't have to do that," his brother-in-law replied. "He's got that lot trained, runs a tight ship at Belfriars, Trueblood does. Everyone toes the line there, everyone."

"And that will undoubtedly include the poor soul who's agreed to become his wife. She must have been hard up to take him."

"Oh, I don't know. He's not a bad catch, you know. A bit old and crotchety but pots of money."

"Pots of money to breed other pots of money and little else."

"That's not quite fair, Charles. You're forgetting about his charitable efforts."

"Which consist, for the most part, of getting money out of other people—I must say he's rather good at that."

"Eunice says you have a positive hatred of the old boy."

"I do, and it's more than he's worth. One of my shortcomings, I'm afraid, is to invest a great deal too much energy in that hearty dislike I have for him, energy that should well be directed to other purposes."

"Eunice said you were like a bear with a sore head yesterday. She thinks you're in love again."

"Even though she's my sister, Eunice lacks originality; she thinks like every other woman I know—if a man's out of humour, it has to be over a woman."

"Well, is it?"

"For God's sake, John, not you now."

"No, sorry old chap, don't mean to pry. It's just that—well, I read about old Philby Staverton going to a watery grave. Sorry to hear of it, of course."

"Very regrettable."

"Yes . . . still, I know you were potty about his wife, at least Eunice always said you were, said she was the reason you went off to the wars."

"Eunice is a hopeless romantic."

"Yes, I know, still I was wondering . . ."

"Well, out with it, wondering what?"

"Well, if you two, eventually would . . . well, you know what I mean, better late than never."

"John," Mortimer's tone was unusually unctuous, "surely you are not suggesting, with the lady only just a widow, that she and I would . . ."

"No, no, of course not. I beg your pardon. I didn't mean to imply anything just now. I just thought that, well, since you knew one another so well, I thought perhaps . . . but probably I shouldn't say what I thought."

"Oh, come off it, John, of course you may say what you think to me. You're part of the family. I couldn't resist pulling your leg a little, that's all. Undoubtedly Georgina and I will marry at the proper time. You can tell Eunice that, but please ask her not to voice it around—I suppose that's like giving a child a hoop and telling him not to play with it. Anyway, enough of all that, I want to tell you about this idea I have been playing around with for storing food in metal containers. It has been done by the French with glass, but I think I've found a tinplate which would do even better."

Eunice, Georgina, everyone was forgotten as he expounded on his latest invention, an invention which took him in to see Wrexford's blacksmith the following morning to discuss the possibility of refining the wrought iron with coke instead of charcoal in order to make it more malleable. It was as he came out of the forge that he ran into the vicar.

"A fine morning, Lord Mortimer, a very fine morning."

"Indeed it is, Mr. Drummond."

"A fine thing to see you looking so well. You are in good health I hear from your dear sister, who keeps me *au courant* with these things."

"My sister is nothing if not *au courant*."

"She tells me it may not be so very long before we have a mistress in residence at Chenwyth as we shall have at Belfriars."

"My sister is a deuced sight too *au courant*, if you'll pardon my French."

"Oh dear me, did I speak out of turn?"

"Not you, sir, it's my sister who spoke out of turn."

"I beg pardon for mentioning it. She did indeed tell me in the strictest confidence, but I saw no harm in speaking of it to you."

"No matter, sir."

"Really, it's a coincidence to run into you this morning, for I had intended calling in at Chenwyth."

"Was it to enquire after my health, the state of my soul, or is our parish in need of some assistance?"

"Our parish is always in need of something, Lord Mortimer."

"I'm well aware of that, but I think in comparison with other parish priests you may find yourself more fortunate by having arch rivals such as Mr. Trueblood and myself as members of your flock."

"I fail to understand, sir."

"But I think you do, and believe me I consider it only good sense—whatever donation you get from me you can always be sure Trueblood will top it. So what is it you need now?"

"I assure you, Lord Mortimer, I wouldn't dream of . . ." but the vicar's eye caught the twinkle in Mortimer's eye and both men laughed.

"Well, out with it, what is it you need? I shall try to be as generous as possible, if only to make Trueblood pay through the nose."

"It's the roof, Lord Mortimer, the roof of St. Oswald's. I fear it will not go through another winter, if we have the rain and snow of last year, not without serious leaks, that is. And there's the matter of the organ; you know the last leak was immediately above the organ and it has wheezed ever since."

"How much do you think you need?"

"I think it will be close to five hundred pounds, even more if the organ cannot be repaired."

"You may tell Trueblood that I shall give three hundred; in that way you should get enough from him to afford the new organ. Come to think of it, he should donate one; for Eunice tells me you're to call the banns for him on Sunday."

"That is so. Mr. Trueblood wrote to me in the matter. He has just arrived at Belfriars, and I am to see him there today."

"I suppose I must drop in and extend my congratulations also."

"I'm sure that would greatly please him. I shall tell him that you said so, if you don't mind, for it will put him in a good humour."

"By all means." Then Mortimer added, by way of afterthought, "The lady, is she from this part of the country?"

"No, she is from Oxfordshire."

"Oxfordshire? Where in Oxfordshire?"

The vicar, hearing a certain urgency in the question, searched his mind for the name of the parish. "Let me see, it's on the tip of my tongue, Springfield, no that's not it. . . ."

"Surely not Mayfield?"

"Mayfield, that's it. The rector there is a man by the name of Osborn, a Cambridge man like myself, though I had not known him, but then he was at Trinity and I'm a King's man." The vicar noticed that Lord Mortimer had grown pale, and he hastened to apologize, "Of course, you were up at Oxford, a fine university, I have nothing at all against it. Anyway to get back to Mr. Trueblood's nuptials, the lady, it seems, is a widow, a certain Mrs. Penelope Bransom. . . ."

The vicar was at a loss to understand why Lord Mortimer, usually the soul of courtesy, should bid him good-day and turn and stride away, leaving him in mid-sentence.

26

*If two men desire the same thing, which nevertheless they
cannot both enjoy, they become enemies.*

Thomas Hobbes
Leviathan, 1651

That she could have chosen Trueblood, a man he despised, a man with no redeeming qualities, a man totally
devoid of humour, a man not far from his dotage, that she
could have chosen such a man over him—resentment
gnawed at his heart. His pride was hurt, he told himself,
that was all, but deep within something told him it was
much more than his pride that was suffering. They had
known one another, known in every sense of that word; he
had believed she had wanted him as he wanted her. It had
been difficult to accept her rejection of his proposal, but less
so than this. That, he had thought, was occasioned by her
wish to be true to a memory and, however warped he might
consider the attitude, it was her right to feel so. But then to
accept a man of vintage years, a dried-up old curmudgeon,
a man who could never give love because he didn't know the
meaning of the word, rather than himself. Why? Again and
again he asked himself that question.

He stayed away from church on Sunday so that he would
not have to hear the reading of those banns linking her
name with Trueblood's, which resulted in another visit
from Eunice and searching enquiries into his fit of the doldrums.

"Mr. Trueblood asked after you. The vicar had told him
that you planned to call at Belfriars to offer your congratu-

lations. He had waited for you, then he looked for you on Sunday. If I didn't know better, I would say you were deliberately avoiding him but, despise him as you may, you've never been unwilling to face the man."

He grew thoughtful. "You're right, Eunice, in reminding me of my duty. I'll go over tomorrow."

At Belfriars, Trueblood showed his unctuous delight. "My dear Mortimer, so glad you dropped by. I had thought you were coming last week, and when you missed church I was afraid you had returned to London. I spoke to your sister about it, and she said she had found you quite out of sorts. I hope that nothing is troubling you, unless it is another affair of the heart. To those I know you are somewhat susceptible."

"No, that is not the case."

"I have heard, however, that we may soon have a new mistress at Chenwyth," and seeing Mortimer's face cloud, he added quickly, "I should not say soon, for I know there is a prescribed period of mourning. You can rely upon my discretion. I only mention it because of the coincidence. I believe you may have heard that I, at last, am to marry, and to marry a lady not unknown to you."

"Yes, I have heard and that is what brings me to Belfriars this morning. I'm sorry I was not here earlier to extend my congratulations to you . . . and to Mrs. Bransom, for that is the lady, I believe."

"Indeed it is."

Mortimer extended his hand, and Trueblood took it in his cold, lifeless grip. There, it was done. He had hated to come; he had hated to extend felicitations in an infelicitous matter, but it was his duty as a neighbour to do so. It was done. He got up, but Trueblood detained him, calling for refreshments, leaning back to talk more expansively than usual.

"I daresay it came as something of a surprise to you. I know there were many who had decided that I would never marry after . . . but we won't talk about that."

Mortimer ignored his comment; to respond could only lead to trouble.

"But you know Mrs. Bransom quite well, I believe,"

Trueblood commented, noticing unusually sharp discernment in Mortimer's eyes as he replied coldly, "Her sister married my friend, as you know. I have met her a few times before that."

"As, yes, I remember now, the society fete. You paid a pretty penny for her watercolour. Just like his father, I remember thinking, no idea of money."

"I'd rather we did not discuss my father, or any member of my family, Trueblood," Mortimer snapped.

"No offense, no offense. I just wanted to say, I am quite willing to buy it from you."

"It's not for sale."

"Well, just the same, now Mrs. Bransom is to be my wife, it does seem more appropriate that it should be here."

"Why are you marrying her?" Mortimer was surprised at his own question. He hadn't meant to ask it; he felt Trueblood would be within his rights to refuse to reply, but he did not.

"Mrs. Bransom is a sensible woman, one who will be able to understand me and my ways. Her previous husband was a gentleman similar, in many respects, to myself, devoted to his charities, well-regarded within his community. She has conducted herself well in perpetuating his memory."

"Is that what you want, someone to perpetuate your memory?"

Mortimer's tone was insolent, but Trueblood only laughed. "Come, Mortimer, you have your own widow, your dear Lady Staverton; you can take her legally at last. You mustn't begrudge me mine. Marry your widow; don't wait around for my demise hoping to pick up both my wife and fortune. I assure you, though I'm old enough to be your father, I'm strong as I ever was and I'll live a good long life. The lady may outlast me, but if she does I'll be as astute as her first husband in the terms of my will."

"Damn your rotten lily-livered hide, you and your ill-gotten gains, earned with cheap products at the expense of men's lives. Do you think I'd want any of it?"

"You and your family have made good use of my money. Where would you have been without it?"

"We have borrowed from you, at usurious rates, every penny of which has been repaid to you, far more, I may say, in interest than ever was received."

"You made no complaint at the time, nor did that father of yours."

"I make no complaint now; I merely repeat the truth. And it was agreed we would not speak of my family."

"I agreed to nothing. You've seen fit to malign me; I see no reason not to speak of that wastrel who took what was mine."

"My father took nothing from you."

"Only the woman I loved."

"I can't speak for you, but I know my mother loved my father and only my father."

"She loved me until he came along, swashbuckling fool that he was, a handsome profile, a name in English history—how sick I got of hearing about the Mortimers and their exploits. She would have married me, she should have married me. . . ."

"But she didn't; she chose to marry my father."

"And lived to regret it. Had it not been for me, your family would have been thrown off your precious Chenwyth."

"You did loan money, for your own purposes. You did not have to do so; you chose to do so."

"I chose to do so for her, for Rosalind."

"You chose to do so to control not only my mother but all of us; it gave you power to have the Mortimers in your grasp, didn't it?"

"You and your precious name, flaunting your so-called gallantry. I could have crushed you any time I wanted to."

"Then why didn't you? I'll tell you why, because you wanted us there in the palm of your hand. Well, never again will you have power over me or anything that is mine, never."

At that moment the manservant entered with the tray of refreshments.

"What in the name of hell do you think you're doing?" Trueblood exploded.

"Serving the refreshments, sir, that you called for."

"I want no refreshments. Lord Mortimer is leaving."

"I'm sorry, sir, but I was told. . . ."

"And you may leave also, for good."

"But sir, I only did as I was told."

"Get out of my sight, do you hear?"

"For God's sake, Trueblood, the man's done nothing. The quarrel is between us."

"A man's a fool who's lax with his servants. Everyone in this house must know who is master."

"Each man, or woman, is entitled to dignity no matter their station in life."

"Dignity scarce becomes a servant," and to the manservant who stood at the door Trueblood yelled again, "Didn't you hear me tell you to get out?"

"Come over to Chenwyth and see me," Mortimer said to the bewildered servant, then, turning back to Trueblood, "This is possibly the first time we have spoken openly to one another; perhaps it was necessary and should have been done before. I have nothing more to say to you, ever."

27

Thank God Bully was coming, Mortimer thought. He had retreated into the garden at Staverton Park to escape from Lambourne's repetitious detailing of why he had played exactly as he had in piquet the night before and Kitty Radcliffe's incessant high-pitched laugh.

Georgina had written begging him to come immediately to Brook Hill, and he had answered her summons not so much because he wished to be there as because he wished to be as far from Wrexford as was possible. He refused to hear those banns read, to look upon Trueblood's gloating face; most particularly he refused to have anything to do with the forthcoming wedding.

Eunice had found it uncivil for him to leave at that particular time; contrarily, Mortimer had found it the only civil thing to do.

But at Staverton Park he had found the house party in progress not altogether to his liking. Georgina, feeling her activities in town circumscribed by her mourning, had gathered around her a group of people she considered bright and interesting, all of whom were known to Mortimer, none of whom he had ever before realized was so utterly devoid of charm and intellect.

"I've never seen you so cross," Georgina complained.

"You've been black as a thundercloud ever since you arrived. I thought you'd find it fun, instead of which you were rude to Kitty this afternoon and you completely cut her husband."

"I found them foolish, and I thought they deserved it."

"Perhaps they are rather tasteless, but that's not the point, Charles. They're my guests."

"You're right, Georgina. I'm sorry. Since I don't find them amusing, perhaps I should go back to London."

"No," she said quickly, "don't do that, Charles. I'll ask Rodney and his wife over to dinner tonight. You always enjoy his company."

Thank God Bully was coming, he reiterated to himself, as he stood waiting for his friend's carriage to come up the drive. But when it came three, not two, figures climbed down at the front door.

"Most beautiful sight I've ever seen," Bully was saying as he gazed out across the view of the Weald. "Don't you agree, Melissa?"

"It's just heavenly."

"Now, Penelope, aren't you glad you came? Doesn't this make it worth while, even though you travelled all day?"

Colonel Bullerton thought at first that it was the Weald's magnificent scene that produced the distracted look on his sister-in-law's face, but following her line of sight, his gaze fell on a most familiar figure.

"By God, Mortimer, you sly dog! You didn't tell me you were coming to Brook Hill, and it seems only yesterday I had a letter from you; it was yesterday, wasn't it, Melissa?"

"No, Rodney, it was the day before because we received two letters by the post—Lord Mortimer's, and Penelope's telling us of her marriage and that she would come and see us before it took place."

"That's right. I suppose it was the surprise of that news that put everything out of mind. You're to have a new neighbour, Mortimer. Now when we come to Shropshire we'll be hard put to decide who to visit first." Noticing an odd look on his friend's face, he asked, "But perhaps you've heard the news already."

"Yes, I have. I spoke to Trueblood."

An embarrassing silence followed, after which Mortimer, making no attempt to convey his congratulations on the forthcoming event—an omission painfully obvious to everyone—remarked drily, after looking down at Penelope's topaz golden pelisse, "So, at last you are truly out of mourning, Mrs. Bransom."

"I am out of mourning, Lord Mortimer," she replied quietly, her discomfort obvious. A few stilted remarks were made by Melissa and Rodney on the fineness of the evening, the house, the view, before Georgina Staverton appeared.

"There, I thought I heard a carriage. Rodney, how nice to see you, and your lovely bride. And Mrs. Bransom, what a surprise. I've just received an invitation to your wedding. My goodness, I'd never have guessed, but I'm pleased. You'll be good for Samuel, don't you think, Charles?"

"I think they deserve one another," he said quite savagely. Since everyone present knew his views on Trueblood, the pause that followed was even more embarrassing.

"Well, do come in. We've a small party. Charles complains they're not sufficiently amusing, but I hope now you're here his temper will improve."

Bully doubted it until Mortimer bent down to kiss Georgina lightly on the cheek and slip his arm through hers. "Perhaps the impatience of a panting lover who came expecting a rendezvous and was greeted by a grand reception may be excused."

Georgina smiled. "You were the one who pleaded patience, Charles."

"True, but then I did not know pain. He that would woo a widow must woo her day and night, it is said."

They went inside, Rodney and Melissa, Charles and Georgina, with Penelope alone until her brother-in-law turned round. "Come now, this isn't fair. We're forgetting Penelope."

"So we are," Mortimer agreed, turning to wait, though his attitude lacked its customary courtesy. Throughout the evening, in fact, he concentrated all his attention upon one widow, neither approaching nor speaking directly to the other.

"There," Kitty Radcliffe remarked to her husband in

triumph, "I told you he was still mad for Georgina, but you would have it that it had cooled. You don't understand these things the way I do."

"I certainly don't understand Mortimer," her husband commented. "Odd chap; first he'll hardly talk at all, now he's all affability."

"All affability except to Mrs. Bransom." Kitty Radcliffe's eyes narrowed thoughtfully.

"Suppose it's because she's marrying that man he can't stand the sight of. He treats him much the same way," he commented.

"I suppose."

On the other side of the room, Colonel Bullerton was asking his friend whether they might stay with him at the time of the wedding.

"You may stay at Chenwyth by all means, but I myself shan't be there."

"Not going to be there! I know you don't care for Trueblood, but after all he is your neighbour. Not too civil of you, old chap."

"I'm deuced fed up with people telling me what's civil and what's uncivil. Wild rhinoceroses wouldn't make me go to that affair."

Mortimer walked away, leaving his friend to reflect that he was behaving most oddly, first to his sister-in-law, now to himself.

After dinner dancing was suggested, the rugs and chairs pulled back and music selected. Penelope offered to play the piano for the assembled company, despite her sister's objections that she had had an exhausting day.

"It will be a recreation for me, not a hardship; besides, I don't dance, but I suspect everyone else is anxious to do so." She did not add that it would be a great relief for her to be apart from at least one member of the company.

She began with a series of country dances, concentrating entirely on the music as she played, never once glancing over at the dancers, not even in the pauses between one dance and the next.

It was during the third dance that she became conscious

of someone standing behind her, but until his hand preceded hers in turning the music she was not entirely sure who it was: even then, she said nothing until he spoke.

"You play well, Mrs. Bransom."

"Thank you, Lord Mortimer. I enjoy playing. I find serenity and a great deal of similarity in the harmony of music and of colour. Both are most pleasing to me."

"Your playing is, I am sure, pleasing to us all."

"Thank you," she said, glad that the conversation, a conversation she had feared, had been so impersonal.

Still he continued to stand behind her, turning the pages of her music as she played, saying nothing until the piece neared its end, when he demanded in a lower, anguished tone, "Why did you do it, Penelope, why did you take that curmudgeon of a man?"

Her fingers faltered for the first time as she replied, "He asked me to marry him and I accepted; that is all."

"I seem to remember you were asked once before, but that time you refused, or was that man too close to your own age, not near enough to his dotage for you? Perhaps you prefer to look forward to another grand funeral, erecting another atrocious monument, another long period of worshipping beside a grave. Is that why you chose Trueblood over me? You're still afraid of life, aren't you?"

Again she faltered, causing the dancers to glance across at her and her sister to leave the set.

"Go away, leave me. I never want to see you again."

"Very well. The feeling is mutual I can assure you."

Mortimer was gone when Missy reached her sister. "You're tired, Penelope, quite exhausted, admit it."

"Yes, Missy, I am more exhausted than I had realized."

"Then we shall leave immediately."

Penelope didn't glance at Mortimer as adieus were made, nor did he bid her good-night.

him fast . . . it was pulling him down, down into the water. He could see Penelope clearly, but he couldn't reach her. He shouted to her, but she didn't move.

Though it was not the first time in his life he was sure he would die, it was the first time he was afraid to die.

"No!" he cried out in fury. "No, God, no—not here, not now. Spare me! Spare me this time, I beg you."

Many times in battle he had heard such pleas—men begging for another day, even another hour on earth, praying for God's mercy, making pacts with God, promises of what they would do in exchange for being spared. Just so did Mortimer plead.

"Free me that I may reach her. If I drown, she must surely drown too. I'll not interfere in her life, only let me live so I can get to her."

His heart grew heavy with fear as he struggled against the suction of the mud and the entangling growth which, all of a sudden, gave to his thrust, allowing him to gain one firm foothold and then pull the other foot free.

Within seconds thereafter he had hold of her, pulling her head out of the water. She was heavy, lifeless, and much of his strength had been spent in fighting the undergrowth. Rather than try to cross it again with his burden, he swam out into midstream and down the river for about a quarter of a mile to a point where the banks were clear. Only then did he attempt to get ashore. His prayers were, indeed, answered, for when his foot gingerly tried the river bottom, it was firm beneath him.

Once ashore, he hastened to ascertain that though Penelope was unconscious she was breathing. He carried her back along the path to where he had left his horse and, wrapping her in his coat, laid her across the saddle. He got up behind her and, holding her firmly to him, made for the road. There he came upon a carter who directed him to the village apothecary.

That portly gentleman was singularly unshaken at the sight of Mortimer's soaking figure and his bedraggled burden.

"The river again, I fear," he said, shaking his head as he

felt Penelope's pulse. "No need to explain, sir, it's the fourth accident I've seen this year."

"How is she? Will she be all right? Will she live?"

"There, there, sir, calm yourself. The pulse is a trifle weak but not erratic. I can't tell anything for sure until I examine her. You're going to catch your death, shivering so. My wife will make you some tea."

"There's nothing at all wrong with me." Mortimer forced the words through teeth clenched to prevent their chattering. "Please help the lady, please."

"I'll do everything I can."

Despite his remonstrances a dry shirt was found and tea prepared for him while the apothecary made his examination. His face, when at last he came out to where Mortimer waited, was grave.

"Well?" Mortimer demanded forcefully in an effort to hide his fear. "Well, how is she? Will she live?"

"Yes, yes, she will live."

"Thank God!"

But Mortimer's relief changed to stupefaction at the apothecary's next words, "My main concern is for the child."

"The child! She is going to have a child?"

"I'm sorry, sir. I took the lady for your wife. I'm afraid there is some mistake on my part."

Mortimer, recovering from his bewilderment, allowed, as he had once before, that Penelope was his wife.

"Then you knew she was with child, I take it?"

"You must excuse me, I am in a state of confusion. I thought only of her; indeed, her life is the more important."

"That is so, but what she is doing is threatening her own life as well as the life of the child."

"Threatening her life, but how?"

"Those ridiculous bandage corsets. It is foolishness, utter foolishness for these ladies to think of preserving their figures when nature demands otherwise. It should not be allowed. You must pardon my frankness, sir, but I must insist that you forbid your wife to wear such a contraption.

2 4 3

28

I have a faint cold fear thrill through my veins
That almost freezes up the heat of life.
Shakespeare
Romeo and Juliet, 1596

His behaviour that evening, particularly towards Penelope Bransom, had been abysmal, entirely unworthy of him. Mortimer was deeply troubled by it; he did not sleep well and the next day could see no recourse but to apologize.

He found Bully at home, his wife also, but the lady he most wished to see did not appear. Though Mortimer's distraction was obvious to his friend, Melissa was full of news she had just received from her friend Emmeline Halstead.

"She's to marry Gerald Wendling. You remember him, of course, at our wedding."

"Yes, yes, of course," Mortimer agreed, though he was sure he would not recognize the gentleman unless he were pointed out to him. "I'm very happy for her, for both of them."

"Lady Halstead is also. She said that when Penelope caught my bouquet as I was leaving that she had handed it to Emmeline, saying I had intended it for her. That was not so, of course, for I had hoped . . ." She broke off and then concluded awkwardly, "I had hoped Penelope would marry again."

"Well, your wish has come true."

"Yes, in a way," Melissa agreed doubtfully.

"Speaking of your sister, I see no sign of her. Is she in?"

"She went down to the river about an hour ago. She had heard there were some late blooming water forget-me-nots."

"Then perhaps if I return to Staverton Park by way of the river I may see her. And if not, please tell her I asked after her."

Though Bully pressed him to remain, he left almost immediately, determined to convey his regrets for his ill humour. But on reaching the river he at first saw no sign of anyone. Then he caught a glimpse of a blur of blue passing between the rushes growing along the river bank, a female figure that paused now and then to examine the water mint or marsh yellow cress that grew in profusion. He knew it must be Penelope, and he urged his horse in that direction along the path that paralleled the bank. In his mind he went over words of apology; none would be easy, none would truly ameliorate his unkindness towards her. She had every right to choose a husband where she would—by what right did he demand her to explain her actions? Yet as he came closer to that figure lost in its world of nature, his thoughts reverted to their time together. Could he forbear to remind her of them, to question whether they would not be happier together than with the partners fate was providing for them?

He lost sight of her briefly at a bend in the river, yet even after rounding that bend he could not see her. Had she left the river to go back by the road, he wondered, turning his horse in that direction, when a cry, or was it only the call of a bird, made him stop and then turn back.

His eyes scanned the water. Surely she could not have fallen in! He could see nothing. Then, there it was, a glimpse of her dress. She was lying face down, oddly still, not very far from the shore. Throwing off his coat, he plunged into the cold water, only to find himself moments later caught in a tangle of rushes and a network of weeds growing beneath the water's surface. He struggled to free himself, but was hampered by the soft mud beneath that made it impossible to gain a foothold. The more he struggled, the more binding the growth became. It held

It prevents proper blood circulation; it impedes breathing and constricts the position of the child in the womb. No matter what the designer of this infernal garment may say in its favour, it is unhealthy and undesirable for both woman and child. In my opinion, if harm has been done, it is from the corset as much as the accident. Undoubtedly it impeded her when she fell."

"I must confess I was surprised by how little she moved in the water."

"It was probably well nigh impossible." The apothecary eyed him sympathetically. "I conjecture your wife to be close to her fifth month, is that right?"

"Her fifth month," Mortimer repeated distractedly, thinking back. "Yes, yes, that would be so."

His mind was racing. Why had she denied it when he asked her if she could be with child? Why, when she knew, had she not told him?

"It's a delicate period. You will talk to her about the garment."

"Please, take it, dispose of it. You may most certainly do so. But may I not see her? She is conscious?"

"Yes, yes, of course. But she has had a terrible shock, and I have administered some laudanum, so if you find her somewhat sleepy, that is probably the cause. Go in, by all means."

Penelope lay still on the bed, her wet hair loose around her head as it lay on the pillow, her face exceptionally pale, her eyes closed. Yet her breathing was regular, and when he held her hand, he was relieved to find it was warm and that she faintly but definitely returned his pressure. When at last she opened her eyes, however, he was not entirely sure that she recognized him.

"The flower," she murmured, "the forget-me-not, I thought I could reach it, but I slipped. . . ."

"I know, I know. Don't talk, Penelope. You're going to be all right. Everything's going to be all right, everything—I promise."

She nodded, but said nothing, then, closing her eyes again, she fell asleep.

246

248

He sat watching her, a thousand questions crossing his mind, questions that needed answering but none as important as the fact that they must marry immediately. He put his head in his hands, thanking God that they were both alive—all alive. What he truly desired was coming about, but he would make no more wishes; it was not that wishes did not come true, they did, but wishes were ever fools, they manifested their truth at unlikely times, in unlikely ways. He wanted a good life for them, a productive life; that life should begin as it would continue, with honour. For that reason, he realized there was something that must be done, something for which he had no relish, but that must be carried out without delay.

"I am obliged to travel north immediately," he informed the apothecary. "My wife's sister and her husband, Colonel Bullerton, are staying nearby. I shall see that they come to her." Then he added thoughtfully, "I wish you would say nothing about the child—they don't yet know of it and I should like to be present when they hear the good news. It may have been our wish to surprise them that led my wife to wear that garment."

"No harm done, for I have heard the child's heartbeat. I do think, however, that should she continue to use any such device . . ."

"I assure you she will not."

"And you, sir, are you well enough to travel immediately?"

"Perfectly recovered, thanks to you and your good wife. I shall see that you are both well rewarded for your timely, inestimable aid."

29

Let your own discretion be your tutor: suit the action to the
word, the word to the action.

Shakespeare
Hamlet, 1601

Still his head ached. Lord, how it ached! He stretched his
long frame in bed, wondering where he was and what fool
had seen fit to open the bed curtains at such an ungodly
hour of the morning.

Slowly he distinguished the outline of Glossop's wiry
frame, glass in hand filled with that vile concoction with its
glutinous egg yolk floating on the surface.

"Go away, Glossop, leave me alone."

"I will, me lord, after you've taken of this."

The singular calm of Glossop's voice served further to
irritate him, but he recognized the tone and knew there
would be only one way to rid himself of it. Steeling his
queasy stomach for the onslaught to come, he closed his
eyes and drank the liquid as swiftly as possible.

"Bloody poison! Now, are you satisfied?"

"Quite, me lord."

"Well then, go away."

"I will, but I will be back in an hour."

"What on earth for?"

"You told me last night to be sure we was on the road no
later than noon."

"Did I? Did I say where we were going?"

"I'm not quite sure. You said something about Timbuktu."

"Timbuktu! Timbuktu's in Africa."

"If you say so, me lord."

"Well, close the curtain. I'll think about it."

"Right you are, me lord."

Glossop's cheery voice and sprightly step eventually faded away. In the dim light of the curtained bed, a bed he slowly realized, as Glossop's potion went to work, was his own at Chenwyth, everything began to come back to him.

In Surrey he had summoned Bully and Melissa to care for Penelope, then set out almost immediately for Shropshire. He had to talk to Trueblood. At first, when he had been told by the apothecary about the child, he thought it only a matter of a special license, a quiet wedding and all would be solved. But he remembered Trueblood; he remembered Trueblood's conviction that his mother had been maliciously stolen from him years before. Might he not believe Mortimer was acting, as he continued to believe his father had acted, out of spite, stealing his bride on the eve of their wedding?

He would tell Trueblood what he had discovered. Trueblood would surely be glad to release a woman who was to bear another man's child. Then they could start their married life free from the fear of having harmed another. The journey to Wrexford and back would require two, at the most three, days; that would give Penelope time to recover from her accident. They would go abroad, to Florence perhaps. There were good doctors there; the birth could be registered at the Consulate, and when mother and child were strong, when they had enjoyed all they wished to of the Italian sunshine, they could return to England to take up their life at Chenwyth in good faith, none the worse for any of it. He saw how it would be, Penelope painting, himself experimenting with those dozens of ideas to improve daily life that teemed through his mind—and children, dozens of children, theirs, their nieces and nephews, eventually grandchildren. That was the life he wanted, a full life, a family life, in harmony with his community, with that one at his side who would make life all that he dreamed. But to have a contented life it should begin in happiness and accord, not in anger and recrimination. His interview with Trueblood, unpleasant though it would be, was mandatory.

Arriving at Belfriars, the house he had vowed never again to enter, to speak to Trueblood, the man he had sworn never again to address, he realized that the owner might refuse to see him. Far from it, however; Trueblood seemed pleased. He positively glowed at Mortimer's apology for his ill manners.

Mortimer went on to explain about the accident, assuring Trueblood that Penelope was safe, before revealing the more delicate matter of the apothecary's disclosure of her pregnancy.

"I thought it only right that you should know," he finished, relieved that it was done, totally unprepared for Trueblood's calm response.

"But I did know. Mrs. Bransom had confided in me. I offered to marry her with that knowledge."

Mortimer was completely taken aback. Was it possible to have so misjudged Trueblood? Was he, in fact, the benefactor that he would have the world believe him to be?

"I believe I may not have always treated you justly," he said at last.

"That I cannot argue with."

Still, Mortimer shook his head. "Perhaps I should not put this question to you, and yet I must. Why, knowing the child is not yours, did you take on the responsibility?"

There was a certain smugness in Trueblood's expression, as though at last he had brought Mortimer to his knees. "Because the child is yours, Mortimer."

So, that was it! He had not, after all, misjudged Trueblood. His act was totally in character with the man he had supposed him to be. His resolve to marry Penelope was to gain control over yet another Mortimer, a Mortimer yet unborn. To own to the truth of his assumption could only firm Trueblood in his resolve, but there was one response that might make him release her—denial.

"You're mad! When I learned of Mrs. Bransom's condition I was astonished, utterly astonished. What on earth could draw you to such a conclusion?"

"Mrs. Bransom herself told me. As for your knowing nothing of it, I knew that also. I had not thought you would discover it until later. I intended, I still intend, to ask you to act as godfather to the child, keeping the matter in the family, so to speak. I hope that you will."

"If it were mine, as you say, the lady would have had no reason not to tell me so."

"Silly heroics, I think, were behind her silence. She thought at last you had a chance to marry the woman you loved, Georgina Staverton."

"That's ridiculous."

"I know. I have suspected, despite what your sister has said to the contrary, that the matter has cooled. But you know how women are, romantics at heart."

"There's not an ounce of romance in you, is there, Trueblood?"

"I leave the swashbuckling to the Mortimers, or I have up until now. The next generation of Truebloods will be interesting, don't you think?"

"I have no idea what you're talking about."

"Don't try subterfuge in an effort to make me release her. I shan't, not now, not ever."

"If you wish to give another man's child your name, that is your affair," Mortimer replied as calmly, as slowly as he could, aware that a confession of the truth was useless.

"Not just another man's child; I should certainly not give my name to any other man's child, but to a Mortimer I shall, and gladly."

"You are sadly mistaken, and I don't know what I can say to convince you of the fact."

"There is nothing you can say that would. I saw that message you wrote on her fan; you used it as a toast at her sister's wedding. I knew then there was something between you."

"There has been something between me and any number of women; discretion may be the better part of valour, but I regret to say that my affairs have not always been particularly discreet. Mrs. Bransom, though, is not exactly the type of woman I would choose."

He thought Trueblood began to waver as he asked swiftly, "Are you saying the lady lied to me?"

"I don't wish to malign her."

"Naturally you don't, because that would go against your code of honour, wouldn't it, Mortimer? Nothing you say is going to convince me that the child she carries is anyone's other than yours."

Mortimer's face was impassive as he shrugged. "That is up to you, then. If you are generous enough to give the child your name, I should certainly be equally generous and act as godfather."

Trueblood was certainly off guard; again Mortimer thought he had won his point, and perhaps something showed in his eyes, for Trueblood snapped, "No, Mortimer, it won't work. I shall marry her, the child shall be mine. I should warn you that if you have any ideas of persuading the lady to run off with you, to leave me at the altar, you won't suffer, but you have my promise that she will. Her marriage to me has been announced. The banns for our wedding are even now being read—it will take place as arranged. Take her from me and I shall show her to the world as a faithless, immoral woman, panting to the tune of a younger, more flamboyant lover. I can so easily take her character from her, Mortimer; society is only too ready to think ill of a woman. When I've finished with her, there'll be no greater hypocrite on earth than Penelope Bransom, promising herself to one, running off with another, while pretending to grieve for a long-departed husband. I'll never willingly release her. That's what you came for, no doubt. Take her if you will, act as your father did, but know yourself to be the cause of her everlasting shame and degradation. When I'm done playing the role of wronged lover, there'll not be a drawing room in England where she'll be welcomed, that I can guarantee."

Mortimer knew that Trueblood meant every word, and that if maliciously he chose to play the part of an older, worthy man, jilted by a woman in favour of one younger, more desirable, he could make good his threat. Society might wink an eye at a child born before it was due, but it showed no similar lenience for a tangle of broken promises, a faithless woman. There had been that *contretemps* over the Paget-Wellesley-Cadogan affair, where the new Lady Paget alone had suffered, and the Holland case that had ostracized only the second Lady Holland—she had been formidable enough to form her own circle, but not every woman could survive such abuse. Penelope was soft and gentle; society could damage not only her reputation but also her spirit. Would his love be enough to offset such harm to one who, until he came into her life, had led such a blame-free existence? Had he, perhaps, not already done her sufficient disservice? Unless Trueblood were to release her voluntarily, their marriage, for her at least, might turn into intolerable isolation rather than perfect bliss.

"I have no intention of running away with Mrs. Bransom," Mortimer said stiffly. "I came to you to give you information I thought you should know. Though I deny the child is mine, I am only glad that you are firm in your resolve to give a lady in a difficult position and a child whose life might otherwise be a misery your protection. Had she come to me, I am not convinced that I would have shown equal magnanimity—perhaps, perhaps not."

He left immediately; he could keep up the pretence no longer. He had played his cards and had lost not only the trick but the entire game.

He sat long over his wine that evening, pondering what must be done, but he could find no solution. He could not stay in Shropshire, that was certain. London held no charm for him. He would leave England, for a time at least—he didn't know for where—anywhere.

30

"There is," said Candide, "a great amount of evil in the world."

Voltaire
Candide, 1759

Samuel Trueblood was convinced that in his battle against the Mortimers he had, at last, won. Mortimer, he was sure, having discovered that Penelope was to have his child, had come to Belfriars for the purpose of making Trueblood release her so that she would be free to marry him. He had asserted it was not his child, but Trueblood had been too clever for such subterfuge. Still, he was not entirely satisfied with the interview. He would have preferred that Mortimer had confessed all to him, that he had begged for her release; instead, he had actually acquiesced to the suggestion that he stand as godfather to the child when it was born. The idea of Mortimer with his family pride standing as godfather to his own child had shaken his conviction and left an uncomfortable seed of doubt gnawing within him. What if the child were not his? Trueblood would not give his good name to any bastard.

There was no one who could confirm the matter better than Penelope Bransom. Accordingly, to assuage his doubts, he wrote saying that he had heard of her accident from Mortimer and proposed to travel to Surrey after a short stay in London. He would, thus, be able to escort her back to Wrexford for the wedding.

As he sealed the letter with magenta wax, he congratulated himself on always knowing how to solve his own problems. He would make sure that his London establishment was in order, cross-examine Penelope, and then be free to marry her without the fear that she might have made a fool of him.

His arrival at his town house only served to confirm the wisdom of his actions, for a number of letters had accumulated there that should most certainly have been forwarded to him at Belfriars. His servants were lazy oafs; he refused to accept their explanation that they expected him to return as, in fact, he had. Servants were not paid to have expectations, only to carry out his wishes. They had been sacked on the spot. He was not sorry; since he would not be using the house for a while, it was foolish to keep such a large staff. Thus he was not concerned that the letters, when he opened them, were of little consequence, invitations that he had no intention of accepting because of his wedding, accounts he had no intention of paying until they were rendered at least three times: money kept longer in his pocket earned money, and only fools paid bills promptly.

There was one letter remarkable only by its illegible scrawl; he was about to throw it away when his eyes deciphered the words "to your advantage." Now Samuel Trueblood was a man who had reached his comfortable financial position by always taking advantage of advantages. He sat down to study the letter, but since he could make little sense of it, he replied suggesting the writer call on him immediately if he did, in fact, have advantageous news, but only in that event.

The next day, quite early in the day, the writer of the letter was shown in to Trueblood, who found him quite as ill-favoured as had been his letter.

"And what do you want, my man? No long tales, for I've little time to spare, and no begging—I do not deal kindly with beggars."

"I don't cadge me bees and 'oney, not even when I'm 'earts of oak. Albert Watkins is no cadger, 'e works for 'is greengages. I 'appen to 'ave summat. . . ."

"My good fellow, what on earth are you talking about—

bees and honey, hearts of oak, greengages—how dare you waste my valuable time with drivel? You said you had something to my advantage to know."

"I 'ave, indeed I 'ave."

"Then get to the point, what is it? You have two minutes, not a second more."

"Then take a butcher's 'ook at this bit of linen draper." Watkins pulled from his pocket a piece of paper which Trueblood took from him with utmost disdain. It was a letter written to a man he knew, a man for whom he had no respect whatsoever, but it was the hand in which it was written that held him transfixed. Unable to believe his eyes, he read and re-read the letter, his face growing first pale, then hot with anger.

"Yours for fifty quid," Watkins said, and when Trueblood repeated, "Fifty pounds it is," without argument, he wished he had asked a hundred.

"Where did you get it?" Trueblood demanded.

"From a gent. I ain't no Noah's ark, you'll get no more out of me. Fifty quid is all I asked."

"Very well." It was unlike Trueblood to part with such a sum to a man who was clearly a scoundrel, yet he did with the merest caution that Watkins should say nothing of the letter to anyone.

"Like I said, Albert Watkins ain't no Noah's ark."

"No, no, of course, I didn't imply you were a Noah's ark," he replied uncomprehendingly, only aware that the knot of doubt he had felt in his stomach after seeing Mortimer had tightened with a vengeance.

Though he had thought to remain in London for several days, that very afternoon saw him setting out for Surrey, and the interview that followed in the front parlour of Colonel Bullerton's house was even more strained than the one that had taken place in Samuel Trueblood's study.

Under other circumstances he might have toyed with Penelope in an effort to make her incriminate herself, but Samuel Trueblood was too angry. He produced the letter immediately.

"You do not deny having written this letter."

She glanced down at it briefly with no show of emotion. "No."

Her calmness was disconcerting, as disconcerting as Mortimer's denials. He had expected, even hoped for tearful denials.

"Where did you get it?" she asked.

"From a dirty knave by the name of Watson who slaughtered the King's English in a most deplorable manner."

"Watkins," Penelope corrected.

"So, you don't deny knowing him."

"No, he is the father—no, that's not right, but anyway, he brought up Meg Watkins who lives with me."

"Meg Watkins, is she that hoyden maid of yours you had me running after all over London . . . the one you found prostituting herself on Bond Street."

"She is no longer my maid, but she does live with me. I discovered she had been fathered by my late husband, Josiah Bransom. That, making her in some manner related to me, entitled her to a better place in my household."

The pained expression Trueblood had worn since his arrival deepened. "Madam, has the world gone quite mad! Are you calmly telling me that that highly-esteemed gentleman had a . . . an illegitimate child?"

"Yes."

"I cannot accept such a thing. He was a pious man, a good man—everyone said so."

"He did, in fact, have a great number of children— fathered by a variety of ladies, I suppose you would refer to them as persons. He left all of them to starve. Since his death I have seen to it that they have had enough to support themselves until such time as they can work."

"Slander, it's pure slander. And all this time I thought you showed the deepest respect for the dead."

"For some, not all. I wore mourning because it was prescribed under the terms of my late husband's will, a will now nullified by our engagement."

"That engagement may well be in the severest jeopardy unless you can give me a clear and entirely satisfactory explanation of that letter you hold in your hands. I should

2 5 7

warn you that I shall not take your word alone but shall seek corroborating evidence from reliable witnesses, so don't attempt to lie to me to save yourself."

"I shouldn't stoop to such a thing."

"You don't deny it is written in your hand."

"No."

"And where was it written?"

"At the Blue Boar, it's an inn at—"

"I am well aware of where the Blue Boar is and the kind of clientele to which it caters. That you, madam, a respectable woman, as I had thought, actually went to such a hostelry, a place of the utmost Bacchanalian revelry. . . ."

"Your description is not inaccurate," Penelope agreed drily.

"You were there, perhaps, changing horses?"

"I was there under an odd set of circumstances. That letter was written in Palfry's room, you see, I—"

But she had no chance to finish her sentence, for he rudely interrupted her, his voice faint with anger, "No more, I shall not listen to another word! How could I possibly give my name to a woman who had been carrying on with such a vile creature as Palfry, known even by rogues and roués with contempt? You are depraved, madam, and a lying hypocrite to boot. No wonder Mortimer denied that your child was his. I thought it bluff, but perhaps you tried to hoodwink him as you did me. Thank God I discovered in time. When he came to me I thought it was because he wanted you. No wonder he said he would be delighted to stand as godfather to the child, laughing all the time up his sleeve, no doubt. What a narrow escape I have had. You are a low, despicable, prevaricating woman."

As he continued to rage at her, Penelope felt an odd detachment from his fury. Only one thing he said had hurt her and that had hurt deeply—that Mortimer had denied the child was his, that he had offered to stand as godfather. Perhaps it had been necessitated because of his future marriage to Lady Staverton—nevertheless, it hurt. But for the rest, as Trueblood continued to heap abuse on her head, all she could see was not him but Josiah Bransom before her. How similar they were.

She was glad she had at last gained the courage to tell Missy the truth about that marriage. It had been a difficult thing for her to do, for she found her own role both during and after the marriage not entirely admirable, but it had been done and she had felt much relieved afterwards. Just as now she felt relieved as Mr. Trueblood was informing her in no uncertain terms that he would never, under any circumstances, consider taking her as his wife.

"I shall stop the calling of the banns immediately. You and that bastard you are carrying may go to the devil, madam; even that is too good for you. I leave you without salutation, neither good-day or good-bye."

The farewell, uttered as he angrily quit the room, had an oddly familiar ring. Then she remembered when she had last heard it, from Edward Bransom. She looked down at the note to Palfry in her hands. Bransom must have passed it to Watkins and instructed him to give it to Trueblood. Though she now had no idea what was to become of her, she was oddly relieved to be free. Little did Edward Bransom know that he had done her a great favour.

31

Fare thee well! and if for ever,
Still for ever, fare thee well.

> Byron
> *Fare Thee Well,* 1816

Passing through the village not far from Staverton Park, a squabbling, rowdy bunch of schoolboys, jostling and yelling, half blocked the roadway, causing Mortimer to slow his horses.

"Watch out there," he shouted. His humour was not good. He was on his way to Dover from Aldford Street, where he had gone from Chenwyth to close his town house and arrange a transfer of funds to the continent. Once abroad, he wasn't altogether sure he knew where he would go—he only knew he did not wish to remain in England.

He had written to his sister announcing his decision to go abroad for a time without detailing reasons. He had written a similar note to Georgina Staverton, but realizing that in going by way of Guildford he would not be far from Staverton Park, he felt it incumbent upon him to tell her of his decision. To deal with her any other way was unworthy. He must, also, tell her of his qualms about their marriage. It was an interview he did not relish, yet to go away avoiding it was a cowardly way of evading the truth. But perhaps he was doing that anyway.

He was cheered only by the thought of leaving England with its unhappy memories and unhappy weather behind him for a time. Thus he had set out once before, because of a woman. Had he really changed? he was thinking, as he came upon the street fight.

"It's mine!" the largest of the boys was yelling.

"It is not. I found it," a smaller voice came from somewhere in the centre of the scrimmage.

"It's not. It's Fred's. I saw him with it."

"I'll cuff you, Tim, if you don't give it to me," the big boy snarled.

"You'll do no such thing. He's much smaller than you, you're a great bully. Leave him alone. Allow me to find out the truth of the matter. You're not to hit him again, do you hear me?"

At the sound of that voice, Mortimer halted his horses abruptly and jumped down.

"What the deuce is happening here?"

The boys turned at his voice, the circle parted, and there, in the midst, kneeling with her arm around the waist of a boy younger and smaller than the rest was Penelope Bransom.

"Mrs. Bransom!"

"Lord Mortimer!"

"Cor, it's Lord Mortimer," said the big boy, staring as though he'd seen a ghost.

"Not the one Mr. Beeson talks about all the time."

"The one who fought Boney."

"The one who beat the daylights out of him."

"Cor," said the small boy, forgetting his bruises as his jaw dropped in amazement.

"What is it? What's happening?" Mortimer squatted down beside Penelope, who explained that the big boy, Fred, had accused the small boy, Timothy, of taking his five-coloured marble, but Timothy denied taking it; he said he'd found it in the gutter and picked it up and was playing with it.

"Then it's simply a case of misunderstanding, isn't it, Fred?" Mortimer said pleasantly. "Tim doesn't seem to be denying it's yours. He found it and thought it was a case of finder's keeper's. You might have done the same thing in a similar situation, don't you suppose?"

"I s'pose I might," Fred allowed, his eyes assiduously

studying Mortimer's face as though to remember every line. "It's not important, really it isn't."

"Then you won't hit Timothy again," Penelope put in.

"Of course he won't," Mortimer concurred. "Fred knows boys don't hit those smaller and weaker than themselves. Only a bully does that."

"I'm not a bully," Fred asserted quickly.

"I'm sure you're not. The only time a fight has any sport in it is when the opponents are equally matched."

Fred dug into his pocket to produce a grubby piece of paper.

"Sir, would you write your name down so I can show it to Mr. Beeson?"

"I shall be very happy to." And Mortimer wrote quite plainly, "To Fred, who plays the game," and he signed it with his best wishes.

The other boys gathered around to see what he had written.

"Cor, wait till Mr. Beeson sees it. He's never going to believe it." One after the other, doffing their caps, the boys hurried away in search of their schoolmaster, all except the youngest, who still hung on to Penelope.

Mortimer reached into his pocket for a coin.

"Why don't you go and buy a five-coloured marble of your own," he suggested gently, but the boy shook his head shyly. "I'd rather you'd sign your name for me," he said.

"I'll do that as well." And Mortimer took a card from his pocket and wrote on the back of it, "To Tim, one of the bravest boys I know." "There, but I insist upon your buying the marble also."

"Right you are, sir!" Tim's face glowed as he ran as fast as his legs would carry him down the village street in the direction of the shop.

They both watched him go, then Mortimer turned to Penelope.

"I suppose if ever I want to find you, all I have to do is to look in the midst of the biggest fracas, wherever some injustice is being done."

"I hate to see the strong taking advantage of the weak."

"I know you do."

He studied her flushed face and looked down at her loose fitting sprig muslin dress, asking anxiously, "Are you sure you're all right? They didn't push you or hurt you in any way?"

"No, I'm quite all right."

"I thought you would be gone by now."

"No," she replied hesitantly. Then, looking beyond him to his coach piled high with luggage, she added, "You're going away then."

"Yes, to the continent—Italy perhaps, I don't know, I don't really care. It doesn't really matter."

"Then you received Rodney's letter already," she exclaimed in surprise.

"A letter from Bully? No, I received nothing."

"I hardly thought it possible, for he only wrote it yesterday. But then, how did you know?"

"Know what?"

"About Philby Staverton."

"What about Philby Staverton?"

"Well, he's alive, he's home. He was picked up at sea by a ship headed around the horn for India—he was saved—he's home. Lady Staverton came with the news yesterday morning, looking as though she'd seen a ghost; in a way she had. She most particularly asked Rodney to write you. She says he is quite changed. Apparently he threw out the guests she had staying with her. He said something about setting his own house in order and running it for a change."

Mortimer grinned. "Good old Staverton—Ulysses home from the wars. I might learn to like him yet."

"But I thought you knew, I thought that was why you were going away. I'm sorry I should be the one to break it to you."

"As a matter of fact it gives me a great sense of relief. I wasn't looking forward to confiding in Georgina what a great mistake I felt we were making in considering marriage in the future."

"But I thought that was what you always wanted."

"Ten years ago, perhaps. Now I know it would have been

2 6 3

a great mistake even then. Neither of us is quite what we thought."

"How often that is the case," Penelope mused. "I should tell you, for though you will undoubtedly hear of it, I'd rather it should come from me. All these years it has been thought I mourned the loss of my husband, whereas in truth I loathed him. I was only complying with his will. It made me a hypocrite in the worst sense of the word."

"Then that mausoleum with its ever fresh floral tributes . . ."

"All his idea, and the window, and the lavish funeral. I simply carried out his wishes so that I might retain my income."

"Well, I suppose it was only sensible. You had to live."

"In my own defence I must say I did it more for the children than for myself."

"Children? I didn't realize he had children—then why did his nephew inherit?"

"All illegitimate, by a variety of girls and women he used. He left them all to starve. I helped them while I could, but now they are again in straitened circumstances." She saw his puzzled look and explained, "The will was nullified at the time I agreed to re-marry."

Mortimer's face hardened. "Since the role of benefactor is one Trueblood relishes, he can undoubtedly include these unfortunates among his flock of waifs and strays, give teas on their behalf and accept thanks from all and sundry for his great benevolence."

"None of that will ever happen." She shook her head. "I'm glad you're not hurt about Georgina Staverton though, I thought you would be."

"Because I'm not hurt about Georgina does not mean that I am not hurt. Why didn't you tell me about the child? Why, Penelope, why?"

Instead of answering, she spoke the thought that had rankled ever since she heard it. "Mr. Trueblood said you had offered to stand as godparent."

"You've seen him then; he told you of our conversation?"
She nodded. "How did you know?"

"The day of the accident."

"Yes, I had forgotten, I suppose the apothecary must have discovered it, though he said nothing to anyone."

"I asked him not to. I didn't want your sister to know, not until I had talked to Trueblood. I thought he would be willing to give you up, but I found he wanted the child because he knew it was mine. I lied, I denied it, I even offered to stand as godparent to convince him, but he knew I was bluffing. He threatened to ruin you if we married. I suppose I shouldn't be telling you any of this now. It's unfair to malign your future husband."

"But I . . . I'm not marrying Samuel Trueblood."

"Not marrying him! I don't understand. It's less than a week since he said nothing would ever persuade him to give up the chance of giving his name to a Mortimer child. What happened?"

"It was my note to Palfry." And she told him everything, the words spilling out one after the other; she told about her humiliation in thinking herself barren, about the fact she had discovered herself to be pregnant only after she had refused him, convinced he had wanted to marry Georgina Staverton, about Trueblood's offer that had seemed to solve everything, about Edward Bransom's treachery, about Palfry at the Blue Boar, about the note she had written, delivered to Trueblood by Watkins. "I suspect he was paid twice for his act, by Edward Bransom and Mr. Trueblood."

"And if he were here now I'd gladly double anything he has already received. In fact I think the first thing I shall do when we return to England is to send him a bank draft for five hundred pounds. Or doesn't it fit your sense of justice to reward an out and out scoundrel?"

But she heard nothing except "When we return to England," and suddenly she felt light-headed, just as though she had inhaled a great cloud of Humphry Davy's laughing gas. She smiled, just as she had smiled on that day at the Royal Institution, though it wasn't laughing gas that caused that smile but the thought of a life filled with unashamed mornings.

He put his arm through hers. "I thought we would go to

Florence. Plenty of English there and doctors who understand our peculiar ways. And flowers, all manner of flowers to please you: mimosa, wisteria, orange blossom—and the colours, blues from cerulean to Prussian, and coquelicot red and bittersweet orange, a riot of colour and warmth for our English eyes. Just what you need to do justice to your graded washes and overpainting technique."

"But Charles, I thought you said you knew nothing about art."

"I have an active mind, and you've awakened a new interest for me, but only as a spectator. However, if our child combines your talent and my pragmatism, what a jewel we may expect."

And there, in the middle of the village street, he kissed her, just as the schoolboys returned, bringing with them their elderly schoolmaster.

"That's him, that's Lord Mortimer," they reassured him as he looked askance at the tall gentleman embracing a lady on a public street.

"Lord Mortimer?" he began timidly, when Mortimer at last looked up.

"Yes?"

"Allow me to present myself. I am Aloysius Beeson. Never did I think the day would come when I should be face to face with England's great hero."

Mortimer thought to direct Mr. Beeson to Glossop, impassively looking on, who knew him on those least heroic days when his faults far outshone his virtues.

"I'm afraid it is only those who believe in heroics who make heroes," he began, but noticing the elderly gentleman's earnest expression, so clearly indicating his desire for a hero—as much as an example for his boys as for himself—Mortimer felt he had no right to deprive him of his illusion. "It is I who am delighted to shake the hand of one who molds our future generation. May it live in peace and prosperity."

Mr. Beeson beamed. "I am sure the boys join me in that same wish for you and your good lady."